CLAUDIA AND THE SAD GOOD-BYE

**Other books by
Ann M. Martin**

Rachel Parker, Kindergarten Show-off
Eleven Kids, One Summer
Ma and Pa Dracula
Yours Turly, Shirley
Ten Kids, No Pets
Slam Book
Just a Summer Romance
Missing Since Monday
With You and Without You
Me and Katie (the Pest)
Stage Fright
Inside Out
Bummer Summer

BABY-SITTERS LITTLE SISTER series
THE BABY-SITTERS CLUB mysteries
THE BABY-SITTERS CLUB series

CLAUDIA AND THE
SAD GOOD-BYE

Ann M. Martin

AN
APPLE
PAPERBACK

SCHOLASTIC INC.
New York Toronto London Auckland Sydney

Cover art by Hodges Soileau

ISBN 0-590-67394-7

12 11 10 9 8 7 6 5 4 3 2   3   6 7 8 9/9 0 1/0

Printed in the U.S.A.   40

This book is for
Margaret Martin Vinsel
With Love

Claudia and the Sad Good-bye

CHAPTER 1

"Mimi! I'm home! I'm home, Mimi!"

"Hello, my Claudia."

My grandmother greeted me at the door when I got home from school. She kissed my forehead and smiled crookedly at me. Mimi is one of my favorite people. She is a second mother to me.

I dropped my book bag and gym shoes on the floor in the hall. Mom or Dad or even my big sister, Janine, would have looked from my stuff to the stairs, as a silent reminder to take the things up to my bedroom instead of leaving them lying around. If that had happened, I would have left the things for ten minutes or so before I took them to my room, to show my family that they can't all boss me around just because I'm the youngest and not a very good student.

But Mimi didn't say anything about dropping my school stuff on the floor. She didn't even look at it. So I immediately picked it up and ran to my room. When I came downstairs again, I found Mimi in the kitchen, fiddling with cups and a tin of tea leaves.

"Special tea, my Claudia?" she asked me.

"Oh, *yes!*" The day was perfect for special tea. For one thing, it was raining. Outside the window there was nothing but drizzle and dreariness, which I don't mind at all. I love mysteries — and drizzle and dreariness are a good backdrop for any mystery. Also, I didn't have any after-school activities planned. Usually I have a baby-sitting job or an art class, but that afternoon I was free. Most important, special tea with Mimi is wonderful any time.

What is special tea? Special tea is when my grandmother prepares Japanese tea and serves it in cups with no handles that she brought with her when she moved from Japan to America. Then she and I sip the tea and talk, just the two of us.

Mimi likes to prepare special tea completely by herself, even though this is difficult for her now, since she had a stroke last summer and can't move around as easily as she used to. In fact, she can't use her right hand at all. Speech is difficult for her, too. Plus, she's been just plain forgetful lately, and has said and done some pretty weird things. But this day seemed to be a good one, and special tea went smoothly.

It is usually as soothing as Mimi herself.

"So, my Claudia," Mimi began (and I should tell you that I am the only one Mimi calls *her* someone), "how school was?"

"Oh, okay. I didn't do so well on that math test."

"How not so well?"

"A C-minus?" I answered with a question, as if I weren't *sure* that was the grade I'd gotten. But it was. One point lower and it would have been a D-plus.

"Oh," said Mimi. "Well. Studied. Studied hard. I remember. Next better time." That garbled message meant that Mimi remembered that I had studied hard with the help of my dad and my big sister, Janine, who is a genius, and that no doubt I would do better on my next test.

"Thanks, Mimi," I replied, smiling. "Guess what I *did* get a good grade on. That history composition," I answered for her.

"The one I help?"

"Yup. The one you helped me with."

"What grade?"

3

"B . . . plus!" I said grandly.

Mimi beamed. She had given me the idea to write a composition on a period in Japanese history, but she had really helped only a little. I had done most of the work myself.

I sipped my tea.

I looked at my hands holding my cup, and at Mimi's hands holding her cup. My hands were smooth and creamy-colored and steady. Mimi's were wrinkled and brown like walnuts, and they shook. Mimi is my mother's mother and she's getting pretty old.

As you have probably guessed, Mimi is Japanese. She came to the United States a long time ago, when she was thirty-two. Her husband was Japanese, too, so of course my mom is Japanese. And so is my dad. Janine and I consider ourselves not just Japanese, but Japanese-American, meaning that we're full-blooded Asian but we've lived all our lives in the U.S. Actually, we've lived all our lives here in Stoneybrook, Connecticut. And Mimi has lived all of *my* life in Stoneybrook, because her husband died after Mom and Dad got married, so she moved in with them. Both of my parents were working. They were doing different things then, but now Dad is a partner in an investment firm in Stamford, Connecticut,

4

which is nearby, and Mom is the head librarian at our public library. Anyway, when my grandfather died, Janine the genius had just been born, so Mimi's moving in seemed like the perfect arrangement. My parents could work, and Mimi could help with the house, watch Janine, and not miss her husband quite so much. Three years later, I was born, and there was Mimi to help raise me. Mimi is my friend and the person who understands me the best in the world, even better than my friends.

I smiled at Mimi over our tea cups and she set hers shakily on the table. "No more talking of school," she said. "Tell me art. Sitting for babies." (She meant baby-sitting.)

So we talked about my art and baby-sitting. And I poured the tea when Mimi's hands shook too much, and helped her with words she couldn't remember.

At last Mimi said, "I start dinner. Now. What do you?"

"I think I'll go upstairs and work on my painting."

Mimi nodded. I left her in the kitchen and went to my room.

I hate school. But here is what I love: reading mysteries, especially Nancy Drews; baby-sitting; art. Not only do I love art, I'm good at it. Really good at it. And thank heavens for that. I better be good at something since Janine is so smart in school. How smart is she? She's smart enough to be a high school junior who takes courses at a college in Stoneybrook. That's right, a *college*. When I say she's a genius, I mean it. Her I.Q. is, like, nine million or something. We used to sort of hate each other, but as we grow up, we get along much better. For one thing, we've been worried about Mimi a lot lately, and that's brought us closer together. Worry and fear can do that.

I looked around my messy room. My room is only messy because I have to keep so many art materials stored in it. I like painting, drawing, pottery, sculpture, crafts, and more. So I've got an easel and paints and charcoals, and boxes and boxes of stuff *everywhere*. My current project is a painting. I'm trying something new. I think of it as "stop-action." Imagine that you're watching a movie on a VCR — a movie with a lot of action — and in the middle of a really exciting scene, you press the pause button. That's how I wanted this picture to look — as if time had halted and people had been stopped with spoons halfway to their mouths, or a dropped object in midair, or a bird about to land on a branch, its feet just inches above it, its wings still outstretched.

I paused in my painting and looked out the window and across the street. I could see Mary Anne's house clearly. Mary Anne Spier is one of a group of my friends who have formed a business called the Baby-sitters Club. I'm the vice-president of the club. Mary Anne is the secretary, and our president is Kristy Thomas. Besides us, there are three other members, plus two associate members (I'll explain about them in a minute), and one member in New York City. (I'll explain about her, too.)

Our club meets three afternoons a week, and although our members are very, *very* different people, we get along well. We're like the pieces of a jigsaw puzzle. Put us all together and we make a great picture.

Let me tell you about my friends, beginning with Kristy, since she's the president. Kristy started the club herself. It was her idea. That's an important thing about Kristy. She's full of ideas. She's also outgoing, sort of bossy, a tomboy, and has a big mouth. Okay, a huge mouth. She's thirteen and in eighth grade, like me and most of the club members. She doesn't care much about clothes or makeup yet. *Some*-times, she'll put on a little mascara, but that's it. And she always wears the same kind of outfit: jeans, a turtleneck, a sweater, and running shoes. Kristy has brown hair (longish), brown eyes, and is the shortest kid in our class. Her family is pretty unusual. Her mom and dad got divorced a long time ago. She has three brothers — two big ones in high school, and David Michael, who is seven. Then her mom married this millionaire (no joke). Watson has two little kids of his own, Karen, who's six, and Andrew, who's four. *And* recently her family adopted Emily Michelle, a two-year-old Vietnamese girl. Then there's Kristy's Nannie, her grandma, who's really neat and decided to move in with them and help care for Emily. The whole family lives in Watson's mansion on the other side of Stoneybrook. (Well, Karen and Andrew only live there every other weekend and for two weeks during the summer. The rest of the time they live with their mom and stepfather, not too far away.)

As I mentioned before, I'm the vice-president of the club. You already know a lot about me, except for a few things. I'm addicted to junk food. Mom and Dad don't really like me to have it, so I have to buy it secretly and hide it around my room. It's everywhere. Despite all the junk I eat, my complexion is pretty nice. Smooth. My friends are always saying I'm so lucky because I don't get pimples. Here's what I look like besides my complexion: dark, almond-shaped eyes and long, *long* silky, black hair that I wear all different ways. And I dress on the wild side. Kristy's outfits and mine are like night and day. Here's an example: At the moment I'm wearing lavender plaid cuffed pants with suspenders over a green shirt with buttons down the front, a matching lavender beret (and *not* just because I'm at my easel), and fleece-lined, high-top sneakers which I must admit are uncomfortably hot, but they *look great*. Also, I've got on earrings shaped like Christmas tree lights that actually blink on and off. I'm not sure why I chose to wear them, since it's nowhere near Christmas, but I love jewelry, like to make my own sometimes, and have pierced ears. (Kristy doesn't. Doesn't have pierced ears, that is.) But I have three — two holes in one ear, and one in the other.

Our club secretary is Mary Anne, who lives across the street. Kristy is one of her best friends. They used to live next door to each other, until Kristy's family moved to Watson's house. Mary Anne is not much like Kristy at

9

all. They sort of illustrate the saying about opposites attracting. Mary Anne is shy and reserved. She's very romantic, cries easily, and hates sports. She's also the only one of *any* of us club members to have a steady boyfriend. His name is Logan Bruno, and he's one of the associate members of the Baby-sitters Club. Mary Anne and Kristy *do* look a little alike, though. Mary Anne also has brown hair and eyes and is on the short side. She used to dress kind of like Kristy, too, but lately her outfits have become trendier. However, Mary Anne doesn't have, and never will have, pierced ears. Mary Anne's family is the smallest of any of the club members. It's just her and her dad. Mrs. Spier died a long time ago. Mary Anne has no brothers or sisters, but she does have a gray kitten named Tigger.

Dawn Schafer is the treasurer of our club. Dawn moved to Stoneybrook with her mother and younger brother, Jeff, about a year ago when her parents got divorced. Mrs. Schafer chose Stoneybrook because she grew up here and her parents still live here, but the move was a shock to Dawn and Jeff since *they* grew up in California. In fact, it was so much of a shock to Jeff that eventually he moved back to California to live with his dad. So now half of

10

Dawn's family lives here, and the other half lives three thousand miles away. Thank goodness Dawn's grandparents are in Stoneybrook. Dawn is the most independent person I know. She's reliable and responsible and organized, but she does things her own way. She never gets swayed by what anyone (or everyone) else is doing. She has her own style of dress, which we call California casual, and she sticks to a total health-food diet, even though some of the kids at school tease her about the weird stuff she eats, and the fact that she won't touch candy or junk food. Dawn lives in an old farmhouse with a secret passage (and maybe a ghost) in it, she has the longest, blondest hair and the bluest eyes I've ever seen, and she's Mary Anne's other best friend. (Her mom and Mr. Spier go out on dates sometimes!)

Our club has two junior officers, Jessi Ramsey and Mallory Pike. While the rest of us are in eighth grade, Jessi and Mal are eleven and in sixth grade. That's why they're junior officers. They're only allowed to baby-sit after school or on weekends; not at night unless they're sitting for their own brothers and sisters. Jessi and Mal are best friends. Like Kristy and Mary Anne, they're similar in some ways and different in some ways. The biggest difference is that Jessi is black and Mallory is white. Also, Jessi has just one younger sister and brother, and Mal has *seven* younger sisters and brothers — and three of the boys are identical triplets! Both girls like to read, especially horse stories, and both feel that their parents aren't letting them grow up fast enough. But Mal loves to write and draw and might want to become a children's book author, while Jessi is a talented, and I mean *talented*, ballet dancer. They're really neat, even if they are a little less mature than the rest of us club members.

Our associate officers are Shannon Kilbourne and Logan Bruno. They don't come to our meetings and no one except Kristy knows Shannon very well because she lives way across town in Kristy's ritzy neighborhood, and doesn't go to Stoneybrook Middle School with the rest of us. We do know Logan, though, and if you were to ask Mary Anne to describe him, all she'd say is, "Incredible." She would mean good-looking, nice, thoughtful, funny, etc., and he is those things. I like him a lot, but no one knows him better than Mary Anne does.

There's one other person I feel I should tell you about. She's only sort of a club member, but she *is* my best friend. Her name is Stacey McGill, and she lived in Stoneybrook for just about one year. She and her parents had lived in New York City, then her dad's company transferred him here, then, after one year, back to New York. Weird, huh? But it was lucky for me, because if none of that had happened, I'd never have met my first and only best friend. Stacey was a club member, of course. And she and I are *so* much alike. We couldn't look more different, but we both love wild clothes and I guess we're a little boy-crazy. Stacey has diabetes, which is a huge drag, but she copes with it pretty well. Now that she's back in New York, she calls herself the New York branch of the Baby-sitters Club, but it isn't the same, and I miss her a *lot*.

I stopped staring out the window and day-dreaming about the Baby-sitters Club and my friends, and went back to work on my painting again. A few minutes later, Mimi came into my room. For someone with a limp, she manages the stairs pretty well — but only sometimes. Other times, they frighten her.

My grandmother stood behind me and studied the painting.

"A beautiful," she said at last.

"Thanks, Mimi," I replied.

Mimi put her arm around me. "Start dinner?" she asked.

Hadn't she started an hour ago? I wondered. But all I said was, "Do you want me to give you a hand?" (I'm used to Mimi's forgetfulness.)

Mimi nodded.

Arm in arm, we walked slowly to the top of the stairs. We walked even more slowly down them. When we reached the kitchen Mimi discovered that she'd forgotten what she'd planned for dinner, so I helped her start over.

Mimi needs lots of help these days.

It's a little bit hard on our family.

14

CHAPTER 2

"Claudia, Claudia!" called an urgent voice, and Mallory Pike burst into my bedroom. She looked close to tears. It was a Wednesday afternoon, just ten minutes before the beginning of a meeting of the Baby-sitters Club. "Mimi just scolded me and told me never to take her shopping again because we have to wait too long to get into the dressing rooms. She sounded really mad at me." (All my friends call my grandmother Mimi. That's what she likes.)

"Sit down," I said, leading Mallory to my bed. "I guess Mimi never yelled at you before, did she?"

"Well," said Mal shakily, "she wasn't exactly yelling, but — "

"I know what you mean." I plopped down next to Mal.

"Anyway, no, she never talked to me that

15

way before — and I never took her shopping. When would I have taken her shopping? And why would she think *I'd* take her shopping instead of you or Janine or one of your parents?''

Before I could answer, Mal rushed on. ''And then she seemed like her old self again. Her voice went back to normal, and she pulled *this* out of her pocket and gave it to me.'' Mallory opened her hand and showed me a small china bird that had been part of Mimi's bird collection for as long as I could remember. ''Mimi said she's known me since I was little and she really wants me to have this. . . . You don't mind, do you? I mean, I didn't ask for it or anything.''

I did mind a little, but not because Mimi had chosen Mal, not me, to have the bird. I minded because for Mimi this was a new weird behavior that I didn't understand. All I said, though, was, ''No, of course not,'' and Mal smiled and looked like she felt better.

Then Kristy came in, or maybe I should say *blew* in, and Mimi was immediately forgotten.

''Hi, you guys!'' cried Kristy. ''Are we the only ones here so far?'' She checked her watch. ''Five minutes till meeting time. Any Oreos, Claud?''

16

I felt winded just listening to Kristy, but I began a search for this package of Oreos which I was pretty sure was inside my hollow book, one of my best hiding places. The other good hiding places are behind a row of Nancy Drews on my shelf, and in boxes under my bed, labeled things like ART SUPLYS. (I am not the world's greatest speller.)

Maybe I better tell you how our club works, before things get underway. Kristy, Mary Anne, Dawn, Mal, Jessi, and I meet Monday, Wednesday, and Friday afternoons from five-thirty until six. We have done a lot of advertising (mostly with fliers and in the newspaper), so people know that these are the times we meet. When they need baby-sitters they call us at those times. We provide the sitters — and get tons of jobs this way.

The club started back at the beginning of seventh grade when Kristy saw how hard it was for her mom to find a sitter for David Michael (who was six then) at a time when neither Kristy nor her older brothers, Sam and Charlie, could watch him. Mrs. Thomas (well, she was Mrs. Thomas then, but now she's Mrs. Watson Brewer) had to make call after call trying to find an available sitter. And Kristy thought to herself, Wouldn't it be great if Mom could make one phone call and find, like, a whole nest of sitters?

That was the beginning of the Baby-sitters Club. She asked Mary Anne, me, and Stacey (who was my new friend then), to join her, and we started advertising to let people know what we were going to do, and when they could reach us. We began receiving calls at our first meeting. We were amazed!

Here's how we run the meetings: officially. As president, Kristy insists on that. She is always a take-charge person, and usually a no-nonsense person. At the beginning of every meeting, she puts a visor on her head, a pencil over one ear, and plunks herself down in my director's chair. (The meetings are held in my room because I have my own phone and my own phone number.) Then she asks Dawn to collect club dues if it's a Monday, and then she just, well, runs things. She makes us keep a club notebook in which each of us is responsible for writing up every job we go on. Once a week, we're supposed to read the past week's entries so that we all know what's happened at the houses where our friends have sat. Plus, we often find good solutions to sitting problems in the notebook. I look at it this way: Kristy deserves to be the president. She's good at being a boss (when she's not actually being *bossy*), she's a natural leader, and besides, the club was her idea.

I'm the vice-president mostly because of my phone. If we held our meetings in anyone else's room we'd have to tie up some adult's phone line three times a week — and get calls for people who aren't club members. Actually, there's a little more to my job than just owning a phone. A lot of times, baby-sitting calls come in while we're not having a meeting. Then I have to take down the information about who needs a sitter when, for how long, and for how many kids, and call my friends to see who's available to take the job.

As secretary, Mary Anne has the most complicated job of all. She's perfect for it, though, because she's organized, precise, and has terribly neat handwriting. What does she do? She keeps our record book up-to-date and in order, and schedules all of our jobs. This includes keeping track of the club members' personal schedules, too — dance lessons, art classes, dentist appointments (or in Mal's case, orthodontist appointments). The record book is the most important feature of our club. It's very official, so of course it was Kristy's idea. Apart from the appointment pages where Mary

Anne does our scheduling, it has pages where she records our clients' names and addresses, the number of children they have, and vital information, such as children who have food allergies or special fears. Also in the record book is space for recording the money we earn, and for keeping track of our treasury. That's Dawn's job, though, so on to Dawn.

Our poor treasurer has the awful job of collecting dues from us club members every week. We hate parting with any of our money, but Dawn (being Dawn) just does her job and isn't bothered by our griping. The money in the treasury is used for several things. First of all, fun stuff — throwing slumber parties or pizza parties from time to time. Our club isn't *all* work. Secondly, to pay Charlie Thomas, Kristy's oldest brother, to drive her to and from meetings now that she lives across town. The third thing we spend the money on is toys for our Kid-Kits. Kid-Kits are boxes that we decorated ourselves (we each have one) and filled with our old games, toys, and books. We take the Kid-Kits with us sometimes when we baby-sit, and the kids love them — which makes *us* popular baby-sitters! Anyway, most of the stuff in the kits, like books and games, never wears out or gets used up. But we do have to replace crayons, activity books, soap bubbles, and things like that. The treasury money is supposed to cover those expenses.

Mallory and Jessi, our junior officers, don't have real duties the way the rest of us do, but they sure help take the pressure off of us. Our club is very successful. We get so many jobs, in fact, that when Stacey (who was our first treasurer — Dawn took over after she left) moved back to New York, we decided to replace her with *two* new club members. It's kind of a pain that Jessi and Mal are too young to sit at night, but at least when they cover more of the afternoon jobs, it frees the rest of us up for the evenings.

Okay, now I'll tell you about Logan Bruno (the love of Mary Anne's life) and Shannon Kilbourne, our two associate club members. They don't come to meetings, but they are good sitters whom we know we can call on if a job comes in that *none* of us is free to take. That might sound unlikely, but it does happen. Just last week, someone needed a sitter on an afternoon when Mallory had an orthodontist appointment, I had an art class, Jessi had a dance rehearsal, and the rest of us were going to be baby-sitting. Whew! Shannon took that job, thank goodness.

Anyway, after some searching around my room on that Wednesday afternoon, I found a new package of Double Stuf Oreos and handed them to Kristy in the director's chair. While she was opening them, Jessi, Dawn, and Mary Anne came in. Mallory moved off the bed to sit on the floor with Jessi, while Mary Anne and Dawn and I settled ourselves in a row on my bed. These are our usual spots for club meetings.

No sooner had Kristy asked if anyone had club business to discuss, than the phone rang.

"I'll get it!" exclaimed Kristy. "First call of the meeting!" Kristy picked up the phone. "Hello, Baby-sitters Club. . . . Yes? . . . Yes?" She sounded puzzled. Then she handed the phone to me and said, cupping her hand over the receiver, "It's Mrs. Addison. Remember her? And she wants to talk to you."

This was not standard club procedure. Usually, whoever answers the phone (and it isn't always Kristy), takes down the information about the job, and then hangs up to give Mary Anne a chance to study our schedule. When we've found someone who's available for the job, we call the client back to tell him or her who the sitter will be.

But our club had baby-sat for the Addison

kids only a couple of times, so maybe Mrs. Addison had forgotten the procedure.

I took the phone from Kristy, feeling curious. "Hi, Mrs. Addison?" I said. Then I listened to her for a long time. When I hung up the phone, I turned to the other girls and said, "Guess what? She doesn't want a baby-sitter, she wants an art teacher."

"Huh?" said Kristy.

"Oh, don't tell me. For Corrie. Or Sean. Right?" spoke up Dawn, who's the only one of us who has sat for the Addisons.

"Yeah, for Corrie," I replied. "How did you know?"

"Because all Mr. and Mrs. Addison want is time for themselves, so they shuttle poor Corrie and Sean from class to class on weekends and after school. Corrie's only nine, and Sean is ten, and I bet they've both already taken basketball, dance, drama, creative writing, football, baseball, and anything else the Addisons can think of."

"Well, now Mrs. Addison's thought of art, and she knows that I'm pretty good at art *and* that I like kids, so she's wondering if I'd give Corrie an art lesson once a week. I guess that would be sort of like a baby-sitting job. . . . Wouldn't it?"

"Sure," replied Kristy. "You'd have to charge more than usual because you'd need to provide materials, but I don't see why — "

"Hey!" I cried, interrupting Kristy. I couldn't help it. For once, I'd had a great idea. "Maybe I could start a little art class. Like on Saturdays in our basement. Gabbie and Myriah Perkins love art projects. So does Jamie Newton. That would be fun. And good experience for me, in case I ever want to be an art teacher."

"And," said Kristy slowly, "it would show people that our club can do more than just baby-sit. I think it would be good for business."

"I'd need some help, though," I said slowly. "I don't know if I could manage a class alone."

"If you hold the class on Saturdays, I could help you," spoke up Mary Anne. "We'll split the money sixty-forty, since you'll be in charge."

It seemed like a great arrangement. If Mrs. Addison agreed, then all systems would be go.

Mrs. Addison did agree. The meeting ended on a happy note.

CHAPTER 3

Sometimes when my friends leave after a club meeting, I feel a little let down. Suddenly my room is quiet again. And it's funny, but that's when I miss Stacey the most. Knowing that my only *best* friend is all the way in New York City makes me feel bad — but just for a few moments. Then I remember that Mimi is home and I can run downstairs and help her fix dinner.

That was just what I did after the meeting when Mary Anne and I decided to hold art classes. Only lately I haven't been just helping Mimi fix dinner, I've pretty much been doing it for her, or at least directing her, if she insists on doing things herself. She's just not too trustworthy in the kitchen anymore. Her hands shake, so I worry when she's using knives or the vegetable peeler. And (I know this is gross, but it's true) she's not very sanitary anymore, either. She's always forgetting to wash her hands before she begins cooking. She doesn't remember to wash food either, like raw chicken pieces or lettuce. And I'm afraid she's going to give us all food poisoning sometime by thawing out a piece of meat, deciding not to serve it after all, and then refreezing it without cooking it first. That's a wonderful way to get salmonella. Plus I worry about matches, the stove, the oven, you name it. Of course, I only need to worry on her bad days. On her good days, no problem. Which is why my parents haven't banned Mimi from the kitchen yet. They know it would take away her sense of usefulness and independence — and that on the bad days, I'll cook or supervise.

"Mimi!" I exclaimed as I entered the kitchen. "I've got a good idea! Let's have a fancy candlelight dinner tonight. You set the table in the dining room with our good china and put out candles and everything."

"Yes. Fine," replied Mimi vaguely.

I was glad she agreed to that. After the business with Mallory that afternoon, I could tell she was having a bad time, and I wanted to make the dinner myself.

During the next hour, my parents came

home from their jobs, and Janine returned from her college course called Advances and Trends in Computerized Biopsychiatry. (Or something like that. I don't know the meaning of any of those words except "and" and "in.")

Everyone was surprised and pleased by our formal dinner. Mimi and I exchanged a secret smile as Mom exclaimed, "Oh, how lovely!" and Janine cried, "Candlelight!" and Dad said, "Chicken and rice, my favorite." (So it wasn't fancy food. At least the meal *looked* fancy.)

My family took our usual places at the table.

I said grandly, "I will serve the first course."

"First course!" repeated Dad.

"Yup," I replied, and then added casually as I was walking around the table with the soup tureen, "By the way, I got a B-plus on my history composition." (I failed to say anything about the math test.)

"Gosh," said Janine, and I couldn't tell whether she was more impressed by the grade or the pea soup, which she was looking at through her thick, round glasses.

I served Mom, then stepped over to Mimi (whom I probably should have served first, but oh, well). Just as I was dipping the ladle into the tureen, Mimi kind of slithered down in her chair.

"Mimi?" I said, hastily setting the hot tureen on the table where it left a mark that we've never been able to get off.

"Do not . . . do not . . . no feel well." Mimi slumped sideways and Dad and Mom both jumped out of their chairs. Dad caught Mimi just before she hit the floor.

"Call the paramedics, Claudia," said Mom in a tone you don't ignore.

I didn't even look back at Mimi. I just raced for the kitchen phone and made the call. The paramedics reached our house in ten minutes. I was waiting outside for them and led them into the dining room, where Mom and Dad had laid Mimi on the floor and covered her with a blanket.

"Is she dead?" I whispered to Janine, who was hovering nearby, not knowing what to do.

"No," replied my sister, sounding surprised. "Listen."

I tried to, over the commotion of the paramedics and their equipment. Mimi wasn't dead. She wasn't even unconscious. She was *talking*. But she was all confused. I heard her mention everything from "the old country" to shopping with Mallory. Sometimes her eyes were closed, sometimes open. She was dis-

28

oriented and probably embarrassed.

"Low blood pressure," I heard one technician say. Then, "Semiconscious. Doesn't know where she is."

A few minutes later the ambulance drove off with Mimi in it. Mom rode with her. Dad and Janine and I followed them in our car. Nobody said a word on the way to the hospital.

What happened next is pretty boring, so I won't even go into it. All you need to know is that Mimi was admitted to a hospital room (it seemed to take a long time), but since she no longer acted too sick, we just stayed with her until she fell asleep, and then we went home. Before we did that, one doctor did give her a shot of something after he examined her briefly, but he didn't hook her up to any machines and no one was rushing around wringing their hands or calling, "Code blue!" So even with Mimi in the hospital, I felt relieved.

Janine and I even went to school the next morning, and Dad went to his office, but Mom took a personal day off from work to be with Mimi at the hospital. And, of course, I went straight to the hospital from school that afternoon. I'd had a baby-sitting job lined up, but

Mallory was able to take it over for me.

I peeked into Mimi's private room, carrying a small teddy bear behind my back that I'd bought at the hospital gift shop. I figured everyone would be sending Mimi flowers, and that flowers are nice to look at, but that she might want something to hug, especially when she was getting a shot, so I bought the bear.

I tiptoed into the room because Mom had her finger to her lips, signaling to me that Mimi was asleep. I nodded. Then I set the bear on her bed, and Mom and I silently left the room.

Out in the hallway, Mom kissed me and smiled. "How was school?" she asked.

"Fine," I replied. "How's Mimi? What's wrong with her?"

Mom shook her head. "The doctors aren't sure. She had some tests today and they think it's a problem with her blood, but they don't know just what."

"Leukemia?" I whispered, terrified.

"No," said Mom. "And not plain old anemia, either."

"Hemophilia?"

My mother smiled. "You have to be born with that."

"Oh." I paused. "You know, if you want to

30

go to work for awhile, you can. Mallory took my baby-sitting job for me. I can stay with Mimi for the rest of the afternoon."

"We-ell . . ." After some hemming and hawing (Mom's term), she took me up on my offer.

So I spent the afternoon with Mimi.

She slept. I held her hand.

Two more days went by. No one could figure out what was wrong with Mimi's blood. They did test after test, and Mimi talked about weirder and weirder things. They even tested her for something called toxoplasmosis, which you get mainly from cats. I told this one doctor that we've never had a cat, but he didn't care.

I spent the afternoons at the hospital with Mimi, since my family all thought *my* activities were less important than *theirs*. I didn't mind much, though. I guess. And I was pleased to be the one who was at Mimi's side when the doctors, as a last resort, decided to give her a couple of pints of fresh, healthy blood. Boy, did that do the trick! Soon we had a new Mimi on our hands, one who wasn't dizzy or faint, whose appetite came back, and who started talking like a normal person again.

The next day they gave her some more blood.

31

"I think I would take little walk," Mimi said.

"You want to take a walk?" I asked her. (Of course, *I* was the one there that afternoon. I was missing an art class.)

"Not outside. Just in hospital. Okay?" said Mimi.

I checked with a nurse. It was okay. Guess where we walked? To the nursery! We stood outside a big glass window and looked at eight babies in their cribs or isolettes or whatever they're called.

"I see Asian baby," said Mimi, pleased.

"Look at all his hair!" I exclaimed. "Or her hair. It stands straight up."

"You look like that. When baby," Mimi told me.

"No, I didn't!" I cried.

"Yes. Yes." Mimi smiled fondly at the memory. She squeezed my hand, and I felt bad for even *thinking* about missing art classes and stuff.

The next day, Thursday, Mimi went home. She'd been in the hospital for just over a week, and no one had a clue as to what was wrong with her, but she wasn't faint or dizzy or weak. She was her old self. Maybe she was like a car that just needed its oil changed.

Maybe.

But I still thought it was weird not to know what was wrong. I think the doctors thought so, too, because they told Mimi to stay in bed as much as possible for awhile. If she was well, why did she have to stay in bed?

So Mimi was home with us again. She could be on her own for short periods of time, but Mom and Dad took turns staying home with her for part of every day, and guess who got to watch her in the afternoons? Me. Janine had a big biopsychiatry test coming up, and my parents let her study for it all she wanted.

One Wednesday afternoon, Mimi asked for special tea. I fixed it and served it to her in bed.

"No!" cried Mimi. "All wrong!"

"*What* is wrong with it?" I asked testily.

Mimi couldn't find the words to explain.

I grabbed up the tray and huffed out of the room with it.

"Sorry, my Claudia," Mimi called after me in a small voice.

I didn't answer.

On Friday, right before a meeting of the Baby-sitters Club, Mimi asked me to help her to the bathroom. When she was back in bed, she asked for a glass of water. Then, as my

33

friends started to arrive, she said, "Bored. Newspaper?"

It was 5:35. Upstairs, Kristy was waiting for me impatiently. I was sure of it. So I gathered up a stack of magazines and newspapers and threw them on the foot of Mimi's bed.

"Anything else?" I asked rudely.

Mimi's gentle eyes filled with tears. She shook her head.

Of course I felt terrible. But I had to go upstairs to the meeting.

"Mimi, I'm sorry," I told her, and fled from her room.

And I was sorry. Very sorry.

I was also sick and tired of being Mimi's maid.

CHAPTER 4

I think that Friday, for me, was the lowest point of Mimi's illness.

It had been awful and scary to see her being loaded onto a stretcher in our dining room, or to see her with bags of blood flowing into her arms, but what I did to her that Friday afternoon was unforgivable. I apologized to her three different times after dinner that night, but I felt only a little better.

Luckily, I have learned that sometimes really awful things are followed by really wonderful things. And guess what — Friday was followed by Saturday (duh), which was the day of the first art class that Mary Anne and I gave. And the art class was wonderful!

Here's who had signed up for it: Corrie Addison (of course), Myriah and Gabbie Perkins, Jamie Newton, Marilyn and Carolyn Arnold (twins!), and Matt Braddock, this wonderful

35

little boy whom Jessi sits for a lot who's totally deaf. We love him to bits, but he and the others, put together, made up an odd class. Mary Anne and I would be teaching five girls and two boys, including twins and a deaf child, ranging in age from two and a half (Gabbie) to nine (Corrie).

Mary Anne and I had decided to hold the art classes in my basement. "That makes the most sense," I said. "All my materials are right upstairs in my room. And Mom said we could use that big utility table down there if we spread newspapers over it and under it. And we have those folding chairs the kids can sit on."

"Perfect," agreed Mary Anne. "Plus, your basement is finished. It's carpeted and heated. Ours is just a dark, old, cold basement with a cement floor that leaks when it rains." Mary Anne paused. "What should we do with the kids at their first lesson?"

"Experiment with paper, paint, and water, I think," I replied. "That's something anyone can do. You know, we'll just let Gabbie mess around. The older kids might want to make watercolor scenes on damp paper. Or do other things. I think the class should be fun and relaxed. We shouldn't tell the kids every little thing to do. We'll let them be creative."

Mary Anne nodded. "Okay," she replied.

Our art class was to be held from eleven o'clock to twelve-thirty each Saturday. I was sure, on that first day, that Mary Anne would get nervous and that she would arrive long before anyone else, especially since she lives right across the street.

But Corrie rang our bell first. It was only 10:45. By the time I opened our front door, Mrs. Addison's car was halfway down the driveway.

"You must be Corrie," I said to the little girl standing on our front steps.

She nodded shyly. Corrie was very pretty, with brownish-blonde hair cut straight across her forehead in bangs, and straight around her shoulders below. Her eyes were framed by long, dark lashes. She was small for her age and had no color at all in her cheeks.

She didn't smile, either. Just nodded and stepped inside when I held the door open for her. "Sorry I'm early," she said in a voice so soft I could barely hear it.

"Hey, no problem," I told her. "Listen, I'm Claudia, and I'm going to be one of your teach-

37

ers. Your other teacher will be Mary Anne. She'll be here soon."

I took Corrie down to the basement. As it turned out, it was a good thing her mother had dropped her off early. By the time Mary Anne and the other kids arrived, Corrie and I had had a chance to talk, she'd chosen a place for herself at the table, and she knew what the day's art project was. She seemed to need to be sure of things in order to feel comfortable.

And so the lesson began. Mary Anne was afraid it would be a mess, but it wasn't. It was just plain fun.

Gabbie Perkins spent most of the morning experimenting with mixing paints in paper cups. She never made a picture. "Look! Look, Claudee Kishi!" she kept exclaiming. "I just made pink!" Or, "I just made . . . made, um . . . a mess." The mess was a greenish-brown color.

Myriah Perkins worked seriously on a picture of Laura, her baby sister, and Matt worked equally seriously at making inkblots. I showed him how to drop paint on one side of a piece of paper, fold it in half, and wind up with symmetrical designs.

"Butterflies," Matt signed to me. (He

doesn't speak. He signs words with his hands.)

Carolyn and Marilyn spent a lot of the lesson trying to fool Jamie Newton. They kept asking him to guess which one of them was which. They weren't dressed alike, and they have different haircuts, but they still look similar; and anyway, Jamie couldn't keep their rhyming names straight.

"You're . . . you're Marilyn," he'd say as Carolyn asked, for the fourteenth time, "Who am I?" Finally he began calling both of them Very Lynn, which they didn't like.

The twins painted identical pictures of just what you'd expect — a house with four windows, a door, a chimney, a curlicue of smoke rising from the chimney, a strip of blue sky across the top of the paper, and a strip of green grass across the bottom of the paper.

Jamie, who is four, used his paints to give a lesson on colors and shapes to Gabbie, who already knows her colors and shapes. She tried to be patient, though.

"You get a J-plus," Jamie told her when, just to make him keep quiet, Gabbie made a red circle for him.

Corrie laughed for the first time since she'd arrived.

All morning I'd been keeping my eye on Corrie's work. She hadn't spoken to the other children, and had worked silently and thoughtfully. She was creating an imaginary landscape and I knew that her work was good — awfully good — for a nine-year-old. So I told her that.

"You know what?" she confided, almost in a whisper. "I like art. I do. I never told Mommy, but I like it. And I don't like ballet or piano lessons or basketball." Awhile later, she asked me (always waiting for me to come peer over her shoulder, never calling to me), "Do you know where my mommy is right now? Do you know what she's doing?"

I shook my head.

"My daddy? Or Sean?"

"Nope. What are they doing?"

"I don't know. Well, Sean is at his tuba lesson, but I don't know about Mommy and Daddy. . . . I wonder why I'm taking art lessons now, too. . . . But I like my painting. . . . When will Mommy be here? I want her to come back."

It was hard to keep up with Corrie. I looked at my watch. "Class is over in five minutes," I announced.

Corrie smiled.

We cleaned up the table.

Mary Anne walked Jamie and the Perkins girls home. Mr. Arnold arrived for the twins, and Haley Braddock, Matt's older sister, walked over to pick him up. Matt signed "butterfly" to me again with a big grin and waved his paper as he trotted off with Haley.

Corrie and I were left waiting on my front steps. We waited and waited. Corrie looked abandoned, like an orphan.

Mrs. Addison finally arrived half an hour late.

Corrie was the only one who took home a dry painting.

CHAPTER 5

Saturday

Our art classes aren't real baby-sitting jobs, but Claudia and I know full well that we have to write about them in the notebook, don't we, Kristy? So here goes. Today was our second lesson. Claud is so good with the kids and with sensing what they're ready for, art-wise. Last week, she saw what they can and can't do, what they like and dislike, and gave them a chance to experiment in their new class. So today she began a real art project, one the kids will work on for several weeks -- papier-mâché puppets. This should be a messy and fun project.

Sure enough, the day started out as fun. The kids were really excited about making puppets. And, as you can imagine, Claudia is going to let each one make whatever he or she wants -- from Jamie's outer space monster to Carrie's Nancy Drew. So the lesson got off to a great start, but it ended in tragedy. I know that sounds corny, but it's true....

I don't know if what Mary Anne wrote is corny — I'm not good at English-class stuff like that — but it sure was true. Every kid who had been at the lesson the week before was back. And when Mary Anne and I told them about the puppets and how to make them, you should have heard the excitement:

"I'm going to make our Cabbage Patch doll," announced Gabbie.

"But why? We already have one," Myriah pointed out. "Caroline Eunice."

"Well, we should have two." Gabbie paused and then said graciously, "You can have the doll for keeps and I'll take the puppet." (The doll is Myriah's anyway.)

"Okay," agreed her sister. "And I'm going to make a rabbit."

"I'm going to make a witch!" said Marilyn Arnold gleefully.

"A space monster . . . grrr!" growled Jamie.

I had a signing session with Matt to make sure he understood what we were doing, and finally he grinned and signed that he was going to make a baseball player.

The ideas flew — except from Corrie, who merely looked thoughtful.

"Corrie?" I said after awhile. "Do you know what you'd like to make?"

"Nancy Drew," she whispered.

"Really? *Nancy Drew?*" I couldn't help exclaiming. "You like Nancy Drew?"

"Yes!" said Corrie, in the most enthusiastic voice I'd ever heard her use. "You like her, too?"

"Sure," I said. "Nancy Drews are my favorite books."

Corrie beamed. And it was then that both Mary Anne and I realized that some sort of bond was growing between Corrie and me. A bond like the one my friend Stacey used to have with Charlotte Johanssen, a kid our club sits for a lot.

So, with the kids' ideas flowing, Mary Anne

helped me set out bowls of water, strips of newspaper we'd cut up the evening before, a jar of flour, and a big tin for dipping the strips into the papier-mâché once it was made.

Then we handed each child a balloon.

"Baby balloons," Gabbie noted.

"She means they're not blown up," Myriah interpreted for us.

"What are they for?" asked Carolyn Arnold.

"Those balloons — after we blow them up — will be the puppets' heads. Well, the forms for the heads," I said. "Then we'll cover them with papier-mâché, then — "

"Claudia! My Claudia!" called a voice.

It was Mimi. She was standing at the top of the steps to the basement. What was she doing there? She wasn't even supposed to be out of bed.

"Mimi!" I called back. "Don't try to come down the stairs." Where was the rest of my family? I knew Mom was at the grocery store. But what about Dad and Janine? Why weren't they keeping an eye on Mimi?

"Don't come down," I said again, but it was too late. Mimi was already halfway down the stairs, and not even holding onto the banister. Had she simply forgotten how teetery she could be?

45

"Why can't she come down?" asked Myriah.

There was no time to answer her question. Mary Anne was dashing up the staircase to Mimi.

It seemed easier to help her the rest of the way down than to try to turn her around and get her back upstairs. So that's what Mary Anne did in her gentle, understanding way. She led Mimi to the art class.

"Claudia and I are giving art lessons," she said. "The kids are making puppets."

"I'm going to make a . . . grrr . . . monster!" said Jamie.

I took over with Mimi and walked her around the table. "We're making papier-mâché," I told her.

"See," said Mimi, nodding wisely.

Since Mimi seemed okay, and the kids who knew her well — Myriah, Gabbie, and Jamie — liked her a lot, I decided it would be okay to let her stay for the class.

"I'll get you a seat, Mimi," I said, eyeing a lawn chair that was folded up in a corner of the basement.

I was struggling to pull the chair out from between the wall and a bicycle, when I heard Mary Anne scream.

I spun around.

Mimi was slithering to the floor at the foot of the stairs. She had fainted again. Luckily she didn't hit her head or anything. The kids looked on in horror, especially Corrie, who kept glancing from Mimi to me. I think she knew somehow that Mimi and I were very close.

And Jamie cried, "Mimi!" and ran to her.

But Mary Anne caught him in her arms and held him in a bear hug for a few seconds to keep him from going near her.

Everything was happening at once. Mary Anne put Corrie, the oldest of the kids, in charge of Jamie. Then she ran to Mimi's side while I dashed upstairs to find my father. As I reached the top step, I could hear Mary Anne say, "Corrie, can you be my helper and take all the kids over to the other side of the room? Ask Jamie to teach you guys his funny song about the big blue frog. Myriah, you help sign to Matt, or he won't understand."

It was amazing. Every kid followed every direction. I know because they were singing and signing, "I'm in love with a big blue frog," when I came back down to the basement with my father.

I had found him in the garage, cleaning up an oil leak from one of our cars. He'd had no idea that Mimi was out of bed, much less dressed and in the basement.

When I found him, I'd cried, "Dad! Dad!" (In my panic, I think I might even have called him "Daddy" like I used to do when I was little.) "Come quick! Right now! Mimi's in the basement and she fainted again."

Dad jumped up in a flash, leaving the oily rag on the floor of the garage. He took the steps down to the basement two at a time, something I'd never seen him do before. When he knelt by Mimi's side (she was still out cold) he began giving orders.

"Claudia, call the paramedics, then find your sister. Mary Anne, take the children home."

He might have sounded cross, but he wasn't. Not really. Just a little panicky.

Mary Anne wisely led the kids out our back basement steps to our side yard. This turned out to be a good decision for two reasons. One, the children didn't have to step over Mimi. Two, they were so fascinated by climbing the flight of dank cement steps, watching Mary Anne push apart the heavy double doors, and emerging into our yard, that they nearly forgot about Mimi.

For the next half hour or so, two things were

going on at once. Mary Anne was dealing with the children, and I was dealing with Mimi. I'll tell you what was going on with Mimi first.

I did just what Dad had told me to do. I ran to the phone in the kitchen and called the paramedics. I was getting pretty good at that. Then I ran through the house, shouting, "Janine! Janine! JANINE!"

"What?" she called. Her voice came from upstairs. She was probably in her room, working on that computer of hers.

"Come downstairs! Mimi's sick again! The ambulance is on its way!"

Sometimes you can't pry Janine away from her computer with a crowbar, but when I told her about Mimi, she came flying out of her room as fast as Dad had left the oil leak in the garage. Then we raced to Mimi.

When Dad saw us coming he said briskly, "You two stay with her, I'll go wait for the ambulance. I think I'll tell the paramedics to use the stairs Mary Anne and the kids used. It'll be easier."

Janine and I stayed with Mimi. I covered her with a blanket that was folded up on the washing machine, and we held her hands and talked to her, just in case she could hear us.

When the paramedics arrived, they lifted

her gently onto the stretcher and carried her up the stairs. I kept waiting for the stretcher to tilt and Mimi to slide off, but somehow the men kept it level.

Meanwhile, Mary Anne and all the children had walked first to Jamie's house and dropped him off, explaining to his parents what had happened. Then they walked back to our neighborhood, where they took Myriah and Gabbie home. Finally, Mary Anne waited outside her house with the remaining kids. It was about time for them to be picked up, and since Mary Anne was just across the street from us, she knew that the parents (or Haley Braddock) would see the children at her house and not come bother us.

However, the children saw the paramedics carry Mimi around from the back of my house and into the ambulance. Mary Anne was glad Jamie and the Perkins girls were at their houses, because they would have been upset. The Arnold twins and Matt were merely curious. But Corrie began to cry.

Mary Anne put her arm around her. "It's going to be okay," she said.

Corrie cried harder. "Claudia must be very sad," she replied.

And Mary Anne thought again that Corrie

50

seemed to be getting awfully attached to me. She had plenty of time to think about it, too, because it was a good forty-five minutes later, long after the ambulance had left, and Marilyn, Carolyn, and Matt had been picked up, that Mrs. Addison finally arrived.

Mary Anne considered discussing Corrie's and my relationship with me — but not then. Only when things got better. She knew I had plenty to worry about besides Corrie.

CHAPTER 6

Guess who rode to the hospital in the ambulance with Mimi? I did. Dad decided to take the car, and Janine stayed behind so she could tell our mother what had happened as soon as Mom came home. Janine offered to go with Mimi, but I really wanted to and there was no time for arguing.

I've been in an ambulance before. The last time, I was the patient. I had broken my leg badly. But this time, I was just a passenger. Sometimes the paramedics make the passenger ride up front next to the driver. Sometimes you can beg to sit in back with the patient, which is what I did, and again, no one took the time to argue with me.

I sat on a ledge across from two paramedics, Mimi on the stretcher between us. While the attendants took her blood pressure and stuff,

I just kept holding Mimi's hand and talking to her.

About halfway to the hospital, Mimi woke up and realized what was going on. She was so embarrassed that she tried to make up for it by acting like a grand lady.

"Do I not know father?" she said to one of the attendants. "The honorable Mr. . . . Mr. . . . um . . ."

"I — I don't think so," replied the man. He fiddled with the gauge on the blood pressure instrument.

"But sure. Yes. Live Bradford Court years long ago."

"No, ma'am."

"It's okay, Mimi," I said.

"Oh, my Claudia. You here," said Mimi, turning her head.

"Yes, I'm here." I squeezed her hand a little harder.

"Dinner is not ready," Mimi told me distinctly.

"Don't worry about it," I said. "It's only lunchtime."

"And I never have enough money for payment. Car loan."

I almost pointed out that Mimi hadn't owned a car in years, but decided not to. Besides, we'd reached the hospital.

Here we go again, I thought.

Things were pretty much the same. Mimi got another private room and, by later in the afternoon, our entire family was crowded into it.

Mimi was already better because, remembering her last stay in the hospital, the doctors had given her some new blood.

"Vampire!" exclaimed Mimi, and we laughed, mostly because if Mimi could joke, that was the best sign of all that she was feeling better.

I laughed, too, even though I was madder than I'd ever been. Not at Mimi, not at anyone else in my family, but at the doctors and nurses. Want to know why? I'll tell you why.

This is what happened when Mimi was first taken to her room. She had seemed to be okay in the ambulance and rolling through the hallways of the hospital on the way to her room, but as soon as the attendants transferred her onto her hospital bed which, really, they tried to do as gently as possible, Mimi screamed.

"Oh! Oh!" she cried.

Her entire body stiffened with pain. Dad and I were standing on either side of her bed and we each grabbed one of her hands and held on tight.

"Will someone please get her some pain-killers or something?" my father shouted to whomever was in the room.

Everyone scurried out, but no one came back except a nurse's aide, who took off Mimi's dress and put on a hospital gown instead. She didn't even bother to close the door to the room, so I gave her a dirty look and did it myself.

Mimi's pain seemed to have gone away by then, but Dad asked for the painkillers again anyway.

"I'll see what I can do," the woman replied.

But the next people who came in were Mom and Janine, Mom looking very upset.

"Mother!" she cried, and ran to Mimi. She bent over her. "How are you feeling?"

I think Mimi was about to say, "Fine," when suddenly she went into another one of those awful spasms of pain.

Mom burst into tears.

Dad and I each grabbed one of Mimi's hands again (it was all we could do), and I signaled to Janine to take Mom out of the room. The last thing Mimi needed was to see that she'd upset her daughter. I'm not sure she would have noticed, though. When the pain came, she would arch her back and squinch up her face, closing her eyes.

That darn nurse's aide hadn't put Mimi's hospital gown on very well, I soon realized. Each time Mimi arched her back, the gown slipped further and further down her chest until she was half naked. And Janine had forgotten to close the door behind her when she took Mom out. Anyone in the hall could see right into the room, see Mimi arching her back and squinching her eyes and crying out, with her gown around her waist. I tried to remember her other ways. I imagined her fully dressed, jewelry and all, smiling at me from across the kitchen table as we shared special tea.

After three or four more spasms of pain, Mimi suddenly lay quietly on the bed. I fixed her hospital gown and drew the sheet up to her chin while Dad rang the bell for a nurse for the eighty-eighth time.

"Hey, you guys," I called to Mom and Janine in the hallway. "Come on in. And close the door."

My mother and sister reappeared, Mom with a paper cup full of coffee she'd gotten from a vending machine. She looked an awful lot calmer, even though coffee is supposed to make you hyper or something.

Mom set her coffee cup on Mimi's bedside table and peered over at her mother.

Mimi smiled at her. "All better," she said, and we laughed nervously.

She wasn't, of course. She was so weak she could barely move. When she tried to raise herself to a sitting position, she got dizzy and had to lie down. So we raised the bed for her.

But the pain was gone.

It seemed like hours before anyone bothered to do anything for Mimi, but finally doctors and nurses began showing up. Each time they did, I made sure the door to her room was closed. No more public indignity if I could help it. It was bad enough that our family was standing around while the doctors examined Mimi.

Anyway, they finally gave her those pints of blood, and very soon she announced that she was feeling better. "TV?" she suggested. And not long after that, "Dinner?"

By the next day, Sunday, Mimi was even better — physically. But her mind didn't seem to be working too well. She kept talking about her things at home, about giving them away, as she'd given Mallory the bird. Only she was subtler than that now. On Sunday afternoon, she said, "My Claudia, I would like please to move plants to room. You room."

"Plants?"

"My plants."

"Oh, at home?"

"Yes. Put in room."

"I'll remember to water them," I assured her. "I don't have to move them."

"No. Not that. You have them. Put in room."

"Okay, okay."

Later she told Janine she was afraid someone would steal her diamond earrings while she was away in the hospital. She told her to take them out of her jewelry box and put them in Janine's jewelry box. Or preferably on Janine's ears. That night, I moved the plants and Janine took the earrings.

Mom and Dad asked me to stay with Mimi the following afternoon. So I went to the hospital, even though I had to miss an art class before our club meeting. Mimi was not the funny person she'd been when she'd made the vampire joke on Saturday, nor the anxious person she'd been the day before. On Monday she was confused and cranky. She wandered into the nurses' station and complained that the price of kitty litter was going way up. Then, back in her bed (I practically had to drag her to it), she said crossly, "Turn on TV, Claudia."

I was startled. She hadn't said, "My Claudia."

I turned it on.

"Change. Change channel. No good."

It was a rerun of *Wheel of Fortune*, which is her favorite, but I changed it anyway.

Soon her supper arrived. (It seems like hospital patients get supper around four-thirty.)

"Mess!" said Mimi, scanning her tray. "Trash!" She actually threw a container of bright yellow pudding at the wall. (Well, I might have done the same thing. The pudding looked like a cup of melted yellow crayons.)

Luckily, a doctor came in then to do some more tests on Mimi, since they still didn't know what was wrong with her. I didn't even care that he interrupted her dinner. I was glad for the distraction.

I didn't understand Mimi at all. Especially not when, after the doctor left, Mimi seemed to be her sweet self again and told me, "My Claudia, never believe what other people say. About you. Never unless you believe it, too. I love you."

"I love you, too, Mimi," I said, forgetting entirely that just a while ago I'd wanted to take her by her shoulders and shake her for being such a baby and throwing her pudding at the wall.

That night, Corrie called me twice. She didn't really have much to say. I think she just wanted to talk. And I wanted somebody who needed my sympathy, since Mimi didn't seem to want much of mine. When I'd left the hospital that afternoon, I'd said, "Feel better soon," and she hadn't even answered. I don't know why.

But guess what happened on Tuesday — the doctors said Mimi could go home the next day! They couldn't figure out what was wrong and didn't see any reason to keep her in the hospital. I was so excited, I called all my friends with the news. I even called Corrie, who said, "Oh, Claudia! That's great! You must be so happy. I can't wait to see you on Saturday!"

Mom and Dad and Janine and I ate a celebratory dinner that night. Later, as Janine and I were cleaning up the kitchen, Janine suddenly turned to me and gave me a hug. We hardly ever hug.

"What's up?" I asked her, smiling.

"I'm relieved about Mimi. Aren't you?"

"Definitely!"

I went to my room to work on my stop-action painting, and a few minutes later, my phone rang.

It was Mimi!

She sounded fine and we chatted for a long time. I told Mimi how the painting was coming along.

At last she said, "Well, let you go now. Do not want to confuse the Muses."

I had no idea what she meant, so I just said, "See you tomorrow, Mimi."

"Good-bye, my Claudia."

CHAPTER 7

On school days, our family gets up at six-thirty. So I was surprised, on Wednesday morning, to hear voices and people moving around, and to look at my digital clock and see that it read 4:52.

Four fifty-two? What was going on?

I had to go to the bathroom anyway, so I got up. But I never even reached the bathroom. The noise and commotion was coming from my parents' bedroom. I stopped at their door. I know it isn't nice, but I listened to their voices for a few moments. All I could catch were snatches of conversation.

I heard Dad say, ". . . arrangements to make."

Then I heard Mom say (and did she sound as if she were crying?) "I can't believe it." (A pause.) ". . . have to tell the girls."

I drew in a deep breath, knowing something

was very wrong, and knocked on their door.

My father opened it. He was dressed except for his socks, which he was struggling to put on, hopping around on one foot, and at the same time, reaching for his wallet and stuffing it in his pocket.

Behind him, my mother was hurriedly pulling a blouse on over her slip. A pair of stockings and her pocketbook had been tossed on the bed, which was unmade.

Maybe I've made a mistake, I thought. Maybe the clock actually said 9:52 and we were all late for work and school. But no. Mom and Dad's clock now said 4:54.

"Mom? Dad?" I said. "What's going on?"

I realized then that my mother *was* crying. She sank into a chair and opened her arms to me, inviting me to sit in her lap, which I hadn't done in years. But I did it then anyway.

Mom took my hand and said, "Claudia, Mimi died during the night. Just a little while ago."

I think my heart stopped beating then. I really do. I think it missed two beats. When it began working properly again, I felt my stomach turn to ice.

"I don't believe it," I whispered. "She was fine last night."

I felt my father's hand on the back of my head. He stroked my hair. "No, she wasn't," he said, and choked on the words. "She wasn't fine, honey. Not really. She was old and she was sick. I think she just wore out."

All I could do was nod my head.

After that, the morning was pandemonium. The early morning, that is. I had to get out of Mom's lap because she and Dad had to finish dressing and rush to the hospital to do whatever you do there when someone you love dies. But first they had to wake up Janine and tell her, so there were more tears and hugs.

When Mom and Dad finally drove off, Janine and I sat at the kitchen table with cups of tea. We did not use Mimi's special cups. In fact, before our tea, I closed the door to Mimi's room so we wouldn't have to look at her things.

Janine and I had been told that we could stay home from school, so we just sat at the table. After a very long silence, I said, "I talked to Mimi on the phone last night. You know what her last words to me were? I mean, before she said, 'Good-bye, my Claudia'?"

Janine shook her head. "What were they?"

"She said she'd let me go now. She didn't want to confuse the Muses."

Janine smiled. "Were you working on a painting or something?"

I nodded. "The stop-action painting. I was telling Mimi about it."

"Mimi meant to say that she didn't want to *disturb* the Muses."

"I don't get it. What are the Muses?"

"The Muses are, well, they're creative forces. They're spirits or powers that are supposed to inspire artists and musicians and writers. Disturbing the Muses means interrupting a creative person at work. Mimi just got the phrase mixed up."

"Oh." I knew Janine would have an explanation. She always does. But I was really thinking about Mimi. She was the only one in my family who had understood about my art and how *very* important it is to me, and how serious I am about it.

And now she was gone.

Suddenly, I felt alone and abandoned, like Corrie waiting on our front steps for her mother. It's funny to feel abandoned with your own sister sitting across the table from you.

Janine looked at her watch. I looked at mine. Mom and Dad had told us that at seven o'clock we should begin phoning relatives and close friends to tell them what had happened. The

65

funeral would be on Saturday, in just three days, and there was a lot to do before then.

So at seven, Janine took over the phone in the kitchen to call our relatives, and I went upstairs to my own phone to call my friends. I knew that if I called just the families of the Baby-sitters Club members, word would travel fast (it always does in a small town), and soon anyone else who should hear the news, like the Newtons, would hear it.

I sat on my bed with my back to the windowsill so I wouldn't have to look at Mimi's plants.

I called Mary Anne first. That was going to be the hardest of the calls because Mary Anne had been almost as close to Mimi as I'd been. Growing up without a mother, she had come to Mimi with skinned knees or for advice or to learn a new knitting stitch.

"Mary Anne?" I said when she picked up the phone, sounding not quite awake. It was 7:03.

"Claud?" she replied. "Is anything wrong?" (Mary Anne has emotional antennae.)

"Mimi died last night." I had to say it that way. I couldn't hedge with Mary Anne. "She died in the hospital. Mom and Dad are over there now," (my voice broke), "getting her things and — and — "

Mary Anne was already crying, so I didn't see any reason to keep talking.

"I'm sorry, Claud," she said, between sobs.

I began to cry again, too. "So am I. I know how close you were."

When Mary Anne calmed down a little, she offered to call the other members of the club for me, which was very nice of her. I let her call Dawn (so Dawn could console Mary Anne) and Jessi and Mal. But I wanted to call Kristy and Stacey myself.

I called Stacey first. Stacey hadn't been close to Mimi at all, but she'd known her and liked her, and besides, Stacey was my best friend. I *had* to call her.

Stacey was getting ready to leave for school when the phone rang in her New York apartment. She was supposed to be out the door twenty minutes from when I was calling. But she stopped and talked anyway. She knew, as soon as she heard my voice at that hour on a weekday, that something was wrong.

"Mimi died early this morning," I told her flatly. Each time I said that, the words came a little more easily — but they didn't seem any

67

more real. I was calling people, telling them Mimi was dead, and not believing it myself.

Maybe that was because I suddenly realized that I didn't know what "dead" meant. Oh, sure, I understood that it meant not breathing or thinking or moving or feeling; the opposite of alive. But what did it *really* mean?

Stacey was comforting at first, and then began asking questions. "When is the funeral? What time? Which church?" She and her parents were going to come, of course, she said, before we got off the phone.

The call to Kristy was easier than the others had been. Kristy is not a crier. She'd known Mimi for as long as Mary Anne and I had, since the three of us had grown up together (at least before Kristy moved), and she loved Mimi, but she wasn't as close to her as Mary Anne and I had been. I guess she hadn't needed her quite as much as we had. Besides, she has Nannie, her own wonderful grandmother.

Still, Kristy was shocked, and after all the "I'm sorry's" and "What can I do's?" she said, "Our club meeting this afternoon is canceled, of course. I'll tell the rest of the members in school today."

"Oh, no! Please," I said hurriedly. "Don't

cancel it. I want to see you guys tonight. Don't stay away from me. I need you. I mean," I babbled on, "even if we don't conduct an official meeting, please let's just all be together. Mom and Dad won't mind. I don't think. We'll stay up in my room."

"Wow, okay," said Kristy, sounding breathless, even though I had just done all the talking. "I didn't mean for you to think we'd, you know, shut you out. We wouldn't do that. I just figured today would be sort of a private one for your family. But if you want us there, we'll be there."

I felt a little better by the time we hung up.

But not much. Before I left my bedroom I took this framed portrait of Mimi that I had once painted down from the wall and slid it under my bed. Then I decided I didn't want Mimi under my bed, so I put her in my closet. But I didn't want her in my closet, either, so I moved her to the attic and left her there.

Kristy had said she thought that day would be a private one for us. She couldn't have been more wrong. Word about Mimi's death spread fast (as I'd thought it would), and people began coming over to our house around eleven o'clock. And everyone who dropped by

69

brought food. Why? Because Mimi had been the cook in our family? That didn't make sense. The rest of us could cook, too. Anyway, our relatives came (with food) and helped Mom and Dad make funeral arrangements and write Mimi's obituary. Our neighbors and friends dropped by to console us.

It was the longest day of my life. If I hadn't believed it before, I became more and more certain, each time the doorbell rang, that Mimi really and truly had died. (Whatever that meant.)

I wished everyone would go away and leave us alone and let me think that a big mistake had been made.

But at five-thirty, my parents left to meet with our minister, all the visitors left, too, and my friends came over. We held a strange meeting. For one thing, Janine sat in on it because she didn't want to be alone. For another thing, it wasn't really a meeting. Kristy didn't conduct business. She didn't wear her visor. She didn't even sit in the director's chair. And no one called because all our clients knew what had happened and figured we wouldn't be holding a meeting. They didn't want to intrude, anyway. So the seven of us sat on the floor. We barely spoke because no one seemed to know what to say after, "I'm sorry," and, "We'll really miss her."

But we were together.

Even so, the longer we sat there, the guiltier I felt. I couldn't help remembering the times I'd lost my temper, wished to be at an art class instead of at the hospital — and especially the time I'd thrown the magazines on Mimi's bed.

I was a horrible person and I knew it, even if no one else did.

CHAPTER 8

Friday

I was surprised that we held our regular club meeting today, but I was glad, too. I was glad because it gave me a chance to see that you really seem okay, Claudia. In fact, you act almost like nothing happened. And that seems fine to me. I'm happy to see you get back to normal so quickly. I was also surprised to hear that you and Mary Ann will be holding your Saturday art class on Sunday, the day after Mimi's funeral, but, hey -- great. Maybe the best thing to do is just jump right back into your routine.

The reason this notebook entry is not about a baby-sitting job is because there hasn't been much to write about the last couple of days.

No one has called us. I think they're being polite and waiting until after the funeral.

Claud, I'm glad you're feeling so much better. If you hadn't been, Friday night might never have happened, and it was such a great night that I wouldn't have missed it for the world....

Despite what Kristy wrote in the notebook, I know she felt a little funny holding a club meeting on Friday, the day before Mimi's funeral, but I really wanted to. Janine and I weren't going back to school until Monday because there was too much to do at home. And with everything all out of order like that, I at *least* wanted to hold regular club meetings, and Mom and Dad had given their permission. I didn't like special attention. I wanted my life to go on as usual, or, as Kristy said, as if nothing had happened. That was pretty difficult when I wasn't going to school, so if we'd stopped our club meetings, I don't know what I'd have done.

Kristy was right. Our Friday meeting was quiet, like the one on Wednesday. No one called. Plus, us club members didn't seem to

73

know what to talk about at first. Finally, Kristy started talking about food fights and bras, trying to make us laugh (Janine was *not* at that meeting), and that worked for awhile.

At ten minutes of six, Mary Anne stood up. "Come on," she said. "I'm starved. There's no point in sitting around here. Let's go to my house now and order the pizzas."

Mary Anne had invited the club members to her house for a pizza dinner, since her dad and Dawn's mom were going out on a *date*, and she had already invited Dawn over to keep her company. Besides, Mary Anne thought I might *need* a pizza supper with my friends on the night before Mimi's funeral. (I think Mary Anne needed it, too. She'd been pretty teary lately. In fact, she seemed even more upset than I did. I hadn't cried since Wednesday morning.)

So the six of us left my house and walked across the street to Mary Anne's dark, empty one. She turned on the porch light, unlocked the front door, turned on the inside hall light, and was greeted by Tigger, her kitten.

Kristy told me later that she thought it must be really lonely sometimes to be Mary Anne. Was it possible, I wondered, that Mary Anne would miss Mimi even more than I would?

"Hiya, Tiggy. Hi there, Mousekin." (Mousekin is also Tigger. Mary Anne has about a zillion nicknames for him.) She picked Tigger up and nuzzled him under her chin. "I bet you're hungry, aren't you? Well, so are we. Kristy, why don't you order the pizzas while I feed Tigger?"

We had to have a very long conversation about what kinds of pizzas to get since we can all be picky about some foods. Dawn wouldn't eat anything but plain or with vegetables like green peppers. No one else likes green peppers. I wanted a pizza with everything, but Jessi gagged at the thought of anchovies. Mary Anne didn't want sausage. We did finally order two pizzas, though, and when they arrived, they were actually hot. (Pizza Express isn't always as express as they advertise.)

We crowded around the Spiers' kitchen table with the open boxes of pizzas in the middle and started grabbing slices, the cheese stringing out from each slice, still attached to the pies. We didn't bother with plates. A pile of napkins was good enough for us.

In the middle of a big bite of pizza, Kristy began to laugh.

"What?" said the rest of us.

Kristy managed to swallow before she answered. "Remember the time Mimi tasted her first pizza?"

No one seemed aghast that Kristy had brought up the subject of Mimi. In fact, it seemed sort of appropriate, especially since this was a particularly good story.

"*I* do!" I cried. "That was so funny."

"Let's tell Mimi stories!" exclaimed Kristy.

"Okay," my friends and I agreed.

"What about the pizza?" asked Mallory.

I looked at Kristy. "You tell," I said. "You were there."

"Okay," she replied. "Well, it was Claudia's eighth birthday, and Mimi's present to her was going to be a meal at a real Japanese restaurant in Stamford. She wanted to take Claudia, her family, and Mary Anne and me. Mary Anne and I were *so excited*. We'd never had Japanese food before. We'd barely even been in a fancy restaurant. So we got all dressed up in, like, birthday party clothes — so did you, Claud — and everyone *else* was dressed up, and *Mimi* was wearing an actual Japanese outfit — "

"Authentic," I said importantly.

"You know, the kimono and the sandals and everything."

76

"We were fascinated," Mary Anne added.

"So," Kristy continued, "we drive all the way to Stamford and the restaurant is *closed*. No one can believe it. So we begin driving around looking for other places to eat."

"Oh, and remember," said Mary Anne, "we passed a Howard Johnson's and Mr. Kishi said we could go in there to eat because he knew the manager personally, and I thought he meant he knew *Howard Johnson*. I was so impressed."

Everyone giggled at that.

"Well," said Kristy, "we couldn't find a place where Claud and Mary Anne and I wanted to eat. I mean, they were all, like, French places with these frou-frou names, and it *was* Claud's birthday, so when she finally said she wanted pizza, Mr. Kishi stopped at the first pizza place he saw. It was kind of sleazy — dark, with a lot of high school kids being loud — and a miniature juke box playing at every booth. But we went in anyway."

"And everyone stared," I said, "because Mimi looked like she was on her way to a costume party, but we ordered two pies anyway, and Mimi ate one slice very bravely."

"*And*," said Kristy, "as we were finally leaving that awful place where everyone had been

77

staring at us, Mimi turned around, faced the people in the restaurant, and announced, "Best Japanese food I have ever eaten!"

Us club members were hysterical. Jessi even dropped a whole slice of pizza on the floor.

"Tell everyone about Russ and Peaches," Mary Anne suddenly said to me.

"Russ and Peaches?" repeated Dawn.

"My aunt and uncle," I replied.

"Mimi had a son and she named him *Russ?*" said Dawn incredulously. "That just sounds so . . . unconventional. I mean, for Mimi. . . . Russ."

"Well, his real name is Russell," I told her, "but he isn't Mimi's son. And he's American. I mean, *American* American."

"So you're saying Mimi named your mother's sister *Peaches?*" squeaked Mallory. "That's even wor — even more unconventional."

"Oh, no," I said quickly. "My aunt has a Japanese name, but Russ started calling her Peaches and she just called him Russ, so everyone else calls them Russ and Peaches, too. Janine and I never even call them 'Aunt' and 'Uncle.' "

"I remember them," said Kristy.

"Yeah, they used to live in Stoneybrook, right?" added Mary Anne.

I nodded. "Until I was about seven. You'll see them at the, um — the funeral tomorrow."

"They were really wild," said Kristy. "It's hard to believe Peaches is Mimi's daughter."

"It's even harder to believe she married Russ," I said. "Remember the time we had that *huge* storm?" I said to Kristy and Mary Anne. "It was practically a hurricane. It closed school, and Stoneybrook didn't have any electricity for two days, and all the phone lines were down."

"Yeah. We were in, what? First grade?" asked Kristy.

"I think so," I replied. "Anyway, Russ wanted to make sure Mimi and our family were okay, only he couldn't drive to our house because trees were down everywhere, and he couldn't walk because he'd broken his ankle in a shelving accident. (Don't ask.) So he rode over in a *golf cart!*"

Everyone burst out laughing.

"I remember another time," I said, "when Mimi could still drive, and she was on her way to the grocery store and an ambulance pulled out in front of her, and suddenly Mimi decided she was going to be an ambulance chaser. So she puts on the speed and follows the ambulance, and where do you think it goes?"

"Where?" asked my friends.

"To Russ and Peaches' house! Peaches had fallen down the stairs. Mimi never chased another ambulance."

More giggling.

"I also remember when we realized that Mimi couldn't be allowed to drive anymore," I went on. "It wasn't so long ago. She was pulling up to an intersection and she slowed down, peered at the stoplight, glanced at Mom, and said, 'Honey, tell me. That light — is it red or is it green?' "

"Tell about the chicken dinner!" Mallory suddenly cried. "I like *that* story."

"Oh, yeah," I said slowly, remembering. "We were having a dinner party — Mal's parents were there — and all the guests were seated in the dining room and Dad very proudly carries in this platter with a beautiful roast chicken on it. But he trips and the chicken slides off the platter and falls on the floor. Mom is turning beet-red, but you know what Mimi does? She just says very calmly, 'That is all right. Bring in other chicken, son.' Well, of course there was no other chicken, but Dad got the message. He scooped the spilled chicken back onto the platter, took it into the kitchen, fixed it up, and returned it to the dining room."

"Mimi saved the day!" said Jessi, grinning.

The phone rang then and Mary Anne answered. She listened for a moment, said, "Okay, just a sec," then cupped her hand over the receiver and whispered, "Claud, it's for you. It's Corrie. She called your house first and found out you were here."

I nodded. When I took the phone from Mary Anne, I said cheerfully to Corrie, "Hi, kid. How are you doing?"

"Fine," said Corrie, not sounding fine at all. "I miss you."

"I miss you, too. But I'll see you on Sunday. Remember? We'll be having our art class on Sunday this weekend instead of Saturday."

"I remember."

"What are you doing?"

"Staying away from our baby-sitter. Mommy and Daddy are at a party. They got this old lady to come over because they didn't want to bother you. I don't like the lady. Neither does Sean. She smells funny."

"Tell her you're tired and that you're going

to bed," I suggested. "Then you can just play in your room. That's what I used to do when I didn't like my baby-sitters."

"Oh, good idea!"

Corrie and I got off the phone, and soon us sitters had to go home. Kristy told me several days later that, as we were leaving, she could feel our spirits sinking. We'd had fun telling Mimi stories. We'd remembered her the way she would have wanted to be remembered. But the next day would be the funeral, and it would not be happy or funny.

How, Kristy wondered, how on *earth* would we get through Mimi's funeral?

I was wondering the same thing.

CHAPTER 9

Saturday

I am writing in my New York branch of the Baby-Sitters Club notebook. (I keep a notebook even though I'm the only one in the club.) I didn't do any sitting today, that's for sure, but I felt that the day should be recorded somehow, and my baby-sitting notebook seemed like a good place to record in, since if it hadn't been for sitting, I probably wouldn't have gotten to know Mimi as well as I did.

Today was Mimi's funeral. It was a very sad, difficult day. I'm sure there are some better, bigger words to describe how Claudia was feeling, but I can't think of any. Just sad, bad, low, etc.

Anyway, the day started when Mom and I left for Stoneybrook this morning.

Stacey and her mother decided to drive to Stoneybrook instead of taking the train. That way, they wouldn't need anyone to pick them up at the train station, and they could go back whenever they wanted. Also, Mr. McGill likes to drive. Only he decided, at the very last minute, not to come to the funeral. I was a little hurt when I saw just Stacey and her mom get out of the car, but then I thought, Well, Mr. McGill hadn't known Mimi very well. It wasn't until later that Stacey told me, pretty reluctantly, that she'd heard her parents arguing the night before. She thought maybe they needed a day apart from each other. Besides, her mother has always liked Stoneybrook better than her father did. He's happier in the city.

Stacey said the ride to Connecticut was pretty quiet. She had a feeling her mother was thinking about her father. And Stacey was thinking about me. Plus, they were both sad about Mimi, of course.

The McGills arrived at the cemetery right on time. Mimi's burial was to be held before the funeral service, so the McGills just joined the long line of cars that were driving slowly through the cemetery and parking by the side of the road. I watched Stacey and her mother climb out and stretch their legs.

All I wanted to do then was run to Stacey and hug her, but a funny thing had happened that morning.

Our family had woken up formal.

We began the day formally, Janine and I following all sorts of somber instructions from our parents, and we spent the rest of the morning being formal.

When Stacey arrived, her first sight was of the plot where Mimi was to be buried. The casket was sitting next to the open grave, and Mom and Dad, Janine and I, Russ and Peaches, and a few other family members were standing nearest to the casket. Friends and neighbors were behind us. I turned my head and saw Stacey, and we looked at each other.

But I could not run to her, and she could not come to me.

She and her mother joined Kristy, her mother, and her older brothers Sam and Charlie, at the back of the crowd.

The burial service began. It was quite short, but Stacey remembers much more about it than I do. All I remember is thinking, as the casket was being lowered into the ground, Mimi's not in there. So I didn't cry. A bunch of men were just putting a box in the ground. That was all. Then Mom made me throw a white rose into the hole. I thought, What's the point? Mimi won't see it. But I did it anyway (since we were being formal).

Stacey remembers more. She remembers the minister saying some words about Mimi and then saying a blessing over the casket. And she remembers that the graveyard was silent, except for the minister, because no one was ready to cry yet. A burial is just too separate from the memory of the dead person.

It is surreal.

Stacey remembers the rest of the service and then everyone slowly walking back to their cars and driving to the church for the funeral.

I don't remember any of that. It is a blank for me. I dropped the silly flower in the hole — and then suddenly I was in the church, in the front pew with my family.

The thing I learned about death that day is that if it's *your* relative, *you* always get to be in front. Maybe that's to help you feel closer to the dead person.

Stacey also remembers the funeral service better than I do. My mom gave the eulogy, and she referred to Mimi as either "Mother" or "Mimi" throughout the whole talk, which was nice because almost everybody knew her simply as Mimi. Everyone who was at the funeral, I mean, and according to Stacey an awful lot of people were there: all the members of the Baby-sitters Club, even Logan (but not Shannon; she didn't know Mimi), and most of their parents. Then there were people like the Newtons and the Perkinses and our next-door neighbors, the Goldmans, and of course all the rest of our relatives. (You could tell how closely related they were to Mimi by how near the front of the church they got to sit.)

Stacey said that not many kids came to the funeral, and I think that's okay. Little children probably wouldn't understand what was going on, and there's plenty of time for them to learn about death when they're older.

Later I wondered who had baby-sat for all those kids. Probably smelly old ladies. I guess we're not the only baby-sitters in Stoneybrook.

Stacey and her mom sat in a pew sort of in the middle of the church. Also in their pew were Mary Anne and her father, Dawn and her mother, Kristy and her mother, and Sam and Charlie. (Watson didn't come because he had barely known Mimi, so he stayed at home and helped Kristy's grandmother watch the little kids.) In the pew in front of Stacey were

Mallory and her parents and Jessi and her parents. Stacey said that, much as she thought the girls in the club needed comfort then, they suddenly found that they could hardly even look at each other. Stacey was seated right next to Mary Anne, who started to cry buckets as soon as my mother began the eulogy, but she didn't reach for Mary Anne's hand and Mary Anne didn't reach for hers — or for her father's. She just cried silently and kept pulling dry tissues out of her purse and dropping wet ones back into it.

Stacey didn't cry. She said she felt like a stone.

That was a very good description. It was exactly how I felt.

And *that* made me feel guilty on top of everything else. All around me, my relatives were crying. Next to me, Janine, who was wearing Mimi's diamond earrings, was sniffling. On the other side of me, my dad even started to cry and then I almost panicked. I'd never seen him cry before. (What do you do when your father cries?) Even my mother cried a little while she was speaking.

I felt like I just didn't have any tears in me, but that I owed it to Mimi to cry, so I thought about how I had thrown the magazines on her bed, which did bring a few tears of shame to my eyes. I dabbed at them with a Kleenex and hoped that if Mimi could see me from somewhere, she would notice me crying, but not know *why* I was crying. Then I began to wonder if she'd want me to be sad in the first place. It was too confusing.

I didn't pay a bit of attention to any of the service. When it was over, I just stood up and filed into an anteroom, following in Janine's formal footsteps.

In the anteroom, our family formed a line and greeted the other mourners. At last Stacey and I could be together — for a few seconds. We hugged, and Stacey said, "See you at your house later."

There was going to be a reception at our house in about an hour, in just enough time for Mom and Dad, Russ and Peaches, Janine and me to finish greeting people, rush home, and set out all the food everyone had been bringing by since Wednesday. I couldn't wait. I was hoping the formality would wear off during the reception and I could be with my friends.

The formality did wear off. Mom and Dad

let us club members go in the den with a platter of food and talk by ourselves. Logan came, too.

But talk? At first no one knew what to say. Stacey told me weeks and weeks later that it was because everything had already been said. At first it had been, "I'm sorry," and, "Oh, how terrible," and, "Poor Claudia. You must feel so awful." Then we had told our Mimi stories. What else was left to say on the subject? Was it okay *not* to talk about Mimi? Was it okay to tell Stacey about school or for Mary Anne to talk about Tigger?

Tentatively, we tried it on, like a dress we weren't sure we wanted to buy. It seemed to fit okay. So we sat in the den with our food, and Mallory said that the weekend before, one of the triplets had secretly stuck a target on the back of Claire's T-shirt and gleefully spent Saturday shooting things at her. We laughed.

Then I said, "Hey, Stace, Dorrie Wallingford is going out with a freshman in *high school!*"

"No!" cried Stacey, with a gasp.

"Well, I'm leaving," said Logan, who always leaves when we start talking about boy-girl things.

Slowly the other club members left, too. They couldn't stay all afternoon. But Stacey was the last to leave. Her mom very nicely let the two of us have a long visit.

"I put Mimi's portrait in the attic," I confessed to Stacey.

"That's okay," she assured me. "Maybe you'll take it out again someday."

"It was like she was watching me or something."

Stacey nodded, but I don't know if she really understood what I meant.

I didn't dwell on that, though. Mrs. McGill came into the den then and said that they really did have to start home.

So Stacey and I hugged and hugged, but when she left, we found that we could not say good-bye.

CHAPTER 10

Back to school.

Usually I hate going back to school after a weekend or a vacation or even after I've been out sick for a few days. But this time I practically couldn't wait to get there. I was tired of people dropping by our house and not knowing what to say about Mimi. I was tired of flowers and sympathy cards. And I thought that if I saw one more pound cake I would barf. I, the junk food addict, had had enough cake and cookies for the first time ever.

All I wanted was something normal — a day like last Tuesday when Mimi was still alive, which was less than a week ago. I wanted to walk to Stoneybrook Middle School with Mary Anne, open the side door, which we sometimes use because it's close to my locker, saunter through the halls, look for the other club members or maybe for Dorrie Wallingford or

Ashley Wyeth or some other friend, and hope that a boy would notice my outfit and smile at me.

That was not exactly what happened.

Mary Anne and I reached school and we separated because she needed to go talk to her English teacher. So I walked to my locker alone. Then, since the first bell wasn't going to ring for about ten more minutes, I sort of toured the halls. I was itching for friends, gossip, boys, anything normal. But something weird was going on.

No one would talk to me. No one would even look at me.

I saw Dorrie down a hall on the second floor and waved to her. She turned and walked in the other direction, pretending she hadn't seen me. I *know* she was pretending. It was obvious.

Then I practically bumped into Ashley Wyeth.

"Hi!" I cried.

Now, I know Ashley's mind is usually on another planet, but I can always bring her back to earth for a conversation.

Not this time.

All she did was sort of mumble, "Oh, hi," and walk away.

She didn't say, "It's good to have you back," or, "I'm sorry about your grandmother," or even just, "I missed you."

I didn't want a lot of sympathy about Mimi. Frankly, I wanted to forget the past five days and the fact that she was dead. But Ashley could have said *some*thing . . . couldn't she? Even, "Here's all the homework you missed," would have been better than, "Oh, hi," and walking away.

But Ashley wasn't the only one who did things like that. It went on all morning with the kids I hadn't seen since Tuesday.

I couldn't wait for lunch, which the older members of the BSC always eat together. If nothing else, they would talk to me.

"What is going *on?*" I exploded as soon as we were settled at our usual table. I told them about Dorrie and Ashley and the morning. "In the halls, people look away from me," I added. "They look at the floor, the walls, their books, everywhere but at me. It's like I'm a leper. Wait a sec. . . . Did my nose fall off or something?" I put my hand up to my face and felt around for it. "Nope. Couldn't be that. My nose is still there."

We giggled. Then Dawn said, "Maybe the kids just don't know what to say. They *do* know how close you and Mimi were. It's almost as if one of your parents had died. Maybe they think *anything* they say won't be enough. Or that it will sound stupid."

"Maybe they think you'll get too much attention," spoke up Kristy. "You know, your teachers will say, 'Take your time making up your work,' and stuff like that."

But it was Mary Anne who said quietly, "Maybe they're afraid something like this will happen to *them* now. They see that people you love *do* die."

We grew silent, thinking about that. Finally, Logan broke the ice by saying, "Well, Claudia's not catching!"

I might as well have been, though. The rest of the week wasn't much better than Monday had been, although by Friday, some kids would at least *look* at me. Maybe in a way, this new problem was good. I know that sounds funny, but it was something to help keep my mind off Mimi. And I was looking for any distraction I could find. I concentrated on my art — my stop-action painting — and babysitting and even my schoolwork. Often, I did my homework without being told. I don't think I did it very well, but at least I did it — usually. When I couldn't concentrate, I painted or called Stacey or thought about Corrie or about how weird the kids at school were being.

Sometimes I forgot that Mimi was dead. Like, one morning, I woke up to the smell of coffee and thought, Mimi's already in the kitchen. And one afternoon I was in a card store and suddenly thought, almost in a panic, Mimi's birthday is only a week away and I don't have a card or a present for her. Each time, the awful truth would then blaze its way back into my brain.

Other times, I wouldn't be thinking about Mimi at all, and her memory would come crashing back to me. Those times were the most inconvenient, because I wanted to forget, not remember. Once, I was listening to the radio, and a song was playing and there was a line in it about a gentle person or a gentle life or something like that, and it brought Mimi to mind right away.

I only let myself cry for a couple of minutes, though.

Boy, was I glad when Saturday rolled around. I'm always glad to see the weekend, but now Saturday also meant the art class and Corrie and all the other kids. Mary Anne and Corrie usually arrived early and around the same time, so I would let Corrie help Mary Anne and me set things up for the lesson. We were still working on the papier-mâché puppets.

That morning, Corrie arrived before Mary Anne did.

"Hi, Claudia," she greeted me at the door. I always get the feeling that Corrie is more excited than she sounds. Like she's holding back, afraid to let people see how she's really feeling. I wondered what Corrie thought would happen if she let go a little bit.

"Hiya!" I said, giving her a quick hug.

"How are you feeling?" asked Corrie. She had been very concerned ever since Mimi died.

"I'm fine. I really am," I replied, even though I wasn't. But I didn't feel like talking about Mimi. I just wanted to work on the puppets.

Corrie looked relieved.

Mary Anne showed up then, so the three of us set out the partly finished puppets, the paint, the papier-mâché, and the odds and ends and scraps. The kids were at all stages with their puppets, some still applying layers of papier-mâché, other beginning to paint on faces.

The rest of the kids trickled in and soon we were hard at work.

"You know what it's time for you to do today?" I said to Jamie.

"What?"

"Pop your balloon." (Once the papier-mâché is dry, you stick a pin in the bottom of the balloon, then pull the balloon out through what will be the neck of the puppet.)

"Oh! Oh, goody!" For some reason, popping the balloons seemed to be everybody's favorite part of the project.

Marilyn had been the first and she had actually squealed with happiness.

Mary Anne had grinned at me after that class. "You'd have thought Marilyn had died and gone to . . ." She'd trailed off, blushing. "Sorry," she'd mumbled.

Now Jamie popped his balloon with great glee.

"Okay, you're ready to paint your puppet's head," I told him. "But be careful. Remember that papier-mâché is fragile. Your puppet's head is hollow."

Jamie nodded solemnly.

"What color are you going to paint him?" asked Gabbie, who had painted the face of her

Cabbage Patch doll a pale shade of blue.

"Green, what else?" replied Jamie.

"How are you doing, Corrie?" I asked, as Mary Anne and I walked slowly around the table, checking on things.

"Fine, thank you," she replied politely. She held up Nancy Drew. "See?" She was working slowly and carefully. She'd even brought along two Nancy Drew books so she could use pictures of her heroine as models.

I don't like making comparisons between kids, and any comparison between Corrie and this group would have been unfair since Corrie was the oldest student, but I have to say that Corrie's puppet was far and away the best one in the class. It was better than most nine-year-olds would have made.

"It's better than I could do," Mary Anne whispered to me.

When class was over, the materials put away, the puppets propped up to dry, and the children — except for Corrie — gone, she and I sat out on our front steps and waited for her mother. We weren't talking, and I caught Corrie smiling a private smile.

I tickled her and she giggled.

"What was making you smile?" I asked her.

"My puppet," she replied. "I love it. I am going to give it to my mother. Not for any special occasion. Just to please her. I know it will please her."

And Corrie smiled happily again.

CHAPTER 11

Kristy's visor was on. Her pencil was over her ear. She was sitting ramrod straight in my director's chair.

You guessed it. Time for another club meeting.

"Order, please," said Kristy, and the rest of us settled down.

It was a Wednesday, so there were no dues to collect.

"Any club business?" asked Kristy.

"I move that I find my bag of Cheetos," I said, and everyone giggled.

I was pretty sure it was under my bed, so I lay down on the floor and began searching around among shoe boxes and things. I remembered hiding Mimi's portrait under there temporarily, but put the thought out of my head right away. I was getting pretty good at that lately, even though I seemed to feel more tired than I'd ever felt in my life.

Maybe I was coming down with the flu. Or leprosy.

"Here they are!" I said, emerging triumphantly with the bag.

"That's club business?" asked Kristy.

"It is when we're all starving," I told her.

Luckily for me, the phone rang then.

We lined up one job, the phone rang a second time, and we lined up another job.

The meeting hit a lull, so I asked Kristy, "How's Emily?"

Kristy looked rapturous, like a woman with her newborn baby. "Oh, she's *wonderful!*" she exclaimed. "She's learning to speak so *fast*. Of course, we're all teaching her, so she's got nine teachers. Even Andrew goes around the house with her, pointing to things, and saying, '*Book*, Emily. Say *book*.' or 'Pen. This is a *pen*, Emily.' I'm not sure how much Vietnamese she could speak, but she's sure learning English fast. Guess what her favorite word is?"

"What?" asked Mallory.

"Cookie," replied Kristy. "And she usually gets one when she says it."

"I hope you're not going to spoil her," said Dawn.

"We're trying not to. Anyway, I don't think

Nannie will let us. I am *so* glad she moved in instead of some housekeeper. At first, I thought a housekeeper would be good. I thought she would make my bed for me and stuff, but we all decided it would be a little weird having a stranger live in our house. Besides, Nannie was tired of living alone, and I don't blame her. She's too vivacious. She needs people around her. So the arrangement works out perfectly. We cleared out the room we would have given the housekeeper, gave it to Nannie instead, she moved her things in, and now Nannie takes care of Emily while Mom and Watson are at work, and the rest of us are at school. After school, us kids are on our own as usual, because Nannie has a million and one things to do: bowling practice, visiting friends, you know."

"It's so funny to see the Pink Clinker parked in Watson's driveway," spoke up Mary Anne.

"I know." (The Pink Clinker is Kristy's grandmother's old car. She really did have it painted pink, and it really does clink around a lot when she drives it, but it seems to be in good shape.)

Kristy knows her grandmother as well as I knew Mimi, although I'm not sure they're as close. Nannie's husband has been dead for quite awhile, and Kristy hardly ever sees her father's parents. (I don't know what she thinks of Watson's parents.)

"Hey," said Mallory suddenly, "Mary Anne, what's going on with your father and Dawn's mother?"

I thought Mal was being a little nosy (even though I was dying to know myself), but Mary Anne and Dawn just looked at each other and grinned.

"Mom is not seeing the Trip-Man as often," Dawn replied gleefully. (Mrs. Schafer has been dating this man nicknamed Trip, whom Dawn can't stand and calls the Trip-Man.)

"And Dad doesn't see anyone but Mrs. Schafer," said Mary Anne with a grin.

"I don't get it, though," said Dawn, frowning suddenly. "Our parents are perfect for each other. Mary Anne and I have always thought so. So why don't they just get married?"

"I guess it isn't that easy," pointed out Kristy. "Look at how long Mom held off before she agreed to marry Watson. She didn't want to make another mistake. She'd already had one bad marriage."

"*Dad* didn't," said Mary Anne.

"But my mom did," said Dawn. "Maybe it's better that they're waiting."

Just then the phone rang and Corrie's mother called. Mallory arranged a sitting job for me and then asked, "How is Corrie these days?"

I'd written a lot about her in the notebook, so the other girls (I mean, besides Mary Anne) were aware of Corrie and her problems.

"You know, I actually think she's a little better," I replied. "Don't you think so, Mary Anne?"

Mary Anne nodded.

"She still doesn't say much, but I almost take it as a good sign that she seems so attached to me. At least she feels comfortable with *some*body. When we first met, she hardly spoke to anyone at all."

"She barely said two words to me the couple of times I sat for her and Sean," said Dawn. "I'm glad she feels she can talk to you."

I nodded. "It was like something just clicked between us. You know how that happens sometimes? There are people you've known a long time and you know you're never really going to like. And there are people that you meet and *grow* to like. Then there are people you meet and you like instantly. Click! That's pretty much the way it was with Corrie and me."

Mary Anne nodded. "You're right. And it *is* good for her. I mean, to see that it's okay to get close to people, that they're not all going to treat her as casually as her mother does. I just hope she doesn't get too attached to you, Claud."

"If she does, you'll handle it," spoke up Dawn. "Remember when Buddy Barrett got so attached to me? I talked to his mother and everything worked out eventually."

"I hardly ever even *see* Mrs. Addison. She drops Corrie off and picks her up so fast she's just a big blur," I joked.

Dawn smiled.

And Kristy said, "Anyway, we usually do seem to solve our sitting problems. And when we don't, the kids do it themselves. Think of the times *they've* come through. Charlotte Johanssen was pretty attached to Stacey, but when Stacey moved, Charlotte handled it."

"Boy," said Jessi, "I've got a problem I wish *I* could handle. I've heard there are going to be auditions for the ballet *Swan Lake* at the Civic Center — "

"Are you going to try out?" squealed Mal, before Jessi could finish.

"Well, that's the thing. Even if the auditions are open to the public — "

"You're not the public," Mallory interrupted again. "You go to a fancy dance school in Stamford. Stoneybrook's Civic Center — "

" — is pretty important," said Jessi, interrupting Mal this time.

(The rest of us were turning our heads from right to left, left to right, as they spoke.)

"In fact, the productions at the Civic Center," Jessi went on, "are practically off-off-Broadway. Anyway, even if I were allowed to audition, would I really want to? And would my parents let me?"

"Why wouldn't you want to?" I asked.

"Because I'd be competing with professional dancers. Or near-professional dancers, anyway," Jessi replied.

"Don't *you* want to be professional one day?" Mal asked.

"Ye-es . . ."

"Then I think you ought to start competing," I interrupted. "Mimi always said — well, she didn't exactly say it this way, but she said something that meant, 'Give it all you've got.' Otherwise you'll never know what you're culpable of."

"Capable of," Mary Anne corrected me.

"Whatever."

Jessi nodded solemnly, but Mal's face broke into a grin. "Mimi," she said dreamily. "Remember the time she didn't want to go to that county fair with your family, Claud, so she pretended she was sick? Just like a kid who doesn't want to go to school."

"Mm-hmm," I replied shortly. I stared down at the bedspread.

Silence. Dead silence, so to speak. I had brought the discussion to a screeching halt.

After a few moments, Mal said tentatively, "Claudia? I — "

"Be quiet," I said softly. "I don't want to talk about Mimi."

"But on the night before her funeral — " Mal persisted.

"Be *quiet!* I just told you I don't want to talk about her."

"Okay, okay."

"Claud," said Kristy, "this may not be the right time to bring this up, but that never stopped me before." Kristy tried to sound light, but nobody laughed.

"Bring what up?" I said testily. "It better

not have anything to do with Mimi."

"Well, it doesn't . . . exactly."

Even I was disappointed when the phone rang right then. My phone is a blessing and a curse. Sometimes we're saved by it, sometimes it can be *so* inconvenient.

A job was arranged for Kristy, the phone rang twice more, and afternoon jobs were lined up for Jessi and Mal.

Then Kristy picked up where she'd left off. "What I want to say, Claud, is more about Corrie than about Mimi. I know you're filling up a hole in Corrie's life. But I think she's doing the same for you."

After a long pause, I whispered, "Mimi's hole?"

Kristy nodded. "And you have to watch it when you let someone fill a hole. Especially when it's being filled by a kid like Corrie. I don't really believe you'd do this, but just think over what I'm going to say: *Don't drop Corrie.* You're going to start feeling better, Claud, and when you do, you won't need Corrie as much. So don't — don't just drop her."

I was about to protest when Kristy went on, "I don't think you'll do that, though. I think you and Corrie are good for each other and just happen to need each other right now. I think each of you can help the other one get stronger. Be careful, that's all. Everyone says little kids don't break, but they do. Inside. I broke when my father walked out on us."

I gulped and nodded, thinking that I felt pretty broken myself. But I saw Kristy's point and told her so.

Kristy may be a loudmouth. She may be bossy sometimes. But I think she understands kids better than any of the rest of us does.

The meeting ended then, and my friends left club headquarters solemnly.

CHAPTER 12

A week passed. My grades were dropping.

My grades aren't too good to begin with, but they're pretty stable. Your average C work with an occasional B or D thrown in. I've been known to fail tests.

But when I dropped to a solid D average, no one seemed surprised or even said anything. And that surprised *me*. Ordinarily, my parents would have hit the roof, and my teachers would have called me in for conferences. They'd have said things like, "We know you can do better. You're a smart girl. You have a high I.Q." (That's true. I do.) Or, "We know you can do better. You're Janine's sister." That was the killer. It was also the point. I'm Janine's *sister*, not *Janine*.

Anyway, except for feeling tired all the time, I wasn't sure why my grades had gone down. I did my homework more often than usual. I read all the chapters that were assigned to us. But I'll admit that it was hard to concentrate. Maybe that was because suddenly it had become hard *not* to think about Mimi. For awhile, I tried to shut her out of my mind. Now I couldn't. But why didn't someone say something to me? Why did they let my grades slide? Just because Mimi had died? Mimi would have wanted me to do well in school, if I could.

I was angry at my teachers and my parents.

At least Dorrie and Ashley and my other classmates were speaking to me again. But they wouldn't talk about Mimi, which was funny, because now I wanted to talk about her. Now if Mallory had said, "Remember the time when Mimi . . ." I would have been all ears.

But I did find some sympathy cards slipped into my locker at school, and in our mailbox at home, from my classmates. Mostly, they were flowery cards with printed messages inside that said things like: *I share your sorrow and extend my sympathy*. Or: *What you have once cherished you will never lose*. Or even poems like: *Sometimes words just aren't enough, but I want you to know*, da-da da-da da-da da-da da-da da-da da-doe. (You know what I mean.) And then

Dorrie or Ashley or whoever would sign her name (or his name) under the message.

I guess it's hard to know what to do when someone dies. I tried to think what I would do if, for instance, Kristy's mother or grandmother or someone close to her died. I would talk to her and hug her — if that was what she wanted. But if Dorrie's mother died I would send her a card and sign my name. Maybe it depends on how well you know the person.

Saturday mornings. I looked forward to them thirstily. They were oases in my desert. The kids and their puppets kept me going.

The puppets were almost done.

In fact, on one particular Saturday, everyone was due to finish their puppets during class, except for Marilyn and Carolyn, who had already finished theirs. The other kids were just putting on the last touches, such as hair.

I watched Corrie solemnly glue yellow yarn to the top of Nancy Drew's head. I watched Jamie glue antennae to his space monster. I watched Gabbie just decorate and decorate her doll. I could tell her puppet wouldn't be finished until class was over because she could always think of one more thing to add. She kept exclaiming, "Oh! I'll put these sparkly things on her dress!" Or, "She needs barrettes in her hair. Mary Anne Spier, can you please help me make barrettes?"

Meanwhile, the twins made collages with the materials the other kids were using on their puppets. While they worked, Marilyn announced, "We know a good joke." She was speaking for herself and her sister.

"Yeah," said Carolyn. "And since there are two of us, we can tell it better. See, once there were these two brothers and their names were Trouble and Shut Up. And one day they went downtown to go shopping and Trouble got lost. Shut Up was scared so he went looking for a policeman, and this is what happened. I'm going to play the part of Shut Up and Marilyn will be the policeman."

"I always have to be the policeman," complained Marilyn.

"That's because you're good at it," Carolyn told her.

Marilyn looked like she wanted to protest, but Carolyn said, "Come *on*. Let's finish the joke."

"Okay," agreed Marilyn sulkily.

The rest of the joke went like this:

Carolyn: "Oh, Mr. Policeman! Mr. Policeman!"

Marilyn: "What's the matter, little boy?"

Carolyn, pretending to cry: "I lost my brother and I can't find him."

Marilyn: "What's your name?"

Carolyn: "Shut Up."

Marilyn: "Are you looking for trouble?"

Carolyn: "Yes, I just told you that."

I think there must have been more to the joke, but the twins stopped telling it because the other kids were laughing so hard, and anyway it was time to clean up. As we put things away, I kept hearing Jamie and Myriah giggle and murmur things like, "Are you looking for TROUBLE?!!"

Half an hour later the kids and their puppets and collages were gone. Except for Corrie and Nancy Drew. Corrie and I sat on our stoop as usual. Time went by. So much time, in fact, that Mary Anne returned from walking Jamie and the Perkins girls home, and joined us on the stoop.

"What are you going to do with Nancy Drew?" Mary Anne asked Corrie.

Corrie glanced at me and smiled. "Give it to my mom," she replied. "She will be so, so pleased. It will be a special present for her, and she will see that I did well in art. That way, I can make her happy."

"I hope *you* like the puppet, too," said Mary Anne.

"Oh, I do," Corrie told her hastily. "But this is for Mommy. I can show her how much I love her."

At that moment, I heard our front door open behind us.

"Claudia?" It was Janine. "Your phone was ringing upstairs, so I answered it. It's Mrs. Addison. She wants to talk to you."

"Thanks, Janine," I said, glancing at Mary Anne. The two of us exchanged a look that plainly said, "What now?" which I hoped Corrie didn't see. Corrie was probably thinking, What now? herself, though.

Janine stepped outside to sit with Corrie and Mary Anne, and I dashed up to my room. I picked up the receiver, which Janine had placed on the bed.

"Hello? Mrs. Addison?" I said.

"Hi, Claudia. Sorry to do this to you. I'm running late, as you can see."

"Yes. Corrie is waiting for you," I said pointedly.

"Well, the thing is, I've been held up doing

my errands." (She did sound like she was calling from a pay phone on the street.) "My bracelet won't be ready at the jewelry store for another half an hour, and the man at the laundry is running late, too." (What a tragedy, I thought.) "So I was wondering if you'd keep Corrie for another hour or so, dear. I'll pay you whatever the rate is for an unexpected call like this."

"Well, I — " I began. Luckily, I was free. But what if I hadn't been? This was pretty pushy of Mrs. Addison. As it was, I'd planned to do some homework that afternoon and finish up a project for my pottery class.

"Oh, that's wonderful," said Mrs. Addison breathily, before I could tell her any of those things. "Tell Corrie I'll be along. Thanks a million. 'Bye!" She hung up.

Oh, brother, I thought. Now I've got to go downstairs and give Corrie this news. I walked slowly to the front door, opened it slowly, and sat down slowly when Corrie, Janine, and Mary Anne squished aside to make room for me.

"Corrie," I said, deciding just to come out and say it, "your mom's running late. She asked me to watch you for another hour or so while she finishes her errands. So why don't you come inside and we'll have some lunch? I don't know about you, but I'm getting hungry. Then I'll show you all the art stuff up in my room."

I just kept talking away as Corrie's face fell. Mary Anne and Janine played along with me nicely, though.

Mary Anne stood up and stretched, as if she heard stories like this every day. Then she said, "I guess I better be going. I'm getting hungry myself. See you next Saturday, Corrie." Then she ran across the street to her house.

And Janine said, "We've got peanut butter and jelly, Corrie. And tunafish, I think. Let's go make sandwiches. Maybe Mom and Dad will let us fix chocolate milk shakes in the blender."

I was surprised. Janine planned to stick with us? Usually she's stuck to her computer. But, I suddenly realized, she hadn't been quite so stuck to it since Mimi had died. She'd spent more time with me. She knew about my stop-action painting, my pottery class, the D I'd gotten on a math quiz, and even where the portrait of Mimi was stashed.

Janine and I rose, and Corrie reluctantly followed us into the house, clutching Nancy

Drew. We made sandwiches and milk shakes, and Mom and Dad knew enough to let the three of us eat alone. People can practically *see* how timid Corrie is.

All during lunch, poor Corrie kept saying things like, "Where's Daddy, I wonder?" and, "Who's watching Sean?" and, "Do you think Mommy will pick up Sean or me first?"

When Mrs. Addison finally did arrive (she honked her car horn from the street more than two hours later), Corrie looked at me tearfully, thanked me for making milk shakes, and handed me Nancy Drew.

"Here. You take her," she said. "I don't want Mommy to have her after all. I want you to have her."

Whoa, I thought as I watched the Addisons drive away. As terrible as I felt about Mimi, I realized one good thing. Mimi was gone, but I'd known her love. I was lucky.

It must, I decided, be awfully difficult to be Corrie Addison.

CHAPTER 13

After Corrie left, I went to my room and tried to catch up on some of the things I was behind on, and to do over some of the things I'd done poorly in the first place. For most of the afternoon I felt like Mimi was watching me, and that was a good feeling. It was as if she were sitting next to me, patiently helping me, just like she used to do. She would say, "No, look at problem again, my Claudia. Read carefully. Slow down. You can find answer."

Sometimes — not often, but sometimes — she used to climb the steps to the second floor, sit in my room, and watch me work on a painting, a collage, a sculpture, a piece of jewelry. Those times she never said anything. She just watched, and occasionally nodded or smiled. Maybe right now she was thinking about the Muses. Maybe Mimi would become my own personal Muse. Whatever she was, it was nice having her with me. I felt as if she hadn't left us after all.

Our family ate dinner together that night, and I wondered whether the Addisons were doing the same thing, or if Corrie and Sean were eating alone while their parents got dressed to go to a fancy party or something.

When dinner was over, Dad and I cleaned up the kitchen, Mom took the newspaper into the living room, and Janine disappeared, maybe to work on her computer. But those days, who knew? When the kitchen was clean, I left it to go back to my homework. On the way to the stairs, I passed Mimi's bedroom.

The door was open. The light was on. And Janine was sitting on Mimi's bed with the contents of Mimi's jewelry box spilled in front of her.

I was shocked. None of us had been able to go into Mimi's room since the morning she'd died and I'd closed the door.

"We'll give her clothes and things away to charities — to the Salvation Army, maybe — someday soon," Mom kept saying. "Then we'll turn this into a nice guest bedroom."

But no one had opened Mimi's door. We couldn't do it.

Now Janine was in there, pawing through Mimi's most precious things.

She looked up and saw me hovering in the doorway. "Oh, Claudia," she said. "Come here. Look at this pin." She held it out to me. "I think Mimi would want you to have it since she gave me her earrings."

I glanced briefly at the pin. It was a simple circle of pearls set on a ring of gold. It was not my kind of jewelry at all. But that wasn't the point.

"What are you doing in here?" I said with a gasp.

Janine sighed. "I knew you would ask," she replied. "It's time somebody did this. Look. Here's a ring I know Mimi wanted Mom to have. And here's a bar pin. Ooh, I bet Dad could have it made into a tie tack. Wow, look at *this* pin. . . . Oh, I remember this bracelet. Mimi wore it to my eighth-grade graduation."

Janine was holding up one piece of jewelry after another. The clincher was when she found a pair of gold earrings and made a grab for them. "Wow! Here are the flower earrings. I'd forgotten about these. I always wanted them, ever since I was little. They'd look great with my white sweater."

Ha! Who was Janine kidding? She doesn't

care how she looks. Even Kristy pays more attention to what she wears than Janine does.

I exploded. "Oh, my lord, Janine. How could you do this? How *could* you?" I didn't give my sister a chance to answer me. I plowed right ahead. "Mimi's hardly been gone at all and here you are picking through her things like someone with a fine-tooth comb."

"You're mixing your metaphors," said Janine through clenched teeth.

I ignored her. "You're like those awful people in *A Christmas Carol* who wait until Mr. Scrooge is just barely dead and then they go through his room and steal all his stuff, even the rings from his bed curtains, and sell them for practically nothing," I told her.

"I do not," said Janine haughtily, "have plans to sell Mimi's things. I just thought Mimi would want us to have them. Peaches and Russ, too."

"Well, I don't think you should be doing this," I shouted. My voice was getting louder and louder, but I couldn't help it. "Why would anyone want Mimi's dumb old stuff anyway? I hate Mimi. *I hate her!*"

"Hey, hey, what's going on in here?" cried Mom.

She and Dad had appeared behind me in

the hallway. I'm sure, from the way I'd been screaming, that they'd expected to find me murdering Janine. As it was, they were pretty surprised just to see Mimi's room lit up, and my sister on the bed in front of the open jewelry box.

"Nothing," I replied.

Needless to say, my parents didn't believe me.

"Into the living room for a family conference," said Dad.

We gathered in the living room. As we were sitting down, I saw Janine stuff something in the pocket of her skirt.

"All right," my mother began. "Would somebody please explain what was going on?"

Janine told Mom and Dad about the jewelry box, and Mom just looked sort of sad and said that we should have had the courage to go into Mimi's room long ago. I opened my mouth to say something, then closed it again.

After a moment of silence, Dad said gently, "Claudia? Is there anything you'd like to tell us? Your mother and I did hear you say that you hate Mimi. Um . . ."

I could see how uncomfortable he was, so I started talking. "Well," I said, "I didn't realize it at first. I mean, I didn't realize it until right now, but I'm — I'm sort of mad at Mimi." My voice had grown so soft that my family had to lean forward to hear me.

"Why?" asked Mom.

"Because . . ." (I was just figuring this out), "because she left us."

"What do you mean?"

"I mean that she wasn't really sick. She was getting better. She was going to come home from the hospital — and then she died. It's like she just gave up. Like she didn't even care about us enough to stay around awhile longer." There. I'd said it. Even though I hadn't known it, I'd been carrying around that big, bad secret — and I'd finally let it out. No wonder I'd felt so tired lately. Keeping bad secrets takes a lot of energy. "I *tried* not to be mad at Mimi," I assured my parents and sister, remembering how comforted I'd felt that afternoon, feeling that Mimi was near me. "I really tried. Plus, how could I be mad at her when she should have been mad at me?"

Everyone looked puzzled again, so I had to explain about the horrible things I'd done that I felt guilty over. "I bet she thought she was a nuisance," I said. And then with horror I added, "Maybe *that* was why she wanted to die. So she wouldn't have to be a nuisance to us anymore."

"Oh, Claudia!" exclaimed my mother. She jumped up from her armchair, crossed the room, and sat down next to me on the couch, enfolding me in her arms.

"Mimi didn't *want* to die," spoke up Janine softly, and we all looked at her. We watched her pull the something from her pocket that she'd slipped in there earlier. It was a rumpled piece of paper.

"I think she just knew her time had come and that she was *going* to die," Janine went on. "She was trying to accept it and deal with it. Look at this." Janine held the paper out to my mother. "I found this at the bottom of her jewelry box."

I peered over at it, and my father came to look at it, too. Written in Mimi's funny handwriting (she'd had to switch to her left hand after her stroke), was an obituary. Mimi had been writing her own obituary — all the stuff about where she was born and who she was survived by. But the weirdest thing was the date of her death. She'd included that, too, and she'd listed it as this year.

"She knew," I whispered.

My mother n... could have held... might have felt like... that didn't have anyt... of her death. She didn... die. It's like Janine said. ... her time had come. And f... gave out. I think she was sic... even the doctors, knew — ex... knew."

"The doctors *should* have know... I cried, exploding again. "They should have done more. They're supposed to be trained. They're supposed to be so smart, but they let Mimi die. They never even figured out what was wrong with her. What a bunch of jerks. They should have saved her, but I bet they didn't even try. They probably thought to themselves, 'Oh, she's just an old lady. It doesn't matter.' Well, it matters to me!"

My family listened to my outburst, and I felt better when I was finished. It was a whole lot easier to be mad at the doctors, since I didn't really know them, than it was to be mad at Mimi. And I felt like I had to be mad at someone.

"Claudia," said my father, "can you remember some nice times you had with Mimi, in-

ays at the end?"

answered, feeling my throat
I thought of the night before the fu-
al, sitting around Mary Anne's kitchen table with my friends. "Yes," I repeated.

Mom and Dad and Janine and I talked about
Mimi a little longer, and Mom said that, now
that the door to Mimi's room was open, we
really should clean it out and fix it up. The
rest of us agreed. In fact, we left the living
room then and went into Mimi's room. Janine
plopped herself down on the bed again, Mom
and Dad stepped inside and began to look
around, and I hovered in the doorway.

"We can't get rid of the things on her walls,"
I said. "The haiku poem and stuff. I think
those should stay here."

My dad agreed. "They'll look very nice in
the guest bedroom," he said. "All we need to
give away are her personal items. Her clothes
and jewelry and things."

Mom hesitated, then opened the door to
Mimi's closet. "I'd kind of like to have her
kimono," she said.

Dad picked up a paperweight from the table.
"I'd like to keep this," he said, turning it over
in his hands. Then, "Hey!" he exclaimed.
"There's a piece of tape on the bottom with

128

my initials on it. I guess Mimi wanted me to have it, too."

The four of us began looking through everything in Mimi's room. Lots of things were labeled. Mimi had been thinking ahead. We took the items that were marked for us, and set aside those for Russ and Peaches.

"The jewelry isn't marked, though," Janine pointed out, and she held the pearl pin toward me.

This time I took it. I knew I would never wear it, but I would always keep it, because it had belonged to Mimi.

CHAPTER 14

Another Saturday, another art class.

With the puppets finished, we were trying something more abstract. Collages — even though Marilyn and Carolyn had each made one already. They didn't mind making seconds, though. Their first ones had been made with feathers and sequins, crepe paper and glitter, scraps of felt and lace. Their new ones were going to be made up solely of words and pictures cut from magazines and were to be in the form of birthday cards for their father.

Everyone was hard at work.

Jamie, remembering the twins' joke about Trouble and Shut Up, had decided to invent a joke of his own. "Why," he asked expansively, "did the little girl slide down the slide on her toenail?"

"Why?" asked Gabbie.

"Because she wanted to!" hooted Jamie.

He didn't quite have the hang of jokes yet, but most of the kids let out giggles anyway, I guess at the ridiculous thought of someone actually sliding down anything on one toenail.

When the giggling died down, Carolyn leaned over and whispered something to Corrie, who nodded.

A few moments later, Corrie whispered something to Jamie, who also nodded.

What was going on? A secret?

I could understand that. I had a secret of my own. I was working on a special project in my room. I worked on it in between school assignments and assignments for my art classes and my stop-action painting and baby-sitting and club meetings. It was slow-going, as you can imagine, because of everything else I had to do, but that didn't matter. What mattered was that I was working on it. But I didn't tell anyone about it. It was a secret from my family and my friends. I didn't even mention it to Stacey when we talked on the phone. And Stacey knew about everything else — about how the kids at school had acted, about Janine and the jewelry box, and being mad at Mimi and the doctors. But she didn't know my secret.

Soon everyone would, though.

"Claud?" said Mary Anne, interrupting my thoughts.

"Yeah?"

"I hate to say this, but I think we're running out of glue."

That morning, with the help of Corrie, our early bird, Mary Anne and I had filled little paper pill cups with glue, one for each kid. Collages take a lot of glue. Even so, it was hard to believe we were already running out. But I looked around the table, and the children were literally scraping the bottoms of the cups.

"Okay," I said, "I'll go get the big glue bottle."

The big glue bottle, unfortunately, was in my room, so I had to run up two long flights of stairs — from the basement to the first floor, then from the first floor to the second floor — in order to get it.

When I returned with the glue, I got the distinct impression that Mary Anne and the kids had been talking about something, but had stopped as soon as I appeared. More secrets?

Before I could ask, Corrie spoke up shyly. "Claudia?" she began. "Could a collage be a mural, too?"

"What's a mural?" asked Gabbie.

"It's a very big picture," I told her, trying to sign to Matt Braddock at the same time so that he wouldn't be left out of the conversation. "You could make a drawing on a long, long piece of paper. For instance, you could draw a picture of going for a drive. You could show your street, then your town, then the countryside and a farm. Something like that."

"Oh," said Gabbie, and the others, who had been listening intently, nodded.

"But could you make a collage mural?" asked Corrie again.

"Well, I guess so," I answered.

"Goody!" exclaimed several of the children.

"Is that what you'd like to try next?" I asked.

"Yes," replied Myriah firmly.

I was pleased. The kids were learning new art forms and trying to combine them on their own. That was important.

"Can we start next week?" asked Marilyn.

"Sure," I replied.

"We'll need *all* these materials," added Carolyn. "The scraps and glitter and stuff *plus* the magazine pictures and the words."

"You know how you guys could help out?" I said, since I was running out of magazines. "You could each bring in a couple of old magazines and even a newspaper, okay?"

I signed to Matt to make sure he understood what we were doing.

Matt nodded, looking excited.

At that moment, the doorbell rang.

"I'll have to get it," I said to Mary Anne. "Dad's gardening in the backyard, and Mom and Janine are out."

"Okay," agreed Mary Anne. The kids were working busily. Everything was under control.

I dashed up the steps two at a time, ran to our front door, and peered out the side window. Was I ever surprised to see Mrs. Addison standing there! The art class wouldn't be over for another fifteen minutes.

I opened the door. "Hi," I said. (I know I sounded as surprised as I felt.)

"Hi," replied Mrs. Addison. "I'm sorry I'm so early. My husband's waiting in the car." (She turned and gave a little wave toward a blue Camaro parked crookedly in our driveway, as if the Addisons were in a big hurry.) "I forgot to tell Corrie this morning that we have tickets to the ice show in Stamford. I mean, tickets for Sean and Corrie. They'll meet a baby-sitter there, and then Mr. Addison and I can enjoy an afternoon to ourselves."

I could feel my temper rising. An afternoon to themselves? Wasn't that all they *ever* had?

Time without their children? Dumping them at lessons, with friends, with sitters? I counted to five before I said slowly and deliberately something that both Mary Anne and I had been wanting to say to the Addisons for a long time. Mary Anne really should have been the one to say it, since she's better with words than I am. But, oh well. There was Mrs. Addison, and there I was. It might be our only chance.

"Mrs. Addison," I began, trying to think of ways to be tactful, "this is the first time you've picked Corrie up early."

"Yes, I — " she began.

But I kept on talking. "Did you know that Corrie is always the last one to leave my house after class is over? And that she's always the first to arrive?"

Mrs. Addison checked her watch impatiently and glanced over her shoulder at the car waiting in our driveway.

"I love having Corrie around," I went on. "She's a terrific kid. But, well, she feels pretty bad about being left here . . . left here longer than any of the other children, I mean."

Mrs. Addison's expression changed. She looked at me curiously.

"Did you notice," I started to ask, "that Corrie hasn't brought home any of her art projects?"

"Well," (Mrs. Addison cleared her throat), "I noticed that just, um, just this morning. And I did wonder why."

"It's because she's been giving them away," I said.

"Giving them away?"

I nodded. "Yes. To me, to Mary Anne Spier, to the other kids. I think," I began (and oh, my lord, I hoped I wasn't butting in where I didn't belong), "that Corrie is a little bit mad at you and Mr. Addison." (What an understatement.) "She wants to please you, but she gets angry and scared when she feels like," (I tried to think of a nice way to say that Corrie felt her parents didn't care about her), "like . . . sometimes other things are more important to you and Mr. Addison than she is."

There. I'd said it. I waited for the fireworks.

But Mrs. Addison merely looked at me with tears in her eyes. She rummaged around in her purse for some Kleenex.

"All Corrie wants," I dared to say, "is to spend more time with you."

Mrs. Addison began to sniffle. "Excuse me," she said hurriedly, and ran out the door and back to her car.

136

Uh-oh, I thought. Now I've done it. I stood at the door on rubbery legs. A few minutes later, Mrs. Addison returned. I was still at the door.

"I think," Mrs. Addison began, "that the baby-sitter probably wouldn't mind if I attended the ice show with Sean and Corrie today. I can pass up my free afternoon."

"You can?!" I grinned. And you should have seen the look on Corrie's face when her mother and father not only gave Corrie the news about the ice show, but took a tour of our makeshift art room. Corrie even presented her parents with her newly finished collage.

"This is for you," she said proudly, hastily scrawling

Love, Corrie

across the back.

A few moments later, the Addisons and Corrie climbed the basement steps.

I watched them go. I knew that Corrie's life wouldn't magically change, that it wouldn't be perfect from then on. But I thought maybe it would be better. And I realized that Mimi was the one who had shown me how it *could* be better. Because Mimi had always been there when I needed her. I never had to fight for her love the way Corrie had to fight for her parents' love. Now Mimi might be gone, but I knew that before she died (*died*, not *left me*), she had made me a strong person, strong enough to stand up to Mrs. Addison for Corrie.

CHAPTER 15

I will now reveal my secret.

My secret was a tribute to Mimi. It was a piece of art. Mimi had always appreciated my art. She liked anything I did, but she especially liked my paintings and collages. And so, since the kids and I seemed to have collage fever, I made a collage for Mimi.

It was not very big — only about twelve inches by twelve inches, and I filled it with small but important things. Maybe I did that because Mimi had always seemed small but important to me. She was tiny — birdlike — but she could help me to solve any problem or make me feel better even when I was at my lowest of lows.

So the collage contained small pictures cut from magazines — of a tea cup and saucer to represent our "special tea"; of a family eating a meal, since Mimi had always cooked for us and insisted that we eat together; and of a woman knitting, since Mimi liked to do needlework before she had her stroke. Then I drew a picture of a Japanese woman cradling a Japanese baby. I added that, too, plus yarn and ribbon, thread and lace. I even glued down tiny charms — scissors and a thimble — and tea leaves and flour.

I hoped the collage was impressive and meaningful, but I wasn't sure. Even so, I backed it, matted it, and had it framed. That cost a lot of baby-sitting money, but I didn't care. It was for Mimi.

And now it was time to unveil it. As far as I knew, nobody had any idea about my secret. I decided to show it to my friends first, then my family. If my friends didn't like it, or thought it was stupid, they would tell me so. I could count on them for that. Then I could change it, or start over, before I showed it to my family. I wanted my family to see the polished, perfect tribute, not something silly or full of mistakes.

So at the next meeting of the Baby-sitters Club, when we were gathered in my room and Kristy said, "Any club business?" I raised my hand tentatively.

Kristy looked at me curiously. Mallory and

Jessi are usually the only ones who bother to raise their hands. In fact, Kristy has never asked us to do that. It's just that Mal and Jessi are younger, and the sixth-grade teachers still drill that stuff about hand-raising into your head at their age. By eighth grade, the teachers have pretty much given up.

"Claud?" said Kristy.

"I — I know this isn't club, um, club business," I stammered, "so if you don't want to hear about it right — right now, that's okay . . . I guess. I mean, this is Mimi business, and you all knew her, and you know how im — important she was to me." (To my horror, I could feel tears welling up in my eyes.) "I want to — to show you something."

I could feel every single person in my room, even Kristy, melting.

And Kristy was the one to say, "Of course we want to see . . . whatever it is. Don't we, you guys?"

The others agreed without hesitating.

I drew in a deep breath, then let it out slowly. "Okay," I began, "what it is, is a tribute to Mimi. I wanted to do something in her memory. *Having* memories is one thing, but I wanted to do something *for* her. Even though she's not — not here, I think she'll know I did

141

it. I know that sounds weird, but I really feel it's true."

I eased myself off the bed, where I'd been sandwiched between Dawn and Mary Anne, crossed the room to my closet, and emerged with the collage. I set it on the bed, and my friends crowded around for a look.

At first nobody said a word, and a cold feeling washed over me. "It's terrible, isn't it?" I said. "It's really dumb."

"Oh, no," breathed Dawn. "It's perfect. It — it says Mimi all over. I mean, it *is* Mimi. It's Mimi the way we want to remember her."

"Yeah," said Kristy, Jessi, and Mal.

And Mary Anne burst into tears. I think that was what finally convinced me that the collage was all right, not all wrong, that I'd done my job. The collage really was a tribute. In Dawn's words, it said Mimi all over.

I decided I could show it to my parents and Janine. And I decided to do so that night after dinner.

I waited until the kitchen had been cleaned up and everyone was about to begin their evening activities. Janine was heading upstairs to her computer, Mom was sitting down at the desk in the living room to pay bills, and Dad was just opening the paper.

142

"You guys?" I said.

My parents and sister turned toward me.

"I have something to show you." Even though my friends had honestly loved the collage, I began to feel nervous again.

"What is it, sweetie?" asked Mom.

"It's something for Mimi," I replied. "And something for us to remember her by. I'll go get it." I ran to my room, retrieved the collage from my closet, and brought it back downstairs. Then I stood before my family with the front of the collage pressed against my chest.

"Well," I said, "um, this is it." I turned it around.

"Why, Claudia, it's *perfect!*" exclaimed my mother, stepping forward for a closer look.

Dad and Janine peered at it, too, and it was Janine who glanced at the fireplace and said, "I think we should hang it over the mantelpiece."

"That's a wonderful idea," agreed Dad.

But I said, "Thanks. Thank you, guys, for wanting to put it in the living room, but I had a different idea. I mean, if you don't mind, I was wondering if we could put the collage in Mimi's room. I know it's going to become our guest room, but it's been Mimi's room for as long as I can remember, and I like leaving

143

the — the flavor of Mimi there."

"Well, of course you can," said Mom and Dad at the same time. (If they'd been any younger they would have had to hook pinkies and say "jinx.")

And so we hung the collage in Mimi's room. We put it right over her (empty) dresser. Then the four of us stood back and looked at it, feeling quite pleased.

"Mimi would have loved it," said Dad.

The next Saturday was art-class day, of course, and two unusual things happened. First of all, Corrie arrived on time, not early. In fact, Myriah and Gabbie were already in the basement by the time Mrs. Addison dropped Corrie off.

Second, when all the children had arrived, Mary Anne announced, "Claudia, today you are not allowed in the basement."

"But I'm the teacher," I protested, surprised.

"And I'm second-in-command," Mary Anne countered, "and the kids are third-in-command. And we say, 'Out.' Today you are on vacation because we're working on something special and secret."

Ah-*ha!* A secret. I knew it.

"Go upstairs and work on your painting or something."

So I did, all the time wondering just what was going on in the basement. I wasn't worried, with Mary Anne in charge, but I was awfully curious.

Just before class was over, Mary Anne called me back down to the basement. I practically flew there. When I hit the bottom step I was greeted by two things: the sound of Jamie, Marilyn, Carolyn, Corrie, Myriah, Gabbie, and Mary Anne shouting, "Surprise!" (while Matt signed to me), and the sight of the kids' mural-collage.

"It's for Mimi! It's for Mimi!" cried Jamie, jumping up and down.

Mary Anne smiled at me. "The kids thought this up on their own. They didn't know a thing about *your* collage for Mimi. They started talking about this two weeks ago. They wanted to do something for Mimi, just like you did."

I leaned over the table to get a good look at the collage. It didn't really have much to do with Mimi herself, and it was kind of messy — blobs of glue here and there, cotton balls hanging by threads, fingerprints, drippy paint, but the kids were terribly proud of it.

"I'll tell you what we're going to do with

145

it," I said, after I had thanked everyone about a million times. "We're going to put it in Mimi's room, where it belongs. But it's so big I'll have to wait until Dad can help me."

That was okay with the kids. It was time to leave anyway. Just as the doorbell started ringing with arriving parents, Corrie tugged at my arm and pulled me to a corner of the basement, away from the others.

"*I* made something for *you*," she said. "Something special. Mimi deserved a — a what do you call it?"

"A tribute?" I suggested.

"Yes, a tribute. And so do you. So this is for you."

Corrie thrust something at me that she'd been hiding behind her back.

I took it carefully. It was a sketch, and I could tell it was a sketch of me. It was very good.

"Thank you, Corrie," I whispered, kneeling down to give her a hug.

"Mrs. Addison's here!" Janine called just then from upstairs.

"Right on time," said Corrie with a grin.

I grinned back. It was nice to know I'd made a difference in Corrie's life. It was even nicer to know who had helped me to make that difference.

Mimi.

As soon as the basement was cleaned up and everyone had gone, there was something I would have to do. So I did it just after the last kid had been ushered out the door.

I climbed the stairs slowly to the second floor and opened the door to the attic. I turned on the light.

My portrait of Mimi was leaning against an old filing cabinet where I'd left it the morning she had died. Now I picked it up, brought it into my room, and hung it in its old spot.

I stood back to look at it.

I couldn't say anything to it because of the big lump in my throat.

I just let Mimi smile down at me. After a few moments, I smiled back.

Dear Reader:

I began working on *Claudia and the Sad Good-bye* shortly after my own grandmother died. She didn't have a stroke like Mimi, but just like Claudia, I was angry at her doctors for not saving her even though there was nothing anyone could have done. She was just too old and ill. Having just been through that experience helped me to describe Claudia's feelings.

I didn't make a tribute to my grandmother like Claudia did, but on the night before her funeral, my sister and my cousins and I gathered to reminisce about Granny. Eventually, we found ourselves laughing and telling stories about funny things Granny had done. It helped us feel a little better. For a long time after the funeral I kept a picture of Granny on my desk so I could look at her while I was working. And that helped, too.

Happy reading,

Ann M Martin

Ann M. Martin

About the Author

ANN MATTHEWS MARTIN was born on August 12, 1955. She grew up in Princeton, NJ, with her parents and her younger sister, Jane.

Although Ann used to be a teacher and then an editor of children's books, she's now a full-time writer. She gets the ideas for her books from many different places. Some are based on personal experiences. Others are based on childhood memories and feelings. Many are written about contemporary problems or events.

All of Ann's characters, even the members of the Baby-sitters Club, are made up. (So is Stoneybrook.) But many of her characters are based on real people. Sometimes Ann names her characters after people she knows, other times she chooses names she likes.

In addition to the Baby-sitters Club books, Ann Martin has written many other books for children. Her favorite is *Ten Kids, No Pets* because she loves big families and she loves animals. Her favorite Baby-sitters Club book is *Kristy's Big Day*. (By the way, Kristy is her favorite baby-sitter!)

Ann M. Martin now lives in New York with her cats, Gussie and Woody. Her hobbies are reading, sewing, and needlework — especially making clothes for children.

Notebook Pages

This Baby-sitters Club book belongs to _____ .

I am _____ years old and in the _____ grade.

The name of my school is _____ .

I got this BSC book from _____ .

I started reading it on _____ and finished reading it on _____ .

The place where I read most of this book is _____ .

My favorite part was when _____ .

If I could change anything in the story, it might be the part when _____ .

My favorite character in the Baby-sitters Club is _____ .

The BSC member I am most like is _____ because _____ .

If I could write a Baby-sitters Club book it would be about _____

#26 Claudia and the Sad Good-bye

Claudia's grandmother Mimi means a lot to her. One family member who means a lot to me is _____ _____ . I love this person because _____ _____ . One of the best times we have had together was when _____ _____ _____ . Mimi is Claudia's maternal grandmother. My maternal grandparents (my mother's parents) are named _____ and _____ . My paternal grandparents (my father's parents) are named _____ _____ and _____ .

Claudia's family tree looks like this:

My family tree looks like this:

••

CLAUDIA'S

Finger painting at 3...

A spooky sitting adventure

Sitting for two of my favorite charges --
Jamie and Lucy Newton.

SCRAPBOOK

...oil painting
at 13!

my family. Mom and Dad, me and
Janine... and we'll never forget Mimi.

Read all the books
about **Claudia**
in the Baby-sitters Club series
by Ann M. Martin

#63 *Claudia's Fr~~ie~~nd Friend*
Claudia and Shea can't spell — but they can be friends!

#71 *Claudia and the Perfect Boy*
Can Claudia find love in her own personals column?

#78 *Claudia and Crazy Peaches*
Claudia's crazy Aunt Peaches is back in town. Let the games begin!

#85 *Claudia Kishi, Live From WSTO!*
Claudia wins a contest to have her own radio show.

#91 *Claudia and the First Thanksgiving*
Claudia's in the middle of a big Thanksgiving controversy!

Mysteries:

6 *The Mystery at Claudia's House*
Claudia's room has been ransacked! Can the baby-sitters track down whodunnit?

#11 *Claudia and the Mystery at the Museum*
Burglaries, forgeries . . . something crooked is going on at the new museum in Stoneybrook!

#16 *Claudia and the Clue in the Photograph*
Has Claudia caught a thief — on film?

#21 *Claudia and the Recipe for Danger*
There's nothing half-baked about the attempts to sabotage a big cooking contest!

Portrait Collection:

Claudia's Book
Claudia's design for living.

THE BABY-SITTERS CLUB®

by Ann M. Martin

More titles... ▶

The Baby-sitters Club titles continued...

❏ MG47011-6	#73 **Mary Anne and Miss Priss**	$3.50
❏ MG47012-4	#74 **Kristy and the Copycat**	$3.50
❏ MG47013-2	#75 **Jessi's Horrible Prank**	$3.50
❏ MG47014-0	#76 **Stacey's Lie**	$3.50
❏ MG48221-1	#77 **Dawn and Whitney, Friends Forever**	$3.50
❏ MG48222-X	#78 **Claudia and Crazy Peaches**	$3.50
❏ MG48223-8	#79 **Mary Anne Breaks the Rules**	$3.50
❏ MG48224-6	#80 **Mallory Pike, #1 Fan**	$3.50
❏ MG48225-4	#81 **Kristy and Mr. Mom**	$3.50
❏ MG48226-2	#82 **Jessi and the Troublemaker**	$3.50
❏ MG48235-1	#83 **Stacey vs. the BSC**	$3.50
❏ MG48228-9	#84 **Dawn and the School Spirit War**	$3.50
❏ MG48236-X	#85 **Claudi Kishi, Live from WSTO**	$3.50
❏ MG48227-0	#86 **Mary Anne and Camp BSC**	$3.50
❏ MG48237-8	#87 **Stacey and the Bad Girls**	$3.50
❏ MG22872-2	#88 **Farewell, Dawn**	$3.50
❏ MG22873-0	#89 **Kristy and the Dirty Diapers**	$3.50
❏ MG45575-3	**Logan's Story Special Edition Readers' Request**	$3.25
❏ MG47118-X	**Logan Bruno, Boy Baby-sitter Special Edition Readers' Request**	$3.50
❏ MG47756-0	**Shannon's Story Special Edition**	$3.50
❏ MG44240-6	**Baby-sitters on Board! Super Special #1**	$3.95
❏ MG44239-2	**Baby-sitters' Summer Vacation Super Special #2**	$3.95
❏ MG43973-1	**Baby-sitters' Winter Vacation Super Special #3**	$3.95
❏ MG42493-9	**Baby-sitters' Island Adventure Super Special #4**	$3.95
❏ MG43575-2	**California Girls! Super Special #5**	$3.95
❏ MG43576-0	**New York, New York! Super Special #6**	$3.95
❏ MG44963-X	**Snowbound Super Special #7**	$3.95
❏ MG44962-X	**Baby-sitters at Shadow Lake Super Special #8**	$3.95
❏ MG45661-X	**Starring the Baby-sitters Club Super Special #9**	$3.95
❏ MG45674-1	**Sea City, Here We Come! Super Special #10**	$3.95
❏ MG47015-9	**The Baby-sitter's Remember Super Special #11**	$3.95
❏ MG48308-0	**Here Come the Bridesmaids Super Special #12**	$3.95

Available wherever you buy books...or use this order form.

Scholastic Inc., P.O. Box 7502, 2931 E. McCarty Street, Jefferson City, MO 65102

Please send me the books I have checked above. I am enclosing $ _____
(please add $2.00 to cover shipping and handling). Send check or money order—no
cash or C.O.D.s please.

Name _____ Birthdate _____

Address _____

City _____ State/Zip _____

Please allow four to six weeks for delivery. Offer good in the U.S. only. Sorry, mail orders are not
available to residents of Canada. Prices subject to change.

THE BABY-SITTERS CLUB®

by Ann M. Martin

Collect and read these exciting BSC Super Specials, Mysteries, and Super Mysteries along with your favorite Baby-sitters Club books!

The Baby-sitters Club books continued...

Now THE BABY-SITTERS CLUB®

★ is a Video Club too!

The Jesus Bible Journal, NIV

sixty-six books. one story. all about one name.

Genesis / Exodus / Leviticus / Numbers / Deuteronomy / Joshua / Judges / Ruth / First Samuel / Second Samuel / First Kings / Second Kings / First Chronicles / Second Chronicles / Ezra / Nehemiah / Esther / Job / Psalms / Proverbs / Ecclesiastes / Song of Songs / Isaiah / Jeremiah / Lamentations / Ezekiel / Daniel / Hosea / Joel / Amos / Obadiah / Jonah / Micah / Nahum / Habakkuk / Zephaniah / Haggai / Zechariah / Malachi / Matthew / Mark / **Luke** / John / Acts / Romans / First Corinthians / Second Corinthians / Galatians / Ephesians / Philippians / Colossians / First Thessalonians / Second Thessalonians / First Timothy / Second Timothy / Titus / Philemon / Hebrews / James / First Peter / Second Peter / First John / Second John / Third John / Jude / Revelation

The Jesus Bible Journal, Luke, NIV
Published by Zondervan, 2020
Grand Rapids, Michigan, USA
All rights reserved

JESUS: OUR GRACIOUS SAVIOR

LUKE

LUKE

TIBERIUS CAESAR IS ROMAN EMPEROR *c. AD 14 – 37*	JOHN THE BAPTIST'S MINISTRY *c. AD 25 – 27*	JESUS' MINISTRY, DEATH, RESURRECTION *c. AD 27 – 30*

Jesus was sent by God to save sinners. Luke was one such sinner saved by the perfect life and substitutionary death of Jesus, the Messiah. Though Luke never met Jesus personally, it is clear that his life was radically transformed by the message he received from those who had.

Luke, a physician by trade, compiled information concerning the Christ from eyewitnesses to his life, death and resurrection. The letter is addressed to Theophilus, presumably a Gentile convert who served among the Christian community established through Jesus' work. This neophyte church was facing persecution, and Luke sought to reassure Theophilus of God's faithfulness throughout history, seen most clearly in the sending of Jesus Christ. God would surely not abandon his people in the face of persecution when he had already gone to such great lengths to secure their salvation through Christ.

Luke's Gospel is the only one with a sequel — the book of Acts. There Luke continues to describe the ongoing acts of God through the power of the Holy Spirit as the church spread throughout the known world of the first century. Through the church's proclamation of Jesus, God continues to seek and save sinners.

This mission is vividly portrayed in the life of Christ seen throughout Luke's Gospel. Jesus was sent by God to fulfill his pledge to save his people from their sin. Though many would fail to trust him, Jesus relentlessly pursued them in his love. This passionate, gracious love is portrayed in the three stories found in Luke 15 — a lost

heep, a lost coin and two lost sons. There Jesus is pictured as a loving Savior who will
o to any length to find what belongs to him.

The message of salvation is available to all through Christ's work. But, as Luke
hows, few will accept this gracious offer. Even his own people, the Jews, turn their
acks on him and reject Jesus and his disciples. The brutal execution of the Son of
jod shows the widening gulf between followers of Jesus and those hardened in rebel-
on. Yet, the grace of God would overcome the height of human folly. In God's wis-
om, the death of Jesus was God's perfect plan to defeat Satan, sin and death once
nd for all. Through this sacrifice, the lost could be saved. Not only the Jews, but
so Gentiles could receive the priceless gift of salvation. God's people could then
ve their lives for the sake of God's mission, the world — a mission that continues
rough the founding of the church in the book of Acts.

THE SPIRIT OF THE LORD IS ON ME,
BECAUSE HE HAS ANOINTED ME TO PROCLAIM
GOOD NEWS TO THE POOR. HE HAS SENT ME
TO PROCLAIM FREEDOM FOR THE PRISONERS
AND RECOVERY OF SIGHT FOR THE BLIND,
TO SET THE OPPRESSED FREE.

Luke 4:18

LUKE

Introduction

1 Many have undertaken to draw up an account of the things that have been fulfilled[a] among us, [2]just as they were handed down to us by those who from the first were eyewitnesses and servants of the word. [3]With this in mind, since I myself have carefully investigated everything from the beginning, I too decided to write an orderly account for you, most excellent Theophilus, [4]so that you may know the certainty of the things you have been taught.

The Birth of John the Baptist Foretold

[5]In the time of Herod king of Judea there was a priest named Zechariah, who belonged to the priestly division of Abijah; his wife Elizabeth was also a descendant of Aaron. [6]Both of them were righteous in the sight of God, observing all the Lord's commands and decrees blamelessly. [7]But they were childless because Elizabeth was not able to conceive, and they were both very old.

[8]Once when Zechariah's division was on duty and he was serving as priest before God, [9]he was chosen by lot, according to the custom of the priesthood, to go into the temple of the Lord and burn incense. [10]And when the time for the burning of incense came, all the assembled worshipers were praying outside.

[11]Then an angel of the Lord appeared to him, standing at the right side of the altar of incense. [12]When Zechariah saw him, he was startled and was gripped with fear. [13]But the angel said to him: "Do not be afraid, Zechariah; your prayer has been heard. Your wife Elizabeth will bear you a son, and you are to call him John. [14]He will be a joy and delight to you, and many will rejoice because of his birth, [15]for he will be great in the sight of the Lord. He is never to take wine or other fermented drink, and he will be filled with the Holy Spirit even before he is born. [16]He will bring back many of the people of Israel to the Lord their God. [17]And he will go on before the Lord, in the spirit and power of Elijah, to turn the hearts of the parents to their children and the disobedient to the wisdom of the righteous—to make ready a people prepared for the Lord."

[18]Zechariah asked the angel, "How can I be sure of this? I am an old man and my wife is well along in years."

[19]The angel said to him, "I am Gabriel. I stand in the presence of God, and I have been sent to speak to you and to tell you this good news. [20]And now you will be silent and not able to speak until the day this happens, because you did not believe my words, which will come true at their appointed time."

[21]Meanwhile, the people were waiting for Zechariah and wondering why he stayed so long in the temple. [22]When he came out, he could not speak to them. They realized he had seen a vision in the temple, for he kept making signs to them but remained unable to speak.

[23]When his time of service was completed, he returned home.

---

[a]1 Or *been surely believed*

²⁴After this his wife Elizabeth became pregnant and for five months remained in seclusion. ²⁵"The Lord has done this for me," she said. "In these days he has shown his favor and taken away my disgrace among the people."

The Birth of Jesus Foretold

²⁶In the sixth month of Elizabeth's pregnancy, God sent the angel Gabriel to Nazareth, a town in Galilee, ²⁷to a virgin pledged to be married to a man named Joseph, a descendant of David. The virgin's name was Mary. ²⁸The angel went to her and said, "Greetings, you who are highly favored! The Lord is with you."

²⁹Mary was greatly troubled at his words and wondered what kind of greeting this might be. ³⁰But the angel said to her, "Do not be afraid, Mary; you have found favor with God. ³¹You will conceive and give birth to a son, and you are to call him Jesus. ³²He will be great and will be called the Son of the Most High. The Lord God will give him the throne of his father David, ³³and he will reign over Jacob's descendants forever; his kingdom will never end."

³⁴"How will this be," Mary asked the angel, "since I am a virgin?"

³⁵The angel answered, "The Holy Spirit will come on you, and the power of the Most High will overshadow you. So the holy one to be born will be called*ᵃ* the Son of God. ³⁶Even Elizabeth your relative is going to have a child in her old age, and she who was said to be unable to conceive is in her sixth month. ³⁷For no word from God will ever fail."

³⁸"I am the Lord's servant," Mary answered. "May your word to me be fulfilled." Then the angel left her.

Mary Visits Elizabeth

³⁹At that time Mary got ready and hurried to a town in the hill country of Judea, ⁴⁰where she entered Zechariah's home and greeted Elizabeth. ⁴¹When Elizabeth heard Mary's greeting, the baby leaped in her womb, and Elizabeth was filled with the Holy Spirit. ⁴²In a loud voice she exclaimed: "Blessed are you among women, and blessed is the child you will bear! ⁴³But why am I so favored, that the mother of my Lord should come to me? ⁴⁴As soon as the sound of your greeting reached my ears, the baby in my womb leaped for joy. ⁴⁵Blessed is she who has believed that the Lord would fulfill his promises to her!"

Mary's Song

⁴⁶And Mary said:

"My soul glorifies the Lord
⁴⁷   and my spirit rejoices in God my Savior,
⁴⁸for he has been mindful
        of the humble state of his servant.
    From now on all generations will call me blessed,
⁴⁹   for the Mighty One has done great things for me —
        holy is his name.
⁵⁰His mercy extends to those who fear him,
        from generation to generation.
⁵¹He has performed mighty deeds with his arm;
        he has scattered those who are proud in their inmost thoughts.

ᵃ 35 Or So the child to be born will be called holy,

52 He has brought down rulers from their thrones
   but has lifted up the humble.
53 He has filled the hungry with good things
   but has sent the rich away empty.
54 He has helped his servant Israel,
   remembering to be merciful
55 to Abraham and his descendants forever,
   just as he promised our ancestors."

56 Mary stayed with Elizabeth for about three months and then returned home.

The Birth of John the Baptist

57 When it was time for Elizabeth to have her baby, she gave birth to a son. 58 Her neighbors and relatives heard that the Lord had shown her great mercy, and they shared her joy.

59 On the eighth day they came to circumcise the child, and they were going to name him after his father Zechariah, 60 but his mother spoke up and said, "No! He is to be called John."

61 They said to her, "There is no one among your relatives who has that name."

62 Then they made signs to his father, to find out what he would like to name the child. 63 He asked for a writing tablet, and to everyone's astonishment he wrote, "His name is John." 64 Immediately his mouth was opened and his tongue set free, and he began to speak, praising God. 65 All the neighbors were filled with awe, and throughout the hill country of Judea people were talking about all these things. 66 Everyone who heard this wondered about it, asking, "What then is this child going to be?" For the Lord's hand was with him.

Zechariah's Song

67 His father Zechariah was filled with the Holy Spirit and prophesied:

68 "Praise be to the Lord, the God of Israel,
   because he has come to his people and redeemed them.
69 He has raised up a horn[a] of salvation for us
   in the house of his servant David
70 (as he said through his holy prophets of long ago),
71 salvation from our enemies
   and from the hand of all who hate us —
72 to show mercy to our ancestors
   and to remember his holy covenant,
73   the oath he swore to our father Abraham:
74 to rescue us from the hand of our enemies,
   and to enable us to serve him without fear
75   in holiness and righteousness before him all our days.

76 And you, my child, will be called a prophet of the Most High;
   for you will go on before the Lord to prepare the way for him,
77 to give his people the knowledge of salvation
   through the forgiveness of their sins,
78 because of the tender mercy of our God,
   by which the rising sun will come to us from heaven

a 69 Horn here symbolizes a strong king.

79 to shine on those living in darkness
and in the shadow of death,
to guide our feet into the path of peace."

80 And the child grew and became strong in spirit[a]; and he lived in the wilderness until he appeared publicly to Israel.

The Birth of Jesus

2 In those days Caesar Augustus issued a decree that a census should be taken of the entire Roman world. 2(This was the first census that took place while[b] Quirinius was governor of Syria.) 3And everyone went to their own town to register.

4So Joseph also went up from the town of Nazareth in Galilee to Judea, to Bethlehem the town of David, because he belonged to the house and line of David. 5He went there to register with Mary, who was pledged to be married to him and was expecting a child. 6While they were there, the time came for the baby to be born, 7and she gave birth to her firstborn, a son. She wrapped him in cloths and placed him in a manger, because there was no guest room available for them.

8And there were shepherds living out in the fields nearby, keeping watch over their flocks at night. 9An angel of the Lord appeared to them, and the glory of the Lord shone around them, and they were terrified. 10But the angel said to them, "Do not be afraid. I bring you good news that will cause great joy for all the people. 11Today in the town of David a Savior has been born to you; he is the Messiah, the Lord. 12This will be a sign to you: You will find a baby wrapped in cloths and lying in a manger."

13Suddenly a great company of the heavenly host appeared with the angel, praising God and saying,

14 "Glory to God in the highest heaven,
and on earth peace to those on whom his favor rests."

15When the angels had left them and gone into heaven, the shepherds said to one another, "Let's go to Bethlehem and see this thing that has happened, which the Lord has told us about."

16So they hurried off and found Mary and Joseph, and the baby, who was lying in the manger. 17When they had seen him, they spread the word concerning what had been told them about this child, 18and all who heard it were amazed at what the shepherds said to them. 19But Mary treasured up all these things and pondered them in her heart. 20The shepherds returned, glorifying and praising God for all the things they had heard and seen, which were just as they had been told.

21On the eighth day, when it was time to circumcise the child, he was named Jesus, the name the angel had given him before he was conceived.

Jesus Presented in the Temple

22When the time came for the purification rites required by the Law of Moses, Joseph and Mary took him to Jerusalem to present him to the Lord 23(as it is written in the Law of the Lord, "Every firstborn male is to be consecrated to the Lord"[c]), 24and to offer a sacrifice in keeping with what is said in the Law of the Lord: "a pair of doves or two young pigeons."[d]

---

[a]80 Or in the Spirit   [b]2 Or This census took place before   [c]23 Exodus 13:2,12
[d]24 Lev. 12:8

LUKE 2:11

SAVIOR, MESSIAH, LORD

The three titles "Savior," "Messiah" and "Lord" summarize the work of Christ to save. What God was called in 1:47 ("Savior"), Jesus is called here. This description includes the related meanings of deliverer, protector or preserver. The word "Messiah" means "anointed one," referring to Jesus' royal position, the One who was promised and long expected. The word "Lord" is the title of a ruler. The use of "Lord" throughout the New Testament is also significant because, out of reverence for God's covenant name, the Greek word for "Lord" stood in place of *Yahweh* in the Greek translation of the Old Testament.

Peter elaborated on the meaning of these words in Acts 2:30–36 where Jesus is pictured as sitting on a throne and distributing the gift of salvation from God's side, ruling with the Father. In this way, Peter connected Jesus with God's promises to give David an everlasting kingdom. To refer to Jesus as a good man or a good teacher falls immeasurably short of reality. Jesus came to save people from their sin, as promised. He came to minister, to suffer and die, to rise again, and rule and reign forever as Lord. This was the outworking of God's grand plan, what the writer of Hebrews would call "so great a salvation" (Heb 2:3).

25Now there was a man in Jerusalem called Simeon, who was righteous and devout. He was waiting for the consolation of Israel, and the Holy Spirit was on him. 26It had been revealed to him by the Holy Spirit that he would not die before he had seen the Lord's Messiah. 27Moved by the Spirit, he went into the temple courts. When the parents brought in the child Jesus to do for him what the custom of the Law required, 28Simeon took him in his arms and praised God, saying:

29"Sovereign Lord, as you have promised,*
    you may now dismiss* your servant in peace.
30 For my eyes have seen your salvation,
31   which you have prepared in the sight of all nations:
32a light for revelation to the Gentiles,
    and the glory of your people Israel."

33The child's father and mother marveled at what was said about him. 34Then Simeon blessed them and said to Mary, his mother: "This child is destined to cause the falling and rising of many in Israel, and to be a sign that will be spoken against, 35so that the thoughts of many hearts will be revealed. And a sword will pierce your own soul too."

36There was also a prophet, Anna, the daughter of Penuel, of the tribe of Asher. She was very old; she had lived with her husband seven years after her marriage, 37and then was a widow until she was eighty-four.* She never left the temple but worshiped night and day, fasting and praying. 38Coming up to them at that very moment, she gave thanks to God and spoke about the child to all who were looking forward to the redemption of Jerusalem.

39When Joseph and Mary had done everything required by the Law of the Lord, they returned to Galilee to their own town of Nazareth. 40And the child grew and became strong; he was filled with wisdom, and the grace of God was on him.

The Boy Jesus at the Temple

41Every year Jesus' parents went to Jerusalem for the Festival of the Passover. 42When he was twelve years old, they went up to the festival, according to the custom. 43After the festival was over, while his parents were returning home, the boy Jesus stayed behind in Jerusalem, but they were unaware of it. 44Thinking he was in their company, they traveled on for a day. Then they began looking for him among their relatives and friends. 45When they did not find him, they went back to Jerusalem to look for him. 46After three days they found him in the temple courts, sitting among the teachers, listening to them and asking them questions. 47Everyone who heard him was amazed at his understanding and his answers. 48When his parents saw him, they were astonished. His mother said to him, "Son, why have you treated us like this? Your father and I have been anxiously searching for you."

49"Why were you searching for me?" he asked. "Didn't you know I had to be in my Father's house?"* 50But they did not understand what he was saying to them.

51Then he went down to Nazareth with them and was obedient to them. But his mother treasured all these things in her heart. 52And Jesus grew in wisdom and stature, and in favor with God and man.

---

a 29 Or *promised, / now dismiss*   *b* 37 Or *then had been a widow for eighty-four years.*
c 49 Or *be about my Father's business*

MY FATHER'S BUSINESS

The Bible provides limited information about Jesus' life as a child. We know his parents took him to the temple when he was eight days old to present him to the Lord, to circumcise him, and to offer a sacrifice as prescribed by the law (Lk 2:21–24). Then when Jesus was age 12, he and his family returned to the temple. There Jesus demonstrated an understanding of the work God had commissioned him to accomplish. This evocative statement in the Greek text is an elliptical clause that leaves out a key word. It reads, "I must be in the ... of my Father," without specifying a place or activity. So what young Jesus proclaimed here is that either he must be in the house of God discussing God's truth as the translation suggests, or he must be busy with the Father's work in another context. In the end, the two possibilities are not very different. Over time, it became clear that Jesus understood fully the work he had to do — preaching the good news while traveling to Jerusalem to be killed and to rise on the third day (Lk 9:22). In anticipation of the day he would begin his earthly ministry, he "grew in wisdom and stature, and in favor with God and man" (Lk 2:52).

John the Baptist Prepares the Way

3 In the fifteenth year of the reign of Tiberius Caesar—when Pontius Pilate was governor of Judea, Herod tetrarch of Galilee, his brother Philip tetrarch of Iturea and Traconitis, and Lysanias tetrarch of Abilene— ²during the high-priesthood of Annas and Caiaphas, the word of God came to John son of Zechariah in the wilderness. ³He went into all the country around the Jordan, preaching a baptism of repentance for the forgiveness of sins. ⁴As it is written in the book of the words of Isaiah the prophet:

"A voice of one calling in the wilderness,
'Prepare the way for the Lord,
  make straight paths for him.
⁵Every valley shall be filled in,
  every mountain and hill made low.
The crooked roads shall become straight,
  the rough ways smooth.
⁶And all people will see God's salvation.'"ᵃ

⁷John said to the crowds coming out to be baptized by him, "You brood of vipers! Who warned you to flee from the coming wrath? ⁸Produce fruit in keeping with repentance. And do not begin to say to yourselves, 'We have Abraham as our father.' For I tell you that out of these stones God can raise up children for Abraham. ⁹The ax is already at the root of the trees, and every tree that does not produce good fruit will be cut down and thrown into the fire."

¹⁰"What should we do then?" the crowd asked.

¹¹John answered, "Anyone who has two shirts should share with the one who has none, and anyone who has food should do the same."

¹²Even tax collectors came to be baptized. "Teacher," they asked, "what should we do?"

¹³"Don't collect any more than you are required to," he told them.

¹⁴Then some soldiers asked him, "And what should we do?"

He replied, "Don't extort money and don't accuse people falsely—be content with your pay."

¹⁵The people were waiting expectantly and were all wondering in their hearts if John might possibly be the Messiah. ¹⁶John answered them all, "I baptize you withᵇ water. But one who is more powerful than I will come, the straps of whose sandals I am not worthy to untie. He will baptize you withᵇ the Holy Spirit and fire. ¹⁷His winnowing fork is in his hand to clear his threshing floor and to gather the wheat into his barn, but he will burn up the chaff with unquenchable fire." ¹⁸And with many other words John exhorted the people and proclaimed the good news to them.

¹⁹But when John rebuked Herod the tetrarch because of his marriage to Herodias, his brother's wife, and all the other evil things he had done, ²⁰Herod added this to them all: He locked John up in prison.

The Baptism and Genealogy of Jesus

²¹When all the people were being baptized, Jesus was baptized too. And as he was praying, heaven was opened ²²and the Holy Spirit descended on him in bodily form like a dove. And a voice came from heaven: "You are my Son, whom I love; with you I am well pleased."

ᵃ6 Isaiah 40:3-5   ᵇ16 Or in

23Now Jesus himself was about thirty years old when he began his ministry. He was the son, so it was thought, of Joseph,

the son of Heli, 24the son of Matthat,
the son of Levi, the son of Melki,
the son of Jannai, the son of Joseph,
25the son of Mattathias, the son of Amos,
the son of Nahum, the son of Esli,
the son of Naggai, 26the son of Maath,
the son of Mattathias, the son of Semein,
the son of Josek, the son of Joda,
27the son of Joanan, the son of Rhesa,
the son of Zerubbabel, the son of Shealtiel,
the son of Neri, 28the son of Melki,
the son of Addi, the son of Cosam,
the son of Elmadam, the son of Er,
29the son of Joshua, the son of Eliezer,
the son of Jorim, the son of Matthat,
the son of Levi, 30the son of Simeon,
the son of Judah, the son of Joseph,
the son of Jonam, the son of Eliakim,
31the son of Melea, the son of Menna,
the son of Mattatha, the son of Nathan,
the son of David, 32the son of Jesse,
the son of Obed, the son of Boaz,
the son of Salmon,*a* the son of Nahshon,
33the son of Amminadab, the son of Ram,*b*
the son of Hezron, the son of Perez,
the son of Judah, 34the son of Jacob,
the son of Isaac, the son of Abraham,
the son of Terah, the son of Nahor,
35the son of Serug, the son of Reu,
the son of Peleg, the son of Eber,
the son of Shelah, 36the son of Cainan,
the son of Arphaxad, the son of Shem,
the son of Noah, the son of Lamech,
37the son of Methuselah, the son of Enoch,
the son of Jared, the son of Mahalalel,
the son of Kenan, 38the son of Enosh,
the son of Seth, the son of Adam,
the son of God.

Jesus Is Tested in the Wilderness

4 Jesus, full of the Holy Spirit, left the Jordan and was led by the Spirit into the wilderness, 2where for forty days he was tempted*c* by the devil. He ate nothing during those days, and at the end of them he was hungry.

3The devil said to him, "If you are the Son of God, tell this stone to become bread."

4Jesus answered, "It is written: 'Man shall not live on bread alone.'*d*"

5The devil led him up to a high place and showed him in an instant all the kingdoms of the world. 6And he said to him, "I will give you all

---

*a*32 Some early manuscripts *Sala*   *b*33 Some manuscripts *Amminadab, the son of Admin, the son of Arni*; other manuscripts vary widely.   *c*2 The Greek for *tempted* can also mean *tested*.   *d*4 Deut. 8:3

LUKE 4:1−13

TEMPTATION AND SCRIPTURE

In his humanity, Jesus experienced every temptation that humans do, yet he was without sin (Heb 4:15). When Satan tempted Jesus in the wilderness, Jesus demonstrated his ability to resist the devil and declared his allegiance to God. What Adam failed to do in the garden, Jesus did in the wilderness. When Satan challenged Jesus' identity and authority, Jesus responded by quoting Scripture (Dt 8:3), a succinct way to demonstrate his refusal to live independently from his Father. Next, when Satan enticed Jesus to avoid the cross and gain power in an easier way, Jesus confronted Satan's exaggerated claims about power and authority with another scriptural quote (Dt 6:13). Finally, Satan suggested that Jesus jump from the highest point on the temple, fighting fire with fire and bolstering this temptation with a Scripture passage (Ps 91:11−12). Refusing to put God to a test, Jesus withstood this last temptation by quoting Scripture once again (Dt 6:16). Satan retreated, defeated for the moment by Jesus, who resisted his advances by submitting humbly to God (Jas 4:7). Using the sword of the Spirit, which is the Word of God, Jesus demonstrated how to defeat the devil's schemes and extinguish the flaming arrows directed at God's children (Eph 6:10−17).

their authority and splendor; it has been given to me, and I can give it to anyone I want to. ⁷If you worship me, it will all be yours."

⁸Jesus answered, "It is written: 'Worship the Lord your God and serve him only.'ᵃ"

⁹The devil led him to Jerusalem and had him stand on the highest point of the temple. "If you are the Son of God," he said, "throw yourself down from here. ¹⁰For it is written:

"'He will command his angels concerning you
    to guard you carefully;
¹¹they will lift you up in their hands,
    so that you will not strike your foot against a stone.'ᵇ"

¹²Jesus answered, "It is said: 'Do not put the Lord your God to the test.'ᶜ"

¹³When the devil had finished all this tempting, he left him until an opportune time.

Jesus Rejected at Nazareth

¹⁴Jesus returned to Galilee in the power of the Spirit, and news about him spread through the whole countryside. ¹⁵He was teaching in their synagogues, and everyone praised him.

¹⁶He went to Nazareth, where he had been brought up, and on the Sabbath day he went into the synagogue, as was his custom. He stood up to read, ¹⁷and the scroll of the prophet Isaiah was handed to him. Unrolling it, he found the place where it is written:

¹⁸"The Spirit of the Lord is on me,
    because he has anointed me
    to proclaim good news to the poor.
He has sent me to proclaim freedom for the prisoners
    and recovery of sight for the blind,
    to set the oppressed free,
¹⁹   to proclaim the year of the Lord's favor."ᵈ

²⁰Then he rolled up the scroll, gave it back to the attendant and sat down. The eyes of everyone in the synagogue were fastened on him. ²¹He began by saying to them, "Today this scripture is fulfilled in your hearing."

²²All spoke well of him and were amazed at the gracious words that came from his lips. "Isn't this Joseph's son?" they asked.

²³Jesus said to them, "Surely you will quote this proverb to me: 'Physician, heal yourself!' And you will tell me, 'Do here in your hometown what we have heard that you did in Capernaum.'"

²⁴"Truly I tell you," he continued, "no prophet is accepted in his hometown. ²⁵I assure you that there were many widows in Israel in Elijah's time, when the sky was shut for three and a half years and there was a severe famine throughout the land. ²⁶Yet Elijah was not sent to any of them, but to a widow in Zarephath in the region of Sidon. ²⁷And there were many in Israel with leprosyᵉ in the time of Elisha the prophet, yet not one of them was cleansed — only Naaman the Syrian."

²⁸All the people in the synagogue were furious when they heard this. ²⁹They got up, drove him out of the town, and took him to the

ᵃ8 Deut. 6:13   ᵇ11 Psalm 91:11,12   ᶜ12 Deut. 6:16   ᵈ19 Isaiah 61:1,2 (see Septuagint); Isaiah 58:6   ᵉ27 The Greek word traditionally translated *leprosy* was used for various diseases affecting the skin.

brow of the hill on which the town was built, in order to throw him off the cliff. ³⁰But he walked right through the crowd and went on his way.

Jesus Drives Out an Impure Spirit

³¹Then he went down to Capernaum, a town in Galilee, and on the Sabbath he taught the people. ³²They were amazed at his teaching, because his words had authority.

³³In the synagogue there was a man possessed by a demon, an impure spirit. He cried out at the top of his voice, ³⁴"Go away! What do you want with us, Jesus of Nazareth? Have you come to destroy us? I know who you are — the Holy One of God!"

³⁵"Be quiet!" Jesus said sternly. "Come out of him!" Then the demon threw the man down before them all and came out without injuring him.

³⁶All the people were amazed and said to each other, "What words these are! With authority and power he gives orders to impure spirits and they come out!" ³⁷And the news about him spread throughout the surrounding area.

Jesus Heals Many

³⁸Jesus left the synagogue and went to the home of Simon. Now Simon's mother-in-law was suffering from a high fever, and they asked Jesus to help her. ³⁹So he bent over her and rebuked the fever, and it left her. She got up at once and began to wait on them.

⁴⁰At sunset, the people brought to Jesus all who had various kinds of sickness, and laying his hands on each one, he healed them. ⁴¹Moreover, demons came out of many people, shouting, "You are the Son of God!" But he rebuked them and would not allow them to speak, because they knew he was the Messiah.

⁴²At daybreak, Jesus went out to a solitary place. The people were looking for him and when they came to where he was, they tried to keep him from leaving them. ⁴³But he said, "I must proclaim the good news of the kingdom of God to the other towns also, because that is why I was sent." ⁴⁴And he kept on preaching in the synagogues of Judea.

Jesus Calls His First Disciples

5 One day as Jesus was standing by the Lake of Gennesaret,ᵃ the people were crowding around him and listening to the word of God. ²He saw at the water's edge two boats, left there by the fishermen, who were washing their nets. ³He got into one of the boats, the one belonging to Simon, and asked him to put out a little from shore. Then he sat down and taught the people from the boat.

⁴When he had finished speaking, he said to Simon, "Put out into deep water, and let down the nets for a catch."

⁵Simon answered, "Master, we've worked hard all night and haven't caught anything. But because you say so, I will let down the nets."

⁶When they had done so, they caught such a large number of fish that their nets began to break. ⁷So they signaled their partners in the other boat to come and help them, and they came and filled both boats so full that they began to sink.

⁸When Simon Peter saw this, he fell at Jesus' knees and said, "Go away from me, Lord; I am a sinful man!" ⁹For he and all his

ᵃ1 That is, the Sea of Galilee

companions were astonished at the catch of fish they had taken, ¹⁰and so were James and John, the sons of Zebedee, Simon's partners.

Then Jesus said to Simon, "Don't be afraid; from now on you will fish for people." ¹¹So they pulled their boats up on shore, left everything and followed him.

Jesus Heals a Man With Leprosy

¹²While Jesus was in one of the towns, a man came along who was covered with leprosy.ᵃ When he saw Jesus, he fell with his face to the ground and begged him, "Lord, if you are willing, you can make me clean."

¹³Jesus reached out his hand and touched the man. "I am willing," he said. "Be clean!" And immediately the leprosy left him.

¹⁴Then Jesus ordered him, "Don't tell anyone, but go, show yourself to the priest and offer the sacrifices that Moses commanded for your cleansing, as a testimony to them."

¹⁵Yet the news about him spread all the more, so that crowds of people came to hear him and to be healed of their sicknesses. ¹⁶But Jesus often withdrew to lonely places and prayed.

Jesus Forgives and Heals a Paralyzed Man

¹⁷One day Jesus was teaching, and Pharisees and teachers of the law were sitting there. They had come from every village of Galilee and from Judea and Jerusalem. And the power of the Lord was with Jesus to heal the sick. ¹⁸Some men came carrying a paralyzed man on a mat and tried to take him into the house to lay him before Jesus. ¹⁹When they could not find a way to do this because of the crowd, they went up on the roof and lowered him on his mat through the tiles into the middle of the crowd, right in front of Jesus.

²⁰When Jesus saw their faith, he said, "Friend, your sins are forgiven."

²¹The Pharisees and the teachers of the law began thinking to themselves, "Who is this fellow who speaks blasphemy? Who can forgive sins but God alone?"

²²Jesus knew what they were thinking and asked, "Why are you thinking these things in your hearts? ²³Which is easier: to say, 'Your sins are forgiven,' or to say, 'Get up and walk'? ²⁴But I want you to know that the Son of Man has authority on earth to forgive sins." So he said to the paralyzed man, "I tell you, get up, take your mat and go home." ²⁵Immediately he stood up in front of them, took what he had been lying on and went home praising God. ²⁶Everyone was amazed and gave praise to God. They were filled with awe and said, "We have seen remarkable things today."

Jesus Calls Levi and Eats With Sinners

²⁷After this, Jesus went out and saw a tax collector by the name of Levi sitting at his tax booth. "Follow me," Jesus said to him, ²⁸and Levi got up, left everything and followed him.

²⁹Then Levi held a great banquet for Jesus at his house, and a large crowd of tax collectors and others were eating with them. ³⁰But the Pharisees and the teachers of the law who belonged to their sect complained to his disciples, "Why do you eat and drink with tax collectors and sinners?"

ᵃ12 The Greek word traditionally translated *leprosy* was used for various diseases affecting the skin.

LUKE 5:24

SON OF MAN

The religious leaders watched to see if Jesus would heal on the Sabbath. Jesus increased the stakes by stating that he, as the Son of Man, had the power and authority to forgive sin. The phrase "Son of Man" was an Aramaic idiom that referred to a human being, meaning "someone" or "I." But in this situation, Jesus referenced a title from Daniel 7:13, something he did regularly during his ministry, especially when he wanted to emphasize the nature of his relationship to the Father (Lk 21:27; 22:69). Daniel used the title "son of man" to describe one who shared authority with the Ancient of Days, a powerful reference to the one true God. By invoking this image, Jesus tapped into the supernatural impression of this figure, for only God rides the clouds (Ex 14:20; Ps 104:3).

The question Jesus posed to the religious leaders was whether he had the authority to forgive sin. By referring to himself as the Son of Man in that context, Jesus claimed the authority to forgive sins with the full understanding that such authority was limited only to God.

³¹Jesus answered them, "It is not the healthy who need a doctor, but the sick. ³²I have not come to call the righteous, but sinners to repentance."

Jesus Questioned About Fasting

³³They said to him, "John's disciples often fast and pray, and so do the disciples of the Pharisees, but yours go on eating and drinking."

³⁴Jesus answered, "Can you make the friends of the bridegroom fast while he is with them? ³⁵But the time will come when the bridegroom will be taken from them; in those days they will fast."

³⁶He told them this parable: "No one tears a piece out of a new garment to patch an old one. Otherwise, they will have torn the new garment, and the patch from the new will not match the old. ³⁷And no one pours new wine into old wineskins. Otherwise, the new wine will burst the skins; the wine will run out and the wineskins will be ruined. ³⁸No, new wine must be poured into new wineskins. ³⁹And no one after drinking old wine wants the new, for they say, 'The old is better.'"

Jesus Is Lord of the Sabbath

6 One Sabbath Jesus was going through the grainfields, and his disciples began to pick some heads of grain, rub them in their hands and eat the kernels. ²Some of the Pharisees asked, "Why are you doing what is unlawful on the Sabbath?"

³Jesus answered them, "Have you never read what David did when he and his companions were hungry? ⁴He entered the house of God, and taking the consecrated bread, he ate what is lawful only for priests to eat. And he also gave some to his companions." ⁵Then Jesus said to them, "The Son of Man is Lord of the Sabbath."

⁶On another Sabbath he went into the synagogue and was teaching, and a man was there whose right hand was shriveled. ⁷The Pharisees and the teachers of the law were looking for a reason to accuse Jesus, so they watched him closely to see if he would heal on the Sabbath. ⁸But Jesus knew what they were thinking and said to the man with the shriveled hand, "Get up and stand in front of everyone." So he got up and stood there.

⁹Then Jesus said to them, "I ask you, which is lawful on the Sabbath: to do good or to do evil, to save life or to destroy it?"

¹⁰He looked around at them all, and then said to the man, "Stretch out your hand." He did so, and his hand was completely restored. ¹¹But the Pharisees and the teachers of the law were furious and began to discuss with one another what they might do to Jesus.

The Twelve Apostles

¹²One of those days Jesus went out to a mountainside to pray, and spent the night praying to God. ¹³When morning came, he called his disciples to him and chose twelve of them, whom he also designated apostles: ¹⁴Simon (whom he named Peter), his brother Andrew, James, John, Philip, Bartholomew, ¹⁵Matthew, Thomas, James son of Alphaeus, Simon who was called the Zealot, ¹⁶Judas son of James, and Judas Iscariot, who became a traitor.

Blessings and Woes

¹⁷He went down with them and stood on a level place. A large crowd of his disciples was there and a great number of people from all over

Judea, from Jerusalem, and from the coastal region around Tyre and Sidon, ¹⁸who had come to hear him and to be healed of their diseases. Those troubled by impure spirits were cured, ¹⁹and the people all tried to touch him, because power was coming from him and healing them all.

²⁰Looking at his disciples, he said:

"Blessed are you who are poor,
for yours is the kingdom of God.
²¹Blessed are you who hunger now,
for you will be satisfied.
Blessed are you who weep now,
for you will laugh.
²²Blessed are you when people hate you,
when they exclude you and insult you
and reject your name as evil,
because of the Son of Man.

²³"Rejoice in that day and leap for joy, because great is your reward in heaven. For that is how their ancestors treated the prophets.

²⁴"But woe to you who are rich,
for you have already received your comfort.
²⁵Woe to you who are well fed now,
for you will go hungry.
Woe to you who laugh now,
for you will mourn and weep.
²⁶Woe to you when everyone speaks well of you,
for that is how their ancestors treated the false prophets.

Love for Enemies

²⁷"But to you who are listening I say: Love your enemies, do good to those who hate you, ²⁸bless those who curse you, pray for those who mistreat you. ²⁹If someone slaps you on one cheek, turn to them the other also. If someone takes your coat, do not withhold your shirt from them. ³⁰Give to everyone who asks you, and if anyone takes what belongs to you, do not demand it back. ³¹Do to others as you would have them do to you.

³²"If you love those who love you, what credit is that to you? Even sinners love those who love them. ³³And if you do good to those who are good to you, what credit is that to you? Even sinners do that. ³⁴And if you lend to those from whom you expect repayment, what credit is that to you? Even sinners lend to sinners, expecting to be repaid in full. ³⁵But love your enemies, do good to them, and lend to them without expecting to get anything back. Then your reward will be great, and you will be children of the Most High, because he is kind to the ungrateful and wicked. ³⁶Be merciful, just as your Father is merciful.

Judging Others

³⁷"Do not judge, and you will not be judged. Do not condemn, and you will not be condemned. Forgive, and you will be forgiven. ³⁸Give, and it will be given to you. A good measure, pressed down, shaken together and running over, will be poured into your lap. For with the measure you use, it will be measured to you."

³⁹He also told them this parable: "Can the blind lead the blind? Will

they not both fall into a pit? ⁴⁰The student is not above the teacher, but everyone who is fully trained will be like their teacher.

⁴¹"Why do you look at the speck of sawdust in your brother's eye and pay no attention to the plank in your own eye? ⁴²How can you say to your brother, 'Brother, let me take the speck out of your eye,' when you yourself fail to see the plank in your own eye? You hypocrite, first take the plank out of your eye, and then you will see clearly to remove the speck from your brother's eye.

A Tree and Its Fruit

⁴³"No good tree bears bad fruit, nor does a bad tree bear good fruit. ⁴⁴Each tree is recognized by its own fruit. People do not pick figs from thornbushes, or grapes from briers. ⁴⁵A good man brings good things out of the good stored up in his heart, and an evil man brings evil things out of the evil stored up in his heart. For the mouth speaks what the heart is full of.

The Wise and Foolish Builders

⁴⁶"Why do you call me, 'Lord, Lord,' and do not do what I say? ⁴⁷As for everyone who comes to me and hears my words and puts them into practice, I will show you what they are like. ⁴⁸They are like a man building a house, who dug down deep and laid the foundation on rock. When a flood came, the torrent struck that house but could not shake it, because it was well built. ⁴⁹But the one who hears my words and does not put them into practice is like a man who built a house on the ground without a foundation. The moment the torrent struck that house, it collapsed and its destruction was complete."

The Faith of the Centurion

7 When Jesus had finished saying all this to the people who were listening, he entered Capernaum. ²There a centurion's servant, whom his master valued highly, was sick and about to die. ³The centurion heard of Jesus and sent some elders of the Jews to him, asking him to come and heal his servant. ⁴When they came to Jesus, they pleaded earnestly with him, "This man deserves to have you do this, ⁵because he loves our nation and has built our synagogue." ⁶So Jesus went with them.

He was not far from the house when the centurion sent friends to say to him: "Lord, don't trouble yourself, for I do not deserve to have you come under my roof. ⁷That is why I did not even consider myself worthy to come to you. But say the word, and my servant will be healed. ⁸For I myself am a man under authority, with soldiers under me. I tell this one, 'Go,' and he goes; and that one, 'Come,' and he comes. I say to my servant, 'Do this,' and he does it."

⁹When Jesus heard this, he was amazed at him, and turning to the crowd following him, he said, "I tell you, I have not found such great faith even in Israel." ¹⁰Then the men who had been sent returned to the house and found the servant well.

Jesus Raises a Widow's Son

¹¹Soon afterward, Jesus went to a town called Nain, and his disciples and a large crowd went along with him. ¹²As he approached the town gate, a dead person was being carried out — the only son of his mother, and she was a widow. And a large crowd from the town was with her. ¹³When the Lord saw her, his heart went out to her and he said, "Don't cry."

LUKE 7:1–10

AUTHORITY

A Roman soldier who was a centurion demonstrated insight into Jesus' authority. After asking Jesus to heal his servant, the soldier exhorted Jesus not to travel to him; Jesus needed only to issue the command for the request to be granted. The centurion reasoned that since he exercised authority over the soldiers he led, Jesus could exercise far greater authority. Upon hearing what the centurion said, Jesus affirmed his great faith (Lk 7:9–10).

This Roman discerned what the spiritual leaders of the day missed as they questioned Jesus repeatedly about his authority (Mt 21:23–27; Lk 20:2). The centurion and the common people recognized Jesus' authority, contrasting his powerful teaching with that of the teachers of the law (Mt 7:29). Before his ascension into heaven, Jesus explained to his disciples that all authority in heaven and on earth had been given to him (Mt 28:18). Years later, the apostle Paul would proclaim that God the Father had placed everything in the present age and the age to come under Jesus' feet (Eph 1:19–21). As a result, acknowledging or denying Jesus' absolute authority changes people's eternal destinies, as well as their lives now.

¹⁴Then he went up and touched the bier they were carrying him on, and the bearers stood still. He said, "Young man, I say to you, get up!" ¹⁵The dead man sat up and began to talk, and Jesus gave him back to his mother.

¹⁶They were all filled with awe and praised God. "A great prophet has appeared among us," they said. "God has come to help his people." ¹⁷This news about Jesus spread throughout Judea and the surrounding country.

Jesus and John the Baptist

¹⁸John's disciples told him about all these things. Calling two of them, ¹⁹he sent them to the Lord to ask, "Are you the one who is to come, or should we expect someone else?"

²⁰When the men came to Jesus, they said, "John the Baptist sent us to you to ask, 'Are you the one who is to come, or should we expect someone else?'"

²¹At that very time Jesus cured many who had diseases, sicknesses and evil spirits, and gave sight to many who were blind. ²²So he replied to the messengers, "Go back and report to John what you have seen and heard: The blind receive sight, the lame walk, those who have leprosy*ᵃ* are cleansed, the deaf hear, the dead are raised, and the good news is proclaimed to the poor. ²³Blessed is anyone who does not stumble on account of me."

²⁴After John's messengers left, Jesus began to speak to the crowd about John: "What did you go out into the wilderness to see? A reed swayed by the wind? ²⁵If not, what did you go out to see? A man dressed in fine clothes? No, those who wear expensive clothes and indulge in luxury are in palaces. ²⁶But what did you go out to see? A prophet? Yes, I tell you, and more than a prophet. ²⁷This is the one about whom it is written:

"'I will send my messenger ahead of you,
who will prepare your way before you.'ᵇ

²⁸I tell you, among those born of women there is no one greater than John; yet the one who is least in the kingdom of God is greater than he."

²⁹(All the people, even the tax collectors, when they heard Jesus' words, acknowledged that God's way was right, because they had been baptized by John. ³⁰But the Pharisees and the experts in the law rejected God's purpose for themselves, because they had not been baptized by John.)

³¹Jesus went on to say, "To what, then, can I compare the people of this generation? What are they like? ³²They are like children sitting in the marketplace and calling out to each other:

"'We played the pipe for you,
and you did not dance;
we sang a dirge,
and you did not cry.'

³³For John the Baptist came neither eating bread nor drinking wine, and you say, 'He has a demon.' ³⁴The Son of Man came eating and drinking, and you say, 'Here is a glutton and a drunkard, a friend of

---

ᵃ22 The Greek word traditionally translated *leprosy* was used for various diseases affecting the skin. ᵇ27 Mal. 3:1

tax collectors and sinners.' ³⁵But wisdom is proved right by all her children."

Jesus Anointed by a Sinful Woman

³⁶When one of the Pharisees invited Jesus to have dinner with him, he went to the Pharisee's house and reclined at the table. ³⁷A woman in that town who lived a sinful life learned that Jesus was eating at the Pharisee's house, so she came there with an alabaster jar of perfume. ³⁸As she stood behind him at his feet weeping, she began to wet his feet with her tears. Then she wiped them with her hair, kissed them and poured perfume on them.

³⁹When the Pharisee who had invited him saw this, he said to himself, "If this man were a prophet, he would know who is touching him and what kind of woman she is — that she is a sinner."

⁴⁰Jesus answered him, "Simon, I have something to tell you."

"Tell me, teacher," he said.

⁴¹"Two people owed money to a certain moneylender. One owed him five hundred denarii,ᵃ and the other fifty. ⁴²Neither of them had the money to pay him back, so he forgave the debts of both. Now which of them will love him more?"

⁴³Simon replied, "I suppose the one who had the bigger debt forgiven."

"You have judged correctly," Jesus said.

⁴⁴Then he turned toward the woman and said to Simon, "Do you see this woman? I came into your house. You did not give me any water for my feet, but she wet my feet with her tears and wiped them with her hair. ⁴⁵You did not give me a kiss, but this woman, from the time I entered, has not stopped kissing my feet. ⁴⁶You did not put oil on my head, but she has poured perfume on my feet. ⁴⁷Therefore, I tell you, her many sins have been forgiven — as her great love has shown. But whoever has been forgiven little loves little."

⁴⁸Then Jesus said to her, "Your sins are forgiven."

⁴⁹The other guests began to say among themselves, "Who is this who even forgives sins?"

⁵⁰Jesus said to the woman, "Your faith has saved you; go in peace."

The Parable of the Sower

8 After this, Jesus traveled about from one town and village to another, proclaiming the good news of the kingdom of God. The Twelve were with him, ²and also some women who had been cured of evil spirits and diseases: Mary (called Magdalene) from whom seven demons had come out; ³Joanna the wife of Chuza, the manager of Herod's household; Susanna; and many others. These women were helping to support them out of their own means.

⁴While a large crowd was gathering and people were coming to Jesus from town after town, he told this parable: ⁵"A farmer went out to sow his seed. As he was scattering the seed, some fell along the path; it was trampled on, and the birds ate it up. ⁶Some fell on rocky ground, and when it came up, the plants withered because they had no moisture. ⁷Other seed fell among thorns, which grew up with it and choked the plants. ⁸Still other seed fell on good soil. It came up and yielded a crop, a hundred times more than was sown."

When he said this, he called out, "Whoever has ears to hear, let them hear."

ᵃ 41 A denarius was the usual daily wage of a day laborer (see Matt. 20:2).

⁹His disciples asked him what this parable meant. ¹⁰He said, "The knowledge of the secrets of the kingdom of God has been given to you, but to others I speak in parables, so that,

" 'though seeing, they may not see;
    though hearing, they may not understand.'ᵃ

¹¹"This is the meaning of the parable: The seed is the word of God. ¹²Those along the path are the ones who hear, and then the devil comes and takes away the word from their hearts, so that they may not believe and be saved. ¹³Those on the rocky ground are the ones who receive the word with joy when they hear it, but they have no root. They believe for a while, but in the time of testing they fall away. ¹⁴The seed that fell among thorns stands for those who hear, but as they go on their way they are choked by life's worries, riches and pleasures, and they do not mature. ¹⁵But the seed on good soil stands for those with a noble and good heart, who hear the word, retain it, and by persevering produce a crop.

A Lamp on a Stand

¹⁶"No one lights a lamp and hides it in a clay jar or puts it under a bed. Instead, they put it on a stand, so that those who come in can see the light. ¹⁷For there is nothing hidden that will not be disclosed, and nothing concealed that will not be known or brought out into the open. ¹⁸Therefore consider carefully how you listen. Whoever has will be given more; whoever does not have, even what they think they have will be taken from them."

Jesus' Mother and Brothers

¹⁹Now Jesus' mother and brothers came to see him, but they were not able to get near him because of the crowd. ²⁰Someone told him, "Your mother and brothers are standing outside, wanting to see you."

²¹He replied, "My mother and brothers are those who hear God's word and put it into practice."

Jesus Calms the Storm

²²One day Jesus said to his disciples, "Let us go over to the other side of the lake." So they got into a boat and set out. ²³As they sailed, he fell asleep. A squall came down on the lake, so that the boat was being swamped, and they were in great danger.

²⁴The disciples went and woke him, saying, "Master, Master, we're going to drown!"

He got up and rebuked the wind and the raging waters; the storm subsided, and all was calm. ²⁵"Where is your faith?" he asked his disciples.

In fear and amazement they asked one another, "Who is this? He commands even the winds and the water, and they obey him."

Jesus Restores a Demon-Possessed Man

²⁶They sailed to the region of the Gerasenes,ᵇ which is across the lake from Galilee. ²⁷When Jesus stepped ashore, he was met by a demon-possessed man from the town. For a long time this man had not worn clothes or lived in a house, but had lived in the tombs. ²⁸When he saw

ᵃ10 Isaiah 6:9   ᵇ26 Some manuscripts Gadarenes; other manuscripts Gergesenes; also in verse 37

JESUS' FAMILY

One of the mysteries of the incarnation (Jesus' coming to earth as a human being without ceasing to be God), is the fact that Jesus had a flesh-and-blood family—a mother, father and siblings (Mt 13:55–56). While many if not all of his family members ultimately became his disciples, the Gospels demonstrate that they did not follow him initially. On one occasion they traveled "to take charge of him" because they believed he was out of his mind (Mk 3:21). Another time, his brothers taunted that he should travel to Jerusalem so his disciples could see his works there. "No one who wants to become a public figure acts in secret. Since you are doing these things, show yourself to the world" (Jn 7:2–4).

Through his life and teachings, Jesus framed the context of family in terms of the kingdom of God. He expanded the concept of family to include all who did the will of his Father in heaven (Mt 12:50). While he rebuked religious leaders who failed to honor their parents for the sake of their traditions, he called his disciples to love him more than all else, including their families (Mt 10:37). Yet from the cross, Jesus assigned his disciple John to care for Mary, his mother, demonstrating his love and concern for her (Jn 19:26–27). For Jesus, family remained important but not ultimate, aligning with his mandate to seek God's kingdom first so that all other realities in life could align correctly (Mt 6:33).

Jesus, he cried out and fell at his feet, shouting at the top of his voice, "What do you want with me, Jesus, Son of the Most High God? I beg you, don't torture me!" 29For Jesus had commanded the impure spirit to come out of the man. Many times it had seized him, and though he was chained hand and foot and kept under guard, he had broken his chains and had been driven by the demon into solitary places.

30Jesus asked him, "What is your name?"

"Legion," he replied, because many demons had gone into him. 31And they begged Jesus repeatedly not to order them to go into the Abyss.

32A large herd of pigs was feeding there on the hillside. The demons begged Jesus to let them go into the pigs, and he gave them permission. 33When the demons came out of the man, they went into the pigs, and the herd rushed down the steep bank into the lake and was drowned.

34When those tending the pigs saw what had happened, they ran off and reported this in the town and countryside, 35and the people went out to see what had happened. When they came to Jesus, they found the man from whom the demons had gone out, sitting at Jesus' feet, dressed and in his right mind; and they were afraid. 36Those who had seen it told the people how the demon-possessed man had been cured. 37Then all the people of the region of the Gerasenes asked Jesus to leave them, because they were overcome with fear. So he got into the boat and left.

38The man from whom the demons had gone out begged to go with him, but Jesus sent him away, saying, 39"Return home and tell how much God has done for you." So the man went away and told all over town how much Jesus had done for him.

Jesus Raises a Dead Girl and Heals a Sick Woman

40Now when Jesus returned, a crowd welcomed him, for they were all expecting him. 41Then a man named Jairus, a synagogue leader, came and fell at Jesus' feet, pleading with him to come to his house 42because his only daughter, a girl of about twelve, was dying.

As Jesus was on his way, the crowds almost crushed him. 43And a woman was there who had been subject to bleeding for twelve years,*a* but no one could heal her. 44She came up behind him and touched the edge of his cloak, and immediately her bleeding stopped.

45"Who touched me?" Jesus asked.

When they all denied it, Peter said, "Master, the people are crowding and pressing against you."

46But Jesus said, "Someone touched me; I know that power has gone out from me."

47Then the woman, seeing that she could not go unnoticed, came trembling and fell at his feet. In the presence of all the people, she told why she had touched him and how she had been instantly healed. 48Then he said to her, "Daughter, your faith has healed you. Go in peace."

49While Jesus was still speaking, someone came from the house of Jairus, the synagogue leader. "Your daughter is dead," he said. "Don't bother the teacher anymore."

50Hearing this, Jesus said to Jairus, "Don't be afraid; just believe, and she will be healed."

---

a 43 Many manuscripts years, and she had spent all she had on doctors

⁵¹When he arrived at the house of Jairus, he did not let anyone go in with him except Peter, John and James, and the child's father and mother. ⁵²Meanwhile, all the people were wailing and mourning for her. "Stop wailing," Jesus said. "She is not dead but asleep."

⁵³They laughed at him, knowing that she was dead. ⁵⁴But he took her by the hand and said, "My child, get up!" ⁵⁵Her spirit returned, and at once she stood up. Then Jesus told them to give her something to eat. ⁵⁶Her parents were astonished, but he ordered them not to tell anyone what had happened.

Jesus Sends Out the Twelve

9 When Jesus had called the Twelve together, he gave them power and authority to drive out all demons and to cure diseases, ²and he sent them out to proclaim the kingdom of God and to heal the sick. ³He told them: "Take nothing for the journey — no staff, no bag, no bread, no money, no extra shirt. ⁴Whatever house you enter, stay there until you leave that town. ⁵If people do not welcome you, leave their town and shake the dust off your feet as a testimony against them." ⁶So they set out and went from village to village, proclaiming the good news and healing people everywhere.

⁷Now Herod the tetrarch heard about all that was going on. And he was perplexed because some were saying that John had been raised from the dead, ⁸others that Elijah had appeared, and still others that one of the prophets of long ago had come back to life. ⁹But Herod said, "I beheaded John. Who, then, is this I hear such things about?" And he tried to see him.

Jesus Feeds the Five Thousand

¹⁰When the apostles returned, they reported to Jesus what they had done. Then he took them with him and they withdrew by themselves to a town called Bethsaida, ¹¹but the crowds learned about it and followed him. He welcomed them and spoke to them about the kingdom of God, and healed those who needed healing.

¹²Late in the afternoon the Twelve came to him and said, "Send the crowd away so they can go to the surrounding villages and countryside and find food and lodging, because we are in a remote place here."

¹³He replied, "You give them something to eat."

They answered, "We have only five loaves of bread and two fish — unless we go and buy food for all this crowd." ¹⁴(About five thousand men were there.)

But he said to his disciples, "Have them sit down in groups of about fifty each." ¹⁵The disciples did so, and everyone sat down. ¹⁶Taking the five loaves and the two fish and looking up to heaven, he gave thanks and broke them. Then he gave them to the disciples to distribute to the people. ¹⁷They all ate and were satisfied, and the disciples picked up twelve basketfuls of broken pieces that were left over.

Peter Declares That Jesus Is the Messiah

¹⁸Once when Jesus was praying in private and his disciples were with him, he asked them, "Who do the crowds say I am?"

¹⁹They replied, "Some say John the Baptist; others say Elijah; and still others, that one of the prophets of long ago has come back to life."

²⁰"But what about you?" he asked. "Who do you say I am?"

Peter answered, "God's Messiah."

Jesus Predicts His Death

²¹Jesus strictly warned them not to tell this to anyone. ²²And he said, "The Son of Man must suffer many things and be rejected by the elders, the chief priests and the teachers of the law, and he must be killed and on the third day be raised to life."

²³Then he said to them all: "Whoever wants to be my disciple must deny themselves and take up their cross daily and follow me. ²⁴For whoever wants to save their life will lose it, but whoever loses their life for me will save it. ²⁵What good is it for someone to gain the whole world, and yet lose or forfeit their very self? ²⁶Whoever is ashamed of me and my words, the Son of Man will be ashamed of them when he comes in his glory and in the glory of the Father and of the holy angels.

²⁷"Truly I tell you, some who are standing here will not taste death before they see the kingdom of God."

The Transfiguration

²⁸About eight days after Jesus said this, he took Peter, John and James with him and went up onto a mountain to pray. ²⁹As he was praying, the appearance of his face changed, and his clothes became as bright as a flash of lightning. ³⁰Two men, Moses and Elijah, appeared in glorious splendor, talking with Jesus. ³¹They spoke about his departure,ᵃ which he was about to bring to fulfillment at Jerusalem. ³²Peter and his companions were very sleepy, but when they became fully awake, they saw his glory and the two men standing with him. ³³As the men were leaving Jesus, Peter said to him, "Master, it is good for us to be here. Let us put up three shelters — one for you, one for Moses and one for Elijah." (He did not know what he was saying.)

³⁴While he was speaking, a cloud appeared and covered them, and they were afraid as they entered the cloud. ³⁵A voice came from the cloud, saying, "This is my Son, whom I have chosen; listen to him." ³⁶When the voice had spoken, they found that Jesus was alone. The disciples kept this to themselves and did not tell anyone at that time what they had seen.

Jesus Heals a Demon-Possessed Boy

³⁷The next day, when they came down from the mountain, a large crowd met him. ³⁸A man in the crowd called out, "Teacher, I beg you to look at my son, for he is my only child. ³⁹A spirit seizes him and he suddenly screams; it throws him into convulsions so that he foams at the mouth. It scarcely ever leaves him and is destroying him. ⁴⁰I begged your disciples to drive it out, but they could not."

⁴¹"You unbelieving and perverse generation," Jesus replied, "how long shall I stay with you and put up with you? Bring your son here."

⁴²Even while the boy was coming, the demon threw him to the ground in a convulsion. But Jesus rebuked the impure spirit, healed the boy and gave him back to his father. ⁴³And they were all amazed at the greatness of God.

Jesus Predicts His Death a Second Time

While everyone was marveling at all that Jesus did, he said to his disciples, ⁴⁴"Listen carefully to what I am about to tell you: The Son of

---

ᵃ 31 Greek *exodos*

JESUS' SECRET

After Simon Peter affirmed that Jesus was God's Messiah, Jesus "strictly warned" his disciples not to tell anyone. This was not the first time Jesus cautioned against sharing his identity. After healing a man from leprosy, he said, "See that you don't tell anyone" (Mt 8:4). When Jesus came down from the mountain after Peter, James and John had seen him transfigured, Jesus told them, "Don't tell anyone what you have seen, until the Son of Man has been raised from the dead" (Mt 17:9).

Scholars have pondered this "Messianic secret," seeking to understand why Jesus commanded his disciples not to share what they knew. The problem was not that the disciples knew too much; it was that they knew too little. For example, on the way to Jerusalem where Jesus would be crucified, James and John became indignant by the way a village of Samaritans treated them. "Lord, do you want us to call fire down from heaven to destroy them?" they asked (Lk 9:54). At that moment, they were prepared to kill those for whom Jesus came to die. Clearly, they needed to know more, to experience more: Jesus' trial, torture, crucifixion, death, resurrection and ascension to heaven. After that, Jesus commanded them to go to the whole world and make disciples, teaching them to obey everything he had commanded them (Mt 28:19–20). Only then, after their understanding had increased, would the disciples be ready and free to share the Good News.

Man is going to be delivered into the hands of men." ⁴⁵But they did not understand what this meant. It was hidden from them, so that they did not grasp it, and they were afraid to ask him about it.

⁴⁶An argument started among the disciples as to which of them would be the greatest. ⁴⁷Jesus, knowing their thoughts, took a little child and had him stand beside him. ⁴⁸Then he said to them, "Whoever welcomes this little child in my name welcomes me; and whoever welcomes me welcomes the one who sent me. For it is the one who is least among you all who is the greatest."

⁴⁹"Master," said John, "we saw someone driving out demons in your name and we tried to stop him, because he is not one of us."

⁵⁰"Do not stop him," Jesus said, "for whoever is not against you is for you."

Samaritan Opposition

⁵¹As the time approached for him to be taken up to heaven, Jesus resolutely set out for Jerusalem. ⁵²And he sent messengers on ahead, who went into a Samaritan village to get things ready for him; ⁵³but the people there did not welcome him, because he was heading for Jerusalem. ⁵⁴When the disciples James and John saw this, they asked, "Lord, do you want us to call fire down from heaven to destroy them*?" ⁵⁵But Jesus turned and rebuked them. ⁵⁶Then he and his disciples went to another village.

The Cost of Following Jesus

⁵⁷As they were walking along the road, a man said to him, "I will follow you wherever you go."

⁵⁸Jesus replied, "Foxes have dens and birds have nests, but the Son of Man has no place to lay his head."

⁵⁹He said to another man, "Follow me."

But he replied, "Lord, first let me go and bury my father."

⁶⁰Jesus said to him, "Let the dead bury their own dead, but you go and proclaim the kingdom of God."

⁶¹Still another said, "I will follow you, Lord; but first let me go back and say goodbye to my family."

⁶²Jesus replied, "No one who puts a hand to the plow and looks back is fit for service in the kingdom of God."

Jesus Sends Out the Seventy-Two

10 After this the Lord appointed seventy-two[b] others and sent them two by two ahead of him to every town and place where he was about to go. ²He told them, "The harvest is plentiful, but the workers are few. Ask the Lord of the harvest, therefore, to send out workers into his harvest field. ³Go! I am sending you out like lambs among wolves. ⁴Do not take a purse or bag or sandals; and do not greet anyone on the road.

⁵"When you enter a house, first say, 'Peace to this house.' ⁶If someone who promotes peace is there, your peace will rest on them; if not, it will return to you. ⁷Stay there, eating and drinking whatever they give you, for the worker deserves his wages. Do not move around from house to house.

⁸"When you enter a town and are welcomed, eat what is offered

---

[a] 54 Some manuscripts *them, just as Elijah did*   [b] 1 Some manuscripts *seventy*; also in verse 17

to you. 9Heal the sick who are there and tell them, 'The kingdom of God has come near to you.' 10But when you enter a town and are not welcomed, go into its streets and say, 11'Even the dust of your town we wipe from our feet as a warning to you. Yet be sure of this: The kingdom of God has come near.' 12I tell you, it will be more bearable on that day for Sodom than for that town.

13"Woe to you, Chorazin! Woe to you, Bethsaida! For if the miracles that were performed in you had been performed in Tyre and Sidon, they would have repented long ago, sitting in sackcloth and ashes. 14But it will be more bearable for Tyre and Sidon at the judgment than for you. 15And you, Capernaum, will you be lifted to the heavens? No, you will go down to Hades.ᵃ

16"Whoever listens to you listens to me; whoever rejects you rejects me; but whoever rejects me rejects him who sent me."

17The seventy-two returned with joy and said, "Lord, even the demons submit to us in your name."

18He replied, "I saw Satan fall like lightning from heaven. 19I have given you authority to trample on snakes and scorpions and to overcome all the power of the enemy; nothing will harm you. 20However, do not rejoice that the spirits submit to you, but rejoice that your names are written in heaven."

21At that time Jesus, full of joy through the Holy Spirit, said, "I praise you, Father, Lord of heaven and earth, because you have hidden these things from the wise and learned, and revealed them to little children. Yes, Father, for this is what you were pleased to do.

22"All things have been committed to me by my Father. No one knows who the Son is except the Father, and no one knows who the Father is except the Son and those to whom the Son chooses to reveal him."

23Then he turned to his disciples and said privately, "Blessed are the eyes that see what you see. 24For I tell you that many prophets and kings wanted to see what you see but did not see it, and to hear what you hear but did not hear it."

The Parable of the Good Samaritan

25On one occasion an expert in the law stood up to test Jesus. "Teacher," he asked, "what must I do to inherit eternal life?"

26"What is written in the Law?" he replied. "How do you read it?"

27He answered, " 'Love the Lord your God with all your heart and with all your soul and with all your strength and with all your mind'ᵇ; and, 'Love your neighbor as yourself.'ᶜ"

28"You have answered correctly," Jesus replied. "Do this and you will live."

29But he wanted to justify himself, so he asked Jesus, "And who is my neighbor?"

30In reply Jesus said: "A man was going down from Jerusalem to Jericho, when he was attacked by robbers. They stripped him of his clothes, beat him and went away, leaving him half dead. 31A priest happened to be going down the same road, and when he saw the man, he passed by on the other side. 32So too, a Levite, when he came to the place and saw him, passed by on the other side. 33But a Samaritan, as he traveled, came where the man was; and when he saw him, he took pity on him. 34He went to him and bandaged his wounds, pouring on

---

ᵃ15 That is, the realm of the dead   ᵇ27 Deut. 6:5   ᶜ27 Lev. 19:18

oil and wine. Then he put the man on his own donkey, brought him to an inn and took care of him. ³⁵The next day he took out two denarii^a and gave them to the innkeeper. 'Look after him,' he said, 'and when I return, I will reimburse you for any extra expense you may have.'

³⁶"Which of these three do you think was a neighbor to the man who fell into the hands of robbers?"

³⁷The expert in the law replied, "The one who had mercy on him." Jesus told him, "Go and do likewise."

At the Home of Martha and Mary

³⁸As Jesus and his disciples were on their way, he came to a village where a woman named Martha opened her home to him. ³⁹She had a sister called Mary, who sat at the Lord's feet listening to what he said. ⁴⁰But Martha was distracted by all the preparations that had to be made. She came to him and asked, "Lord, don't you care that my sister has left me to do the work by myself? Tell her to help me!"

⁴¹"Martha, Martha," the Lord answered, "you are worried and upset about many things, ⁴²but few things are needed — or indeed only one.^b Mary has chosen what is better, and it will not be taken away from her."

Jesus' Teaching on Prayer

11 One day Jesus was praying in a certain place. When he finished, one of his disciples said to him, "Lord, teach us to pray, just as John taught his disciples."

²He said to them, "When you pray, say:

"'Father,^c
hallowed be your name,
your kingdom come.^d
³Give us each day our daily bread.
⁴Forgive us our sins,
for we also forgive everyone who sins against us.^e
And lead us not into temptation.^f'"

⁵Then Jesus said to them, "Suppose you have a friend, and you go to him at midnight and say, 'Friend, lend me three loaves of bread; ⁶a friend of mine on a journey has come to me, and I have no food to offer him.' ⁷And suppose the one inside answers, 'Don't bother me. The door is already locked, and my children and I are in bed. I can't get up and give you anything.' ⁸I tell you, even though he will not get up and give you the bread because of friendship, yet because of your shameless audacity^g he will surely get up and give you as much as you need.

⁹"So I say to you: Ask and it will be given to you; seek and you will find; knock and the door will be opened to you. ¹⁰For everyone who asks receives; the one who seeks finds; and to the one who knocks, the door will be opened.

¹¹"Which of you fathers, if your son asks for^h a fish, will give him a snake instead? ¹²Or if he asks for an egg, will give him a scorpion?

---

^a35 A denarius was the usual daily wage of a day laborer (see Matt. 20:2).
^b42 Some manuscripts but only one thing is needed   ^c2 Some manuscripts Our Father in heaven   ^d2 Some manuscripts come. May your will be done on earth as it is in heaven.   ^e4 Greek everyone who is indebted to us   ^f4 Some manuscripts temptation, but deliver us from the evil one   ^g8 Or yet to preserve his good name   ^h11 Some manuscripts for bread, will give him a stone? Or if he asks for

¹³If you then, though you are evil, know how to give good gifts to your children, how much more will your Father in heaven give the Holy Spirit to those who ask him!"

Jesus and Beelzebul

¹⁴Jesus was driving out a demon that was mute. When the demon left, the man who had been mute spoke, and the crowd was amazed. ¹⁵But some of them said, "By Beelzebul, the prince of demons, he is driving out demons." ¹⁶Others tested him by asking for a sign from heaven.

¹⁷Jesus knew their thoughts and said to them: "Any kingdom divided against itself will be ruined, and a house divided against itself will fall. ¹⁸If Satan is divided against himself, how can his kingdom stand? I say this because you claim that I drive out demons by Beelzebul. ¹⁹Now if I drive out demons by Beelzebul, by whom do your followers drive them out? So then, they will be your judges. ²⁰But if I drive out demons by the finger of God, then the kingdom of God has come upon you.

²¹"When a strong man, fully armed, guards his own house, his possessions are safe. ²²But when someone stronger attacks and overpowers him, he takes away the armor in which the man trusted and divides up his plunder.

²³"Whoever is not with me is against me, and whoever does not gather with me scatters.

²⁴"When an impure spirit comes out of a person, it goes through arid places seeking rest and does not find it. Then it says, 'I will return to the house I left.' ²⁵When it arrives, it finds the house swept clean and put in order. ²⁶Then it goes and takes seven other spirits more wicked than itself, and they go in and live there. And the final condition of that person is worse than the first."

²⁷As Jesus was saying these things, a woman in the crowd called out, "Blessed is the mother who gave you birth and nursed you."

²⁸He replied, "Blessed rather are those who hear the word of God and obey it."

The Sign of Jonah

²⁹As the crowds increased, Jesus said, "This is a wicked generation. It asks for a sign, but none will be given it except the sign of Jonah. ³⁰For as Jonah was a sign to the Ninevites, so also will the Son of Man be to this generation. ³¹The Queen of the South will rise at the judgment with the people of this generation and condemn them, for she came from the ends of the earth to listen to Solomon's wisdom; and now something greater than Solomon is here. ³²The men of Nineveh will stand up at the judgment with this generation and condemn it, for they repented at the preaching of Jonah; and now something greater than Jonah is here.

The Lamp of the Body

³³"No one lights a lamp and puts it in a place where it will be hidden, or under a bowl. Instead they put it on its stand, so that those who come in may see the light. ³⁴Your eye is the lamp of your body. When your eyes are healthy,ᵃ your whole body also is full of light. But when they are unhealthy,ᵇ your body also is full of darkness. ³⁵See to

---

ᵃ 34 The Greek for *healthy* here implies *generous*.   ᵇ 34 The Greek for *unhealthy* here implies *stingy*.

LUKE 11:20

THE KINGDOM OF GOD

Jesus proclaimed and explained the kingdom of God — God's rule over all things. In the Old Testament, God established his kingdom politically under David. When the Babylonians destroyed Jerusalem, the prophets continued to speak of the reestablishment of the kingdom of God under the coming Messiah (Isa 9:6–7). When Jesus came to earth, he preached that the kingdom of God had arrived (Mt 4:17; 5:3; Lk 11:20). With Jesus' coming, God's redemptive rule has freed men and women from Satan's power. When Jesus cast out demons, he demonstrated the reality of the kingdom. And through his parables, Jesus described what the kingdom was like (Mt 25).

What we know from Jesus' own accounts of the kingdom is that, from an earthly perspective, it turns worldly values and priorities upside down. In God's kingdom, the poor are rich; those who mourn will be comforted; the meek are powerful; and seekers, mercy-givers, peacemakers and those who are persecuted are the ones who will inherit the kingdom (Mt 5:3–12). Jesus' ministry on earth ushered in the kingdom; the coming of the Spirit (Ac 2:1–13) brought it into a new phase; and someday, when the dead in Christ are raised and Jesus comes again to establish his earthly kingdom, it will be fully realized in all of its splendor, justice and perfection (Rev 22:1–5).

it, then, that the light within you is not darkness. [36]Therefore, if your whole body is full of light, and no part of it dark, it will be just as full of light as when a lamp shines its light on you."

Woes on the Pharisees and the Experts in the Law

[37]When Jesus had finished speaking, a Pharisee invited him to eat with him; so he went in and reclined at the table. [38]But the Pharisee was surprised when he noticed that Jesus did not first wash before the meal.

[39]Then the Lord said to him, "Now then, you Pharisees clean the outside of the cup and dish, but inside you are full of greed and wickedness. [40]You foolish people! Did not the one who made the outside make the inside also? [41]But now as for what is inside you — be generous to the poor, and everything will be clean for you.

[42]"Woe to you Pharisees, because you give God a tenth of your mint, rue and all other kinds of garden herbs, but you neglect justice and the love of God. You should have practiced the latter without leaving the former undone.

[43]"Woe to you Pharisees, because you love the most important seats in the synagogues and respectful greetings in the marketplaces.

[44]"Woe to you, because you are like unmarked graves, which people walk over without knowing it."

[45]One of the experts in the law answered him, "Teacher, when you say these things, you insult us also."

[46]Jesus replied, "And you experts in the law, woe to you, because you load people down with burdens they can hardly carry, and you yourselves will not lift one finger to help them.

[47]"Woe to you, because you build tombs for the prophets, and it was your ancestors who killed them. [48]So you testify that you approve of what your ancestors did; they killed the prophets, and you build their tombs. [49]Because of this, God in his wisdom said, 'I will send them prophets and apostles, some of whom they will kill and others they will persecute.' [50]Therefore this generation will be held responsible for the blood of all the prophets that has been shed since the beginning of the world, [51]from the blood of Abel to the blood of Zechariah, who was killed between the altar and the sanctuary. Yes, I tell you, this generation will be held responsible for it all.

[52]"Woe to you experts in the law, because you have taken away the key to knowledge. You yourselves have not entered, and you have hindered those who were entering."

[53]When Jesus went outside, the Pharisees and the teachers of the law began to oppose him fiercely and to besiege him with questions, [54]waiting to catch him in something he might say.

Warnings and Encouragements

12 Meanwhile, when a crowd of many thousands had gathered, so that they were trampling on one another, Jesus began to speak first to his disciples, saying: "Be[a] on your guard against the yeast of the Pharisees, which is hypocrisy. [2]There is nothing concealed that will not be disclosed, or hidden that will not be made known. [3]What you have said in the dark will be heard in the daylight, and what you have whispered in the ear in the inner rooms will be proclaimed from the roofs.

[a]1 Or speak to his disciples, saying: "First of all, be

4"I tell you, my friends, do not be afraid of those who kill the body and after that can do no more. 5But I will show you whom you should fear: Fear him who, after your body has been killed, has authority to throw you into hell. Yes, I tell you, fear him. 6Are not five sparrows sold for two pennies? Yet not one of them is forgotten by God. 7Indeed, the very hairs of your head are all numbered. Don't be afraid; you are worth more than many sparrows.

8"I tell you, whoever publicly acknowledges me before others, the Son of Man will also acknowledge before the angels of God. 9But whoever disowns me before others will be disowned before the angels of God. 10And everyone who speaks a word against the Son of Man will be forgiven, but anyone who blasphemes against the Holy Spirit will not be forgiven.

11"When you are brought before synagogues, rulers and authorities, do not worry about how you will defend yourselves or what you will say, 12for the Holy Spirit will teach you at that time what you should say."

The Parable of the Rich Fool

13Someone in the crowd said to him, "Teacher, tell my brother to divide the inheritance with me."

14Jesus replied, "Man, who appointed me a judge or an arbiter between you?" 15Then he said to them, "Watch out! Be on your guard against all kinds of greed; life does not consist in an abundance of possessions."

16And he told them this parable: "The ground of a certain rich man yielded an abundant harvest. 17He thought to himself, 'What shall I do? I have no place to store my crops.'

18"Then he said, 'This is what I'll do. I will tear down my barns and build bigger ones, and there I will store my surplus grain. 19And I'll say to myself, "You have plenty of grain laid up for many years. Take life easy; eat, drink and be merry."'

20"But God said to him, 'You fool! This very night your life will be demanded from you. Then who will get what you have prepared for yourself?'

21"This is how it will be with whoever stores up things for themselves but is not rich toward God."

Do Not Worry

22Then Jesus said to his disciples: "Therefore I tell you, do not worry about your life, what you will eat; or about your body, what you will wear. 23For life is more than food, and the body more than clothes. 24Consider the ravens: They do not sow or reap, they have no storeroom or barn; yet God feeds them. And how much more valuable you are than birds! 25Who of you by worrying can add a single hour to your life*a*? 26Since you cannot do this very little thing, why do you worry about the rest?

27"Consider how the wild flowers grow. They do not labor or spin. Yet I tell you, not even Solomon in all his splendor was dressed like one of these. 28If that is how God clothes the grass of the field, which is here today, and tomorrow is thrown into the fire, how much more will he clothe you — you of little faith! 29And do not set your heart on what you will eat or drink; do not worry about it. 30For the pagan world runs

a 25 Or single cubit to your height

BLASPHEMY

Jesus' critics accused him of blasphemy, the act of showing contempt or lack of reverence for God. In the Old Testament, blaspheming God was a crime punishable by death (Lev 24:15–16). Blasphemy violated the third of the Ten Commandments, which required people to uphold the name and reputation of the Lord (Ex 20:7). The unbelieving Jewish leaders of Jesus' day charged Jesus with blasphemy since, in their view, he was a man who falsely claimed to be God's Son (Mt 9:3).

Actually, the Jewish leaders' own lawlessness and hypocrisy caused God's name to be blasphemed among the Gentiles (Ro 2:24). Also, their bitter opposition to Jesus and his gospel blasphemed God (Ac 18:6), and Jesus confronted their blasphemy as they attributed the work of the Holy Spirit to Satan (Mt 12:31–32). In the Scripture, Christians are commanded to avoid words or actions that blaspheme the Lord's name and teaching (1Ti 6:1). Rejecting Jesus' gracious gift of salvation remains the ultimate form of blasphemy, one with eternal repercussions.

after all such things, and your Father knows that you need them. [31]But seek his kingdom, and these things will be given to you as well.

[32]"Do not be afraid, little flock, for your Father has been pleased to give you the kingdom. [33]Sell your possessions and give to the poor. Provide purses for yourselves that will not wear out, a treasure in heaven that will never fail, where no thief comes near and no moth destroys. [34]For where your treasure is, there your heart will be also.

Watchfulness

[35]"Be dressed ready for service and keep your lamps burning, [36]like servants waiting for their master to return from a wedding banquet, so that when he comes and knocks they can immediately open the door for him. [37]It will be good for those servants whose master finds them watching when he comes. Truly I tell you, he will dress himself to serve, will have them recline at the table and will come and wait on them. [38]It will be good for those servants whose master finds them ready, even if he comes in the middle of the night or toward daybreak. [39]But understand this: If the owner of the house had known at what hour the thief was coming, he would not have let his house be broken into. [40]You also must be ready, because the Son of Man will come at an hour when you do not expect him."

[41]Peter asked, "Lord, are you telling this parable to us, or to everyone?"

[42]The Lord answered, "Who then is the faithful and wise manager, whom the master puts in charge of his servants to give them their food allowance at the proper time? [43]It will be good for that servant whom the master finds doing so when he returns. [44]Truly I tell you, he will put him in charge of all his possessions. [45]But suppose the servant says to himself, 'My master is taking a long time in coming,' and he then begins to beat the other servants, both men and women, and to eat and drink and get drunk. [46]The master of that servant will come on a day when he does not expect him and at an hour he is not aware of. He will cut him to pieces and assign him a place with the unbelievers.

[47]"The servant who knows the master's will and does not get ready or does not do what the master wants will be beaten with many blows. [48]But the one who does not know and does things deserving punishment will be beaten with few blows. From everyone who has been given much, much will be demanded; and from the one who has been entrusted with much, much more will be asked.

Not Peace but Division

[49]"I have come to bring fire on the earth, and how I wish it were already kindled! [50]But I have a baptism to undergo, and what constraint I am under until it is completed! [51]Do you think I came to bring peace on earth? No, I tell you, but division. [52]From now on there will be five in one family divided against each other, three against two and two against three. [53]They will be divided, father against son and son against father, mother against daughter and daughter against mother, mother-in-law against daughter-in-law and daughter-in-law against mother-in-law."

Interpreting the Times

[54]He said to the crowd: "When you see a cloud rising in the west, immediately you say, 'It's going to rain,' and it does. [55]And when the

south wind blows, you say, 'It's going to be hot,' and it is. 56Hypocrites! You know how to interpret the appearance of the earth and the sky. How is it that you don't know how to interpret this present time?

57"Why don't you judge for yourselves what is right? 58As you are going with your adversary to the magistrate, try hard to be reconciled on the way, or your adversary may drag you off to the judge, and the judge turn you over to the officer, and the officer throw you into prison. 59I tell you, you will not get out until you have paid the last penny."

Repent or Perish

13 Now there were some present at that time who told Jesus about the Galileans whose blood Pilate had mixed with their sacrifices. 2Jesus answered, "Do you think that these Galileans were worse sinners than all the other Galileans because they suffered this way? 3I tell you, no! But unless you repent, you too will all perish. 4Or those eighteen who died when the tower in Siloam fell on them — do you think they were more guilty than all the others living in Jerusalem? 5I tell you, no! But unless you repent, you too will all perish."

6Then he told this parable: "A man had a fig tree growing in his vineyard, and he went to look for fruit on it but did not find any. 7So he said to the man who took care of the vineyard, 'For three years now I've been coming to look for fruit on this fig tree and haven't found any. Cut it down! Why should it use up the soil?'

8"'Sir,' the man replied, 'leave it alone for one more year, and I'll dig around it and fertilize it. 9If it bears fruit next year, fine! If not, then cut it down.'"

Jesus Heals a Crippled Woman on the Sabbath

10On a Sabbath Jesus was teaching in one of the synagogues, 11and a woman was there who had been crippled by a spirit for eighteen years. She was bent over and could not straighten up at all. 12When Jesus saw her, he called her forward and said to her, "Woman, you are set free from your infirmity." 13Then he put his hands on her, and immediately she straightened up and praised God.

14Indignant because Jesus had healed on the Sabbath, the synagogue leader said to the people, "There are six days for work. So come and be healed on those days, not on the Sabbath."

15The Lord answered him, "You hypocrites! Doesn't each of you on the Sabbath untie your ox or donkey from the stall and lead it out to give it water? 16Then should not this woman, a daughter of Abraham, whom Satan has kept bound for eighteen long years, be set free on the Sabbath day from what bound her?"

17When he said this, all his opponents were humiliated, but the people were delighted with all the wonderful things he was doing.

The Parables of the Mustard Seed and the Yeast

18Then Jesus asked, "What is the kingdom of God like? What shall I compare it to? 19It is like a mustard seed, which a man took and planted in his garden. It grew and became a tree, and the birds perched in its branches."

20Again he asked, "What shall I compare the kingdom of God to? 21It is like yeast that a woman took and mixed into about sixty pounds*a* of flour until it worked all through the dough."

---

a 21 Or about 27 kilograms

The Narrow Door

²²Then Jesus went through the towns and villages, teaching as he made his way to Jerusalem. ²³Someone asked him, "Lord, are only a few people going to be saved?"

He said to them, ²⁴"Make every effort to enter through the narrow door, because many, I tell you, will try to enter and will not be able to. ²⁵Once the owner of the house gets up and closes the door, you will stand outside knocking and pleading, 'Sir, open the door for us.'

"But he will answer, 'I don't know you or where you come from.'

²⁶"Then you will say, 'We ate and drank with you, and you taught in our streets.'

²⁷"But he will reply, 'I don't know you or where you come from. Away from me, all you evildoers!'

²⁸"There will be weeping there, and gnashing of teeth, when you see Abraham, Isaac and Jacob and all the prophets in the kingdom of God, but you yourselves thrown out. ²⁹People will come from east and west and north and south, and will take their places at the feast in the kingdom of God. ³⁰Indeed there are those who are last who will be first, and first who will be last."

Jesus' Sorrow for Jerusalem

³¹At that time some Pharisees came to Jesus and said to him, "Leave this place and go somewhere else. Herod wants to kill you."

³²He replied, "Go tell that fox, 'I will keep on driving out demons and healing people today and tomorrow, and on the third day I will reach my goal.' ³³In any case, I must press on today and tomorrow and the next day — for surely no prophet can die outside Jerusalem!

³⁴"Jerusalem, Jerusalem, you who kill the prophets and stone those sent to you, how often I have longed to gather your children together, as a hen gathers her chicks under her wings, and you were not willing. ³⁵Look, your house is left to you desolate. I tell you, you will not see me again until you say, 'Blessed is he who comes in the name of the Lord.'ᵃ"

Jesus at a Pharisee's House

14 One Sabbath, when Jesus went to eat in the house of a prominent Pharisee, he was being carefully watched. ²There in front of him was a man suffering from abnormal swelling of his body. ³Jesus asked the Pharisees and experts in the law, "Is it lawful to heal on the Sabbath or not?" ⁴But they remained silent. So taking hold of the man, he healed him and sent him on his way.

⁵Then he asked them, "If one of you has a childᵇ or an ox that falls into a well on the Sabbath day, will you not immediately pull it out?" ⁶And they had nothing to say.

⁷When he noticed how the guests picked the places of honor at the table, he told them this parable: ⁸"When someone invites you to a wedding feast, do not take the place of honor, for a person more distinguished than you may have been invited. ⁹If so, the host who invited both of you will come and say to you, 'Give this person your seat.' Then, humiliated, you will have to take the least important place. ¹⁰But when you are invited, take the lowest place, so that when your host comes, he will say to you, 'Friend, move up to a better place.' Then you will be honored in the presence of all the other guests. ¹¹For all

---

ᵃ35 Psalm 118:26   ᵇ5 Some manuscripts *donkey*

PROPHETS DYING IN JERUSALEM

Near the end of Jesus' earthly ministry, he moved purposefully toward Jerusalem knowing that he would be mocked, flogged and crucified in that city (Mt 20:18–20). Jesus followed a long line of prophets who were executed in the nation's capital (1Ki 18:4; 2Ch 24:21). During the last week before his death, Jesus looked out over the city and cried, "Jerusalem, Jerusalem" (v. 34). Repeating the name twice was a sign of intense sorrow, like one mourning the loss of a child (2Sa 18:33). Jesus' emotion expressed his love for the people despite the bitter experience that he knew was coming by way of their hands. In the end, like the prophets of old, Jesus issued a declaration of judgment on the city, calling it a house that would be desolated (v. 35). Unlike the prophets of old who died as martyrs, Jesus' death and resurrection brought everlasting life—life that would explode in resurrection power (Php 3:10).

those who exalt themselves will be humbled, and those who humble themselves will be exalted."

¹²Then Jesus said to his host, "When you give a luncheon or dinner, do not invite your friends, your brothers or sisters, your relatives, or your rich neighbors; if you do, they may invite you back and so you will be repaid. ¹³But when you give a banquet, invite the poor, the crippled, the lame, the blind, ¹⁴and you will be blessed. Although they cannot repay you, you will be repaid at the resurrection of the righteous."

The Parable of the Great Banquet

¹⁵When one of those at the table with him heard this, he said to Jesus, "Blessed is the one who will eat at the feast in the kingdom of God."

¹⁶Jesus replied: "A certain man was preparing a great banquet and invited many guests. ¹⁷At the time of the banquet he sent his servant to tell those who had been invited, 'Come, for everything is now ready.'

¹⁸"But they all alike began to make excuses. The first said, 'I have just bought a field, and I must go and see it. Please excuse me.'

¹⁹"Another said, 'I have just bought five yoke of oxen, and I'm on my way to try them out. Please excuse me.'

²⁰"Still another said, 'I just got married, so I can't come.'

²¹"The servant came back and reported this to his master. Then the owner of the house became angry and ordered his servant, 'Go out quickly into the streets and alleys of the town and bring in the poor, the crippled, the blind and the lame.'

²²"'Sir,' the servant said, 'what you ordered has been done, but there is still room.'

²³"Then the master told his servant, 'Go out to the roads and country lanes and compel them to come in, so that my house will be full. ²⁴I tell you, not one of those who were invited will get a taste of my banquet.'"

The Cost of Being a Disciple

²⁵Large crowds were traveling with Jesus, and turning to them he said: ²⁶"If anyone comes to me and does not hate father and mother, wife and children, brothers and sisters — yes, even their own life — such a person cannot be my disciple. ²⁷And whoever does not carry their cross and follow me cannot be my disciple.

²⁸"Suppose one of you wants to build a tower. Won't you first sit down and estimate the cost to see if you have enough money to complete it? ²⁹For if you lay the foundation and are not able to finish it, everyone who sees it will ridicule you, ³⁰saying, 'This person began to build and wasn't able to finish.'

³¹"Or suppose a king is about to go to war against another king. Won't he first sit down and consider whether he is able with ten thousand men to oppose the one coming against him with twenty thousand? ³²If he is not able, he will send a delegation while the other is still a long way off and will ask for terms of peace. ³³In the same way, those of you who do not give up everything you have cannot be my disciples.

³⁴"Salt is good, but if it loses its saltiness, how can it be made salty again? ³⁵It is fit neither for the soil nor for the manure pile; it is thrown out.

"Whoever has ears to hear, let them hear."

LUKE 14:25 – 34

THE COST OF DISCIPLESHIP

Jesus paid an incalculable price for the salvation of sinners. As the Romans executed him on trumped-up charges (Lk 23:22), the Father substituted the death of his innocent Son for the lives of all believers, who are justly charged with the capital offense of sinning against a holy God. This substitution made it possible for a just God to forgive guilty sinners. This divine pardon cannot be bought or earned but only received by grace through faith (Eph 2:8). The miracle of the gospel is that God would accept sinners because of what Jesus did through his life, death and resurrection.

The high cost Jesus paid for salvation demands a high price for discipleship. Jesus clarified this truth when he said that whoever wanted to be his disciples must take up their cross and follow him (Lk 9:23). Jesus' disciples were to surrender completely to God and his will, just as Jesus submitted completely to his Father's will (Jn 5:19). Then, as now, the ones who desire to follow Jesus must obey him (Jn 14:15).

Robust discipleship reflects a realistic understanding of salvation: the price paid, the pain borne and the great gift delivered. Those who seek to follow Jesus casually have failed to think deeply about his death on the cross. While God gives sinners salvation freely, living a life of discipleship costs everything, as what is required is daily and complete surrender to God and his will.

The Parable of the Lost Sheep

15 Now the tax collectors and sinners were all gathering around to hear Jesus. [2]But the Pharisees and the teachers of the law muttered, "This man welcomes sinners and eats with them."

[3]Then Jesus told them this parable: [4]"Suppose one of you has a hundred sheep and loses one of them. Doesn't he leave the ninety-nine in the open country and go after the lost sheep until he finds it? [5]And when he finds it, he joyfully puts it on his shoulders [6]and goes home. Then he calls his friends and neighbors together and says, 'Rejoice with me; I have found my lost sheep.' [7]I tell you that in the same way there will be more rejoicing in heaven over one sinner who repents than over ninety-nine righteous persons who do not need to repent.

The Parable of the Lost Coin

[8]"Or suppose a woman has ten silver coins[a] and loses one. Doesn't she light a lamp, sweep the house and search carefully until she finds it? [9]And when she finds it, she calls her friends and neighbors together and says, 'Rejoice with me; I have found my lost coin.' [10]In the same way, I tell you, there is rejoicing in the presence of the angels of God over one sinner who repents."

The Parable of the Lost Son

[11]Jesus continued: "There was a man who had two sons. [12]The younger one said to his father, 'Father, give me my share of the estate.' So he divided his property between them.

[13]"Not long after that, the younger son got together all he had, set off for a distant country and there squandered his wealth in wild living. [14]After he had spent everything, there was a severe famine in that whole country, and he began to be in need. [15]So he went and hired himself out to a citizen of that country, who sent him to his fields to feed pigs. [16]He longed to fill his stomach with the pods that the pigs were eating, but no one gave him anything.

[17]"When he came to his senses, he said, 'How many of my father's hired servants have food to spare, and here I am starving to death! [18]I will set out and go back to my father and say to him: Father, I have sinned against heaven and against you. [19]I am no longer worthy to be called your son; make me like one of your hired servants.' [20]So he got up and went to his father.

"But while he was still a long way off, his father saw him and was filled with compassion for him; he ran to his son, threw his arms around him and kissed him.

[21]"The son said to him, 'Father, I have sinned against heaven and against you. I am no longer worthy to be called your son.'

[22]"But the father said to his servants, 'Quick! Bring the best robe and put it on him. Put a ring on his finger and sandals on his feet. [23]Bring the fattened calf and kill it. Let's have a feast and celebrate. [24]For this son of mine was dead and is alive again; he was lost and is found.' So they began to celebrate.

[25]"Meanwhile, the older son was in the field. When he came near the house, he heard music and dancing. [26]So he called one of the servants and asked him what was going on. [27]'Your brother has come,' he

---

[a]8 Greek *ten drachmas*, each worth about a day's wages

replied, 'and your father has killed the fattened calf because he has him back safe and sound.'

²⁸"The older brother became angry and refused to go in. So his father went out and pleaded with him. ²⁹But he answered his father, 'Look! All these years I've been slaving for you and never disobeyed your orders. Yet you never gave me even a young goat so I could celebrate with my friends. ³⁰But when this son of yours who has squandered your property with prostitutes comes home, you kill the fattened calf for him!'

³¹"'My son,' the father said, 'you are always with me, and everything I have is yours. ³²But we had to celebrate and be glad, because this brother of yours was dead and is alive again; he was lost and is found.'"

The Parable of the Shrewd Manager

16 Jesus told his disciples: "There was a rich man whose manager was accused of wasting his possessions. ²So he called him in and asked him, 'What is this I hear about you? Give an account of your management, because you cannot be manager any longer.'

³"The manager said to himself, 'What shall I do now? My master is taking away my job. I'm not strong enough to dig, and I'm ashamed to beg — ⁴I know what I'll do so that, when I lose my job here, people will welcome me into their houses.'

⁵"So he called in each one of his master's debtors. He asked the first, 'How much do you owe my master?'

⁶"'Nine hundred gallons*a* of olive oil,' he replied.

"The manager told him, 'Take your bill, sit down quickly, and make it four hundred and fifty.'

⁷"Then he asked the second, 'And how much do you owe?'

"'A thousand bushels*b* of wheat,' he replied.

"He told him, 'Take your bill and make it eight hundred.'

⁸"The master commended the dishonest manager because he had acted shrewdly. For the people of this world are more shrewd in dealing with their own kind than are the people of the light. ⁹I tell you, use worldly wealth to gain friends for yourselves, so that when it is gone, you will be welcomed into eternal dwellings.

¹⁰"Whoever can be trusted with very little can also be trusted with much, and whoever is dishonest with very little will also be dishonest with much. ¹¹So if you have not been trustworthy in handling worldly wealth, who will trust you with true riches? ¹²And if you have not been trustworthy with someone else's property, who will give you property of your own?

¹³"No one can serve two masters. Either you will hate the one and love the other, or you will be devoted to the one and despise the other. You cannot serve both God and money."

¹⁴The Pharisees, who loved money, heard all this and were sneering at Jesus. ¹⁵He said to them, "You are the ones who justify yourselves in the eyes of others, but God knows your hearts. What people value highly is detestable in God's sight.

Additional Teachings

¹⁶"The Law and the Prophets were proclaimed until John. Since that time, the good news of the kingdom of God is being preached, and

---

a 6 Or about 3,000 liters   *b* 7 Or about 30 tons

everyone is forcing their way into it. [17]It is easier for heaven and earth to disappear than for the least stroke of a pen to drop out of the Law.

[18]"Anyone who divorces his wife and marries another woman commits adultery, and the man who marries a divorced woman commits adultery.

The Rich Man and Lazarus

[19]"There was a rich man who was dressed in purple and fine linen and lived in luxury every day. [20]At his gate was laid a beggar named Lazarus, covered with sores [21]and longing to eat what fell from the rich man's table. Even the dogs came and licked his sores.

[22]"The time came when the beggar died and the angels carried him to Abraham's side. The rich man also died and was buried. [23]In Hades, where he was in torment, he looked up and saw Abraham far away, with Lazarus by his side. [24]So he called to him, 'Father Abraham, have pity on me and send Lazarus to dip the tip of his finger in water and cool my tongue, because I am in agony in this fire.'

[25]"But Abraham replied, 'Son, remember that in your lifetime you received your good things, while Lazarus received bad things, but now he is comforted here and you are in agony. [26]And besides all this, between us and you a great chasm has been set in place, so that those who want to go from here to you cannot, nor can anyone cross over from there to us.'

[27]"He answered, 'Then I beg you, father, send Lazarus to my family, [28]for I have five brothers. Let him warn them, so that they will not also come to this place of torment.'

[29]"Abraham replied, 'They have Moses and the Prophets; let them listen to them.'

[30]"'No, father Abraham,' he said, 'but if someone from the dead goes to them, they will repent.'

[31]"He said to him, 'If they do not listen to Moses and the Prophets, they will not be convinced even if someone rises from the dead.'"

Sin, Faith, Duty

17 Jesus said to his disciples: "Things that cause people to stumble are bound to come, but woe to anyone through whom they come. [2]It would be better for them to be thrown into the sea with a millstone tied around their neck than to cause one of these little ones to stumble. [3]So watch yourselves.

"If your brother or sister[a] sins against you, rebuke them; and if they repent, forgive them. [4]Even if they sin against you seven times in a day and seven times come back to you saying 'I repent,' you must forgive them."

[5]The apostles said to the Lord, "Increase our faith!"

[6]He replied, "If you have faith as small as a mustard seed, you can say to this mulberry tree, 'Be uprooted and planted in the sea,' and it will obey you.

[7]"Suppose one of you has a servant plowing or looking after the sheep. Will he say to the servant when he comes in from the field, 'Come along now and sit down to eat'? [8]Won't he rather say, 'Prepare my supper, get yourself ready and wait on me while I eat and drink; after that you may eat and drink'? [9]Will he thank the servant because

---

[a]3 The Greek word for *brother or sister* (*adelphos*) refers here to a fellow disciple, whether man or woman.

he did what he was told to do? 10So you also, when you have done everything you were told to do, should say, 'We are unworthy servants; we have only done our duty.'"

Jesus Heals Ten Men With Leprosy

11Now on his way to Jerusalem, Jesus traveled along the border between Samaria and Galilee. 12As he was going into a village, ten men who had leprosy*a* met him. They stood at a distance 13and called out in a loud voice, "Jesus, Master, have pity on us!"

14When he saw them, he said, "Go, show yourselves to the priests." And as they went, they were cleansed.

15One of them, when he saw he was healed, came back, praising God in a loud voice. 16He threw himself at Jesus' feet and thanked him — and he was a Samaritan.

17Jesus asked, "Were not all ten cleansed? Where are the other nine? 18Has no one returned to give praise to God except this foreigner?" 19Then he said to him, "Rise and go; your faith has made you well."

The Coming of the Kingdom of God

20Once, on being asked by the Pharisees when the kingdom of God would come, Jesus replied, "The coming of the kingdom of God is not something that can be observed, 21nor will people say, 'Here it is,' or 'There it is,' because the kingdom of God is in your midst."*b*

22Then he said to his disciples, "The time is coming when you will long to see one of the days of the Son of Man, but you will not see it. 23People will tell you, 'There he is!' or 'Here he is!' Do not go running off after them. 24For the Son of Man in his day*c* will be like the lightning, which flashes and lights up the sky from one end to the other. 25But first he must suffer many things and be rejected by this generation.

26"Just as it was in the days of Noah, so also will it be in the days of the Son of Man. 27People were eating, drinking, marrying and being given in marriage up to the day Noah entered the ark. Then the flood came and destroyed them all.

28"It was the same in the days of Lot. People were eating and drinking, buying and selling, planting and building. 29But the day Lot left Sodom, fire and sulfur rained down from heaven and destroyed them all.

30"It will be just like this on the day the Son of Man is revealed. 31On that day no one who is on the housetop, with possessions inside, should go down to get them. Likewise, no one in the field should go back for anything. 32Remember Lot's wife! 33Whoever tries to keep their life will lose it, and whoever loses their life will preserve it. 34I tell you, on that night two people will be in one bed; one will be taken and the other left. 35Two women will be grinding grain together; one will be taken and the other left." [36]*d*

37"Where, Lord?" they asked.

He replied, "Where there is a dead body, there the vultures will gather."

The Parable of the Persistent Widow

18 Then Jesus told his disciples a parable to show them that they should always pray and not give up. 2He said: "In a certain town there was a judge who neither feared God nor cared what people

---

a 12 The Greek word traditionally translated *leprosy* was used for various diseases affecting the skin.   *b* 21 Or *is within you*   *c* 24 Some manuscripts do not have *in his day*.   *d* 36 Some manuscripts include here words similar to Matt. 24:40.

LUKE 17:20-21

THE KINGDOM OF GOD IN YOUR MIDST

In Jesus' day, people wanted to know about the kingdom of God, and they asked Jesus about it. Jesus confounded their assumptions by asserting that the kingdom of God was already in their midst. Clearly, an aspect of the kingdom promise was fulfilled in Jesus' first coming. The kingdom of God operates among earthly kingdoms today, but one day, God's kingdom will swallow up all rival kingdoms (Rev 11:15).

The kingdom of God is not the same as the church, though the church is part of the kingdom. The kingdom now is the presence of God alongside earthly kingdoms. The power of God is shown now in the distribution and work of the Holy Spirit (Heb 2:4). One day, however, Jesus will rule over all, and he will share that rule with his people (Rev 5:9-10). Until then, believers wait in anticipation for God's kingdom rule to be complete.

thought. ³And there was a widow in that town who kept coming to him with the plea, 'Grant me justice against my adversary.'

⁴"For some time he refused. But finally he said to himself, 'Even though I don't fear God or care what people think, ⁵yet because this widow keeps bothering me, I will see that she gets justice, so that she won't eventually come and attack me!'"

⁶And the Lord said, "Listen to what the unjust judge says. ⁷And will not God bring about justice for his chosen ones, who cry out to him day and night? Will he keep putting them off? ⁸I tell you, he will see that they get justice, and quickly. However, when the Son of Man comes, will he find faith on the earth?"

The Parable of the Pharisee and the Tax Collector

⁹To some who were confident of their own righteousness and looked down on everyone else, Jesus told this parable: ¹⁰"Two men went up to the temple to pray, one a Pharisee and the other a tax collector. ¹¹The Pharisee stood by himself and prayed: 'God, I thank you that I am not like other people — robbers, evildoers, adulterers — or even like this tax collector. ¹²I fast twice a week and give a tenth of all I get.'

¹³"But the tax collector stood at a distance. He would not even look up to heaven, but beat his breast and said, 'God, have mercy on me, a sinner.'

¹⁴"I tell you that this man, rather than the other, went home justified before God. For all those who exalt themselves will be humbled, and those who humble themselves will be exalted."

The Little Children and Jesus

¹⁵People were also bringing babies to Jesus for him to place his hands on them. When the disciples saw this, they rebuked them. ¹⁶But Jesus called the children to him and said, "Let the little children come to me, and do not hinder them, for the kingdom of God belongs to such as these. ¹⁷Truly I tell you, anyone who will not receive the kingdom of God like a little child will never enter it."

The Rich and the Kingdom of God

¹⁸A certain ruler asked him, "Good teacher, what must I do to inherit eternal life?"

¹⁹"Why do you call me good?" Jesus answered. "No one is good — except God alone. ²⁰You know the commandments: 'You shall not commit adultery, you shall not murder, you shall not steal, you shall not give false testimony, honor your father and mother.'ᵃ"

²¹"All these I have kept since I was a boy," he said.

²²When Jesus heard this, he said to him, "You still lack one thing. Sell everything you have and give to the poor, and you will have treasure in heaven. Then come, follow me."

²³When he heard this, he became very sad, because he was very wealthy. ²⁴Jesus looked at him and said, "How hard it is for the rich to enter the kingdom of God! ²⁵Indeed, it is easier for a camel to go through the eye of a needle than for someone who is rich to enter the kingdom of God."

²⁶Those who heard this asked, "Who then can be saved?"

²⁷Jesus replied, "What is impossible with man is possible with God."

²⁸Peter said to him, "We have left all we had to follow you!"

ᵃ 20 Exodus 20:12-16; Deut. 5:16-20

LUKE 18:9–14

JESUS AND MERCY

The Greek word translated "have mercy" can also mean "to be favorably inclined." This word is used only one other time in the New Testament, and there it describes how Christ made reconciliation possible between God and humanity by his sacrifice on the cross (Heb 2:17). The noun form appears in 1 John 2:2 and 4:10; in both places, Jesus is called the atoning sacrifice for our sins. Jesus, as our sacrifice, paid the price our sins required, thereby making it possible for God to turn aside his righteous wrath.

The tax collector in Jesus' story understood his sinful condition and asked God for mercy. Thankfully, God does not save people because of their righteous acts but solely through his rich mercy (Eph 2:4–5; Titus 3:5). Later, the apostle Peter would write that in God's great mercy, he has given believers new birth into a living hope through the resurrection of Jesus Christ from the dead (1Pe 1:3). When people cry out to God for mercy, God's merciful response is Jesus.

29"Truly I tell you," Jesus said to them, "no one who has left home or wife or brothers or sisters or parents or children for the sake of the kingdom of God 30will fail to receive many times as much in this age, and in the age to come eternal life."

Jesus Predicts His Death a Third Time

31Jesus took the Twelve aside and told them, "We are going up to Jerusalem, and everything that is written by the prophets about the Son of Man will be fulfilled. 32He will be delivered over to the Gentiles. They will mock him, insult him and spit on him; 33they will flog him and kill him. On the third day he will rise again."

34The disciples did not understand any of this. Its meaning was hidden from them, and they did not know what he was talking about.

A Blind Beggar Receives His Sight

35As Jesus approached Jericho, a blind man was sitting by the roadside begging. 36When he heard the crowd going by, he asked what was happening. 37They told him, "Jesus of Nazareth is passing by."

38He called out, "Jesus, Son of David, have mercy on me!"

39Those who led the way rebuked him and told him to be quiet, but he shouted all the more, "Son of David, have mercy on me!"

40Jesus stopped and ordered the man to be brought to him. When he came near, Jesus asked him, 41"What do you want me to do for you?"

"Lord, I want to see," he replied.

42Jesus said to him, "Receive your sight; your faith has healed you." 43Immediately he received his sight and followed Jesus, praising God. When all the people saw it, they also praised God.

Zacchaeus the Tax Collector

19 Jesus entered Jericho and was passing through. 2A man was there by the name of Zacchaeus; he was a chief tax collector and was wealthy. 3He wanted to see who Jesus was, but because he was short he could not see over the crowd. 4So he ran ahead and climbed a sycamore-fig tree to see him, since Jesus was coming that way.

5When Jesus reached the spot, he looked up and said to him, "Zacchaeus, come down immediately. I must stay at your house today." 6So he came down at once and welcomed him gladly.

7All the people saw this and began to mutter, "He has gone to be the guest of a sinner."

8But Zacchaeus stood up and said to the Lord, "Look, Lord! Here and now I give half of my possessions to the poor, and if I have cheated anybody out of anything, I will pay back four times the amount."

9Jesus said to him, "Today salvation has come to this house, because this man, too, is a son of Abraham. 10For the Son of Man came to seek and to save the lost."

The Parable of the Ten Minas

11While they were listening to this, he went on to tell them a parable, because he was near Jerusalem and the people thought that the kingdom of God was going to appear at once. 12He said: "A man of noble birth went to a distant country to have himself appointed king and then to return. 13So he called ten of his servants and gave them ten minas.a 'Put this money to work,' he said, 'until I come back.'

a 13 A mina was about three months' wages.

¹⁴"But his subjects hated him and sent a delegation after him to say, 'We don't want this man to be our king.'

¹⁵"He was made king, however, and returned home. Then he sent for the servants to whom he had given the money, in order to find out what they had gained with it.

¹⁶"The first one came and said, 'Sir, your mina has earned ten more.'

¹⁷"'Well done, my good servant!' his master replied. 'Because you have been trustworthy in a very small matter, take charge of ten cities.'

¹⁸"The second came and said, 'Sir, your mina has earned five more.'

¹⁹"His master answered, 'You take charge of five cities.'

²⁰"Then another servant came and said, 'Sir, here is your mina; I have kept it laid away in a piece of cloth. ²¹I was afraid of you, because you are a hard man. You take out what you did not put in and reap what you did not sow.'

²²"His master replied, 'I will judge you by your own words, you wicked servant! You knew, did you, that I am a hard man, taking out what I did not put in, and reaping what I did not sow? ²³Why then didn't you put my money on deposit, so that when I came back, I could have collected it with interest?'

²⁴"Then he said to those standing by, 'Take his mina away from him and give it to the one who has ten minas.'

²⁵"'Sir,' they said, 'he already has ten!'

²⁶"He replied, 'I tell you that to everyone who has, more will be given, but as for the one who has nothing, even what they have will be taken away. ²⁷But those enemies of mine who did not want me to be king over them — bring them here and kill them in front of me.'"

Jesus Comes to Jerusalem as King

²⁸After Jesus had said this, he went on ahead, going up to Jerusalem. ²⁹As he approached Bethphage and Bethany at the hill called the Mount of Olives, he sent two of his disciples, saying to them, ³⁰"Go to the village ahead of you, and as you enter it, you will find a colt tied there, which no one has ever ridden. Untie it and bring it here. ³¹If anyone asks you, 'Why are you untying it?' say, 'The Lord needs it.'"

³²Those who were sent ahead went and found it just as he had told them. ³³As they were untying the colt, its owners asked them, "Why are you untying the colt?"

³⁴They replied, "The Lord needs it."

³⁵They brought it to Jesus, threw their cloaks on the colt and put Jesus on it. ³⁶As he went along, people spread their cloaks on the road.

³⁷When he came near the place where the road goes down the Mount of Olives, the whole crowd of disciples began joyfully to praise God in loud voices for all the miracles they had seen:

³⁸"Blessed is the king who comes in the name of the Lord!"ᵃ

"Peace in heaven and glory in the highest!"

³⁹Some of the Pharisees in the crowd said to Jesus, "Teacher, rebuke your disciples!"

⁴⁰"I tell you," he replied, "if they keep quiet, the stones will cry out."

⁴¹As he approached Jerusalem and saw the city, he wept over it ⁴²and said, "If you, even you, had only known on this day what would bring you peace — but now it is hidden from your eyes. ⁴³The days will come

---

ᵃ38 Psalm 118:26

LUKE 19:28–44

THE TRIUMPHAL ENTRY

Jesus' entry into Jerusalem bears the unmistakable marks of a royal procession — the arrival of a king greeted by his people with celebration and joy. In the space of a few verses, Luke deftly weaves together historical allusions and nods to prophecy to emphasize that Jesus was indeed Israel's promised king. The ride on the colt strongly resembles Solomon's journey to Gihon where he was to be proclaimed king (1Ki 1:33–35). The description of people eagerly spreading their outer garments to create a pathway for Jesus (roughly equivalent to "rolling out the red carpet" today) recalls the scene of Jehu's coronation (2Ki 9:13). Luke's account of Christ's triumphal entry culminates with a citation from Psalm 118:26, adding the title of "king" so as to leave no doubt: Jesus was the long-awaited King who would bring peace between people and God.

upon you when your enemies will build an embankment against you and encircle you and hem you in on every side. ⁴⁴They will dash you to the ground, you and the children within your walls. They will not leave one stone on another, because you did not recognize the time of God's coming to you."

Jesus at the Temple

⁴⁵When Jesus entered the temple courts, he began to drive out those who were selling. ⁴⁶"It is written," he said to them, " 'My house will be a house of prayer'ᵃ; but you have made it 'a den of robbers.'ᵇ"

⁴⁷Every day he was teaching at the temple. But the chief priests, the teachers of the law and the leaders among the people were trying to kill him. ⁴⁸Yet they could not find any way to do it, because all the people hung on his words.

The Authority of Jesus Questioned

20 One day as Jesus was teaching the people in the temple courts and proclaiming the good news, the chief priests and the teachers of the law, together with the elders, came up to him. ²"Tell us by what authority you are doing these things," they said. "Who gave you this authority?"

³He replied, "I will also ask you a question. Tell me: ⁴John's baptism — was it from heaven, or of human origin?"

⁵They discussed it among themselves and said, "If we say, 'From heaven,' he will ask, 'Why didn't you believe him?' ⁶But if we say, 'Of human origin,' all the people will stone us, because they are persuaded that John was a prophet."

⁷So they answered, "We don't know where it was from."

⁸Jesus said, "Neither will I tell you by what authority I am doing these things."

The Parable of the Tenants

⁹He went on to tell the people this parable: "A man planted a vineyard, rented it to some farmers and went away for a long time. ¹⁰At harvest time he sent a servant to the tenants so they would give him some of the fruit of the vineyard. But the tenants beat him and sent him away empty-handed. ¹¹He sent another servant, but that one also they beat and treated shamefully and sent away empty-handed. ¹²He sent still a third, and they wounded him and threw him out.

¹³"Then the owner of the vineyard said, 'What shall I do? I will send my son, whom I love; perhaps they will respect him.'

¹⁴"But when the tenants saw him, they talked the matter over. 'This is the heir,' they said. 'Let's kill him, and the inheritance will be ours.' ¹⁵So they threw him out of the vineyard and killed him.

"What then will the owner of the vineyard do to them? ¹⁶He will come and kill those tenants and give the vineyard to others."

When the people heard this, they said, "God forbid!"

¹⁷Jesus looked directly at them and asked, "Then what is the meaning of that which is written:

" 'The stone the builders rejected
    has become the cornerstone'ᶜ?

ᵃ46 Isaiah 56:7   ᵇ46 Jer. 7:11   ᶜ17 Psalm 118:22

¹⁸Everyone who falls on that stone will be broken to pieces; anyone on whom it falls will be crushed."

¹⁹The teachers of the law and the chief priests looked for a way to arrest him immediately, because they knew he had spoken this parable against them. But they were afraid of the people.

Paying Taxes to Caesar

²⁰Keeping a close watch on him, they sent spies, who pretended to be sincere. They hoped to catch Jesus in something he said, so that they might hand him over to the power and authority of the governor. ²¹So the spies questioned him: "Teacher, we know that you speak and teach what is right, and that you do not show partiality but teach the way of God in accordance with the truth. ²²Is it right for us to pay taxes to Caesar or not?"

²³He saw through their duplicity and said to them, ²⁴"Show me a denarius. Whose image and inscription are on it?"

"Caesar's," they replied.

²⁵He said to them, "Then give back to Caesar what is Caesar's, and to God what is God's."

²⁶They were unable to trap him in what he had said there in public. And astonished by his answer, they became silent.

The Resurrection and Marriage

²⁷Some of the Sadducees, who say there is no resurrection, came to Jesus with a question. ²⁸"Teacher," they said, "Moses wrote for us that if a man's brother dies and leaves a wife but no children, the man must marry the widow and raise up offspring for his brother. ²⁹Now there were seven brothers. The first one married a woman and died childless. ³⁰The second ³¹and then the third married her, and in the same way the seven died, leaving no children. ³²Finally, the woman died too. ³³Now then, at the resurrection whose wife will she be, since the seven were married to her?"

³⁴Jesus replied, "The people of this age marry and are given in marriage. ³⁵But those who are considered worthy of taking part in the age to come and in the resurrection from the dead will neither marry nor be given in marriage, ³⁶and they can no longer die; for they are like the angels. They are God's children, since they are children of the resurrection. ³⁷But in the account of the burning bush, even Moses showed that the dead rise, for he calls the Lord 'the God of Abraham, and the God of Isaac, and the God of Jacob.'ᵃ ³⁸He is not the God of the dead, but of the living, for to him all are alive."

³⁹Some of the teachers of the law responded, "Well said, teacher!" ⁴⁰And no one dared to ask him any more questions.

Whose Son Is the Messiah?

⁴¹Then Jesus said to them, "Why is it said that the Messiah is the son of David? ⁴²David himself declares in the Book of Psalms:

"'The Lord said to my Lord:
    "Sit at my right hand
⁴³until I make your enemies
    a footstool for your feet."'ᵇ

⁴⁴David calls him 'Lord.' How then can he be his son?"

ᵃ37 Exodus 3:6   ᵇ43 Psalm 110:1

LUKE 20:19 – 26

"WHOSE IMAGE?"

Jesus and his teachings posed a direct challenge to Jewish religious leaders. Yet, because of Jesus' popularity, the chief priests and scribes remained wary of taking direct action against either Jesus or his teachings. Instead, they watched and waited, hoping Jesus' words would be his own downfall. In this passage, the religious leaders set a subtle trap for Jesus by asking a question for which there was no easy answer: Should Jews pay a citizenship tax to Caesar? If Jesus said yes, this would indicate his acceptance of foreign rule and undermine his standing with the people. If Jesus said no, he would sound like a political revolutionary.

But Jesus knew their hearts and risked neither losing the support of the people or being handed over to the Roman governor for sedition. Jesus sidestepped the trap — and set a trap of his own. When Jesus asked for a coin, the Pharisees produced a Roman denarius, proving that they already recognized Roman sovereignty. Jesus pointed out that since this coin bore the image of Caesar, it belonged to Caesar. Caesar had the right to require taxes, and the Jews were not exempt. But Jesus went a step further, taking the opportunity to turn a political debate into a spiritual lesson. Alluding to the fact that human beings are "stamped" with the image of God (Ge 1:26 – 27), Jesus reminded the religious leaders of the vital importance of giving to God what is due to him. God's people, as bearers of God's image, belong to him alone.

Warning Against the Teachers of the Law

⁴⁵While all the people were listening, Jesus said to his disciples, ⁴⁶"Beware of the teachers of the law. They like to walk around in flowing robes and love to be greeted with respect in the marketplaces and have the most important seats in the synagogues and the places of honor at banquets. ⁴⁷They devour widows' houses and for a show make lengthy prayers. These men will be punished most severely."

The Widow's Offering

21 As Jesus looked up, he saw the rich putting their gifts into the temple treasury. ²He also saw a poor widow put in two very small copper coins. ³"Truly I tell you," he said, "this poor widow has put in more than all the others. ⁴All these people gave their gifts out of their wealth; but she out of her poverty put in all she had to live on."

The Destruction of the Temple and Signs of the End Times

⁵Some of his disciples were remarking about how the temple was adorned with beautiful stones and with gifts dedicated to God. But Jesus said, ⁶"As for what you see here, the time will come when not one stone will be left on another; every one of them will be thrown down."

⁷"Teacher," they asked, "when will these things happen? And what will be the sign that they are about to take place?"

⁸He replied: "Watch out that you are not deceived. For many will come in my name, claiming, 'I am he,' and, 'The time is near.' Do not follow them. ⁹When you hear of wars and uprisings, do not be frightened. These things must happen first, but the end will not come right away."

¹⁰Then he said to them: "Nation will rise against nation, and kingdom against kingdom. ¹¹There will be great earthquakes, famines and pestilences in various places, and fearful events and great signs from heaven.

¹²"But before all this, they will seize you and persecute you. They will hand you over to synagogues and put you in prison, and you will be brought before kings and governors, and all on account of my name. ¹³And so you will bear testimony to me. ¹⁴But make up your mind not to worry beforehand how you will defend yourselves. ¹⁵For I will give you words and wisdom that none of your adversaries will be able to resist or contradict. ¹⁶You will be betrayed even by parents, brothers and sisters, relatives and friends, and they will put some of you to death. ¹⁷Everyone will hate you because of me. ¹⁸But not a hair of your head will perish. ¹⁹Stand firm, and you will win life.

²⁰"When you see Jerusalem being surrounded by armies, you will know that its desolation is near. ²¹Then let those who are in Judea flee to the mountains, let those in the city get out, and let those in the country not enter the city. ²²For this is the time of punishment in fulfillment of all that has been written. ²³How dreadful it will be in those days for pregnant women and nursing mothers! There will be great distress in the land and wrath against this people. ²⁴They will fall by the sword and will be taken as prisoners to all the nations. Jerusalem will be trampled on by the Gentiles until the times of the Gentiles are fulfilled.

²⁵"There will be signs in the sun, moon and stars. On the earth, nations will be in anguish and perplexity at the roaring and tossing of

LUKE 21:5–6

FULFILLED PROPHECY

When Jesus prophesied the destruction of the temple, he was standing on the grounds of that magnificently adorned place of worship. The temple was at the heart of Israel's religious life, and Herod the Great had initiated an extravagant refurbishing process: Residents and tourists saw gold- and silver-plated gates, golden grapevine clusters that decorated the courtyard, and ornate Babylonian linen tapestries that hung from the temple veil. Even a Roman historian, Tacitus, was impressed, declaring it to be an "immensely opulent temple."

Jesus' prediction must have seemed unlikely, even unthinkable, to the people listening. Not only was the temple itself impressive, but Jesus lived during a time when Judaism was experiencing great Messianic fervor, with high expectations of national deliverance from Roman rule. How could it be that this building that stood at the center of Jewish life and hope would be reduced to a heap of rubble? But just a few short decades later, in AD 70, Roman forces attacked the city of Jerusalem and ransacked, demolished and burned the temple.

Despite the tragic nature of this episode in history, it highlights a great truth: Jesus' words are reliable. As God's people now live in the hope of Jesus' return, the final resurrection and all the other promises of Jesus that have yet to come to pass, they can find reassurance in knowing that Jesus' prophecies have proven reliable time and time again. Christian hope is well founded on the One who does not change (Mal 3:6; Jas 1:17).

the sea. 26People will faint from terror, apprehensive of what is coming on the world, for the heavenly bodies will be shaken. 27At that time they will see the Son of Man coming in a cloud with power and great glory. 28When these things begin to take place, stand up and lift up your heads, because your redemption is drawing near."

29He told them this parable: "Look at the fig tree and all the trees. 30When they sprout leaves, you can see for yourselves and know that summer is near. 31Even so, when you see these things happening, you know that the kingdom of God is near.

32"Truly I tell you, this generation will certainly not pass away until all these things have happened. 33Heaven and earth will pass away, but my words will never pass away.

34"Be careful, or your hearts will be weighed down with carousing, drunkenness and the anxieties of life, and that day will close on you suddenly like a trap. 35For it will come on all those who live on the face of the whole earth. 36Be always on the watch, and pray that you may be able to escape all that is about to happen, and that you may be able to stand before the Son of Man."

37Each day Jesus was teaching at the temple, and each evening he went out to spend the night on the hill called the Mount of Olives, 38and all the people came early in the morning to hear him at the temple.

Judas Agrees to Betray Jesus

22 Now the Festival of Unleavened Bread, called the Passover, was approaching, 2and the chief priests and the teachers of the law were looking for some way to get rid of Jesus, for they were afraid of the people. 3Then Satan entered Judas, called Iscariot, one of the Twelve. 4And Judas went to the chief priests and the officers of the temple guard and discussed with them how he might betray Jesus. 5They were delighted and agreed to give him money. 6He consented, and watched for an opportunity to hand Jesus over to them when no crowd was present.

The Last Supper

7Then came the day of Unleavened Bread on which the Passover lamb had to be sacrificed. 8Jesus sent Peter and John, saying, "Go and make preparations for us to eat the Passover."

9"Where do you want us to prepare for it?" they asked.

10He replied, "As you enter the city, a man carrying a jar of water will meet you. Follow him to the house that he enters, 11and say to the owner of the house, 'The Teacher asks: Where is the guest room, where I may eat the Passover with my disciples?' 12He will show you a large room upstairs, all furnished. Make preparations there."

13They left and found things just as Jesus had told them. So they prepared the Passover.

14When the hour came, Jesus and his apostles reclined at the table. 15And he said to them, "I have eagerly desired to eat this Passover with you before I suffer. 16For I tell you, I will not eat it again until it finds fulfillment in the kingdom of God."

17After taking the cup, he gave thanks and said, "Take this and divide it among you. 18For I tell you I will not drink again from the fruit of the vine until the kingdom of God comes."

19And he took bread, gave thanks and broke it, and gave it to them, saying, "This is my body given for you; do this in remembrance of me."

²⁰In the same way, after the supper he took the cup, saying, "This cup is the new covenant in my blood, which is poured out for you.ᵃ ²¹But the hand of him who is going to betray me is with mine on the table. ²²The Son of Man will go as it has been decreed. But woe to that man who betrays him!" ²³They began to question among themselves which of them it might be who would do this.

²⁴A dispute also arose among them as to which of them was considered to be greatest. ²⁵Jesus said to them, "The kings of the Gentiles lord it over them; and those who exercise authority over them call themselves Benefactors. ²⁶But you are not to be like that. Instead, the greatest among you should be like the youngest, and the one who rules like the one who serves. ²⁷For who is greater, the one who is at the table or the one who serves? Is it not the one who is at the table? But I am among you as one who serves. ²⁸You are those who have stood by me in my trials. ²⁹And I confer on you a kingdom, just as my Father conferred one on me, ³⁰so that you may eat and drink at my table in my kingdom and sit on thrones, judging the twelve tribes of Israel.

³¹"Simon, Simon, Satan has asked to sift all of you as wheat. ³²But I have prayed for you, Simon, that your faith may not fail. And when you have turned back, strengthen your brothers."

³³But he replied, "Lord, I am ready to go with you to prison and to death."

³⁴Jesus answered, "I tell you, Peter, before the rooster crows today, you will deny three times that you know me."

³⁵Then Jesus asked them, "When I sent you without purse, bag or sandals, did you lack anything?"

"Nothing," they answered.

³⁶He said to them, "But now if you have a purse, take it, and also a bag; and if you don't have a sword, sell your cloak and buy one. ³⁷It is written: 'And he was numbered with the transgressors'ᵇ; and I tell you that this must be fulfilled in me. Yes, what is written about me is reaching its fulfillment."

³⁸The disciples said, "See, Lord, here are two swords."

"That's enough!" he replied.

Jesus Prays on the Mount of Olives

³⁹Jesus went out as usual to the Mount of Olives, and his disciples followed him. ⁴⁰On reaching the place, he said to them, "Pray that you will not fall into temptation." ⁴¹He withdrew about a stone's throw beyond them, knelt down and prayed, ⁴²"Father, if you are willing, take this cup from me; yet not my will, but yours be done." ⁴³An angel from heaven appeared to him and strengthened him. ⁴⁴And being in anguish, he prayed more earnestly, and his sweat was like drops of blood falling to the ground.ᶜ

⁴⁵When he rose from prayer and went back to the disciples, he found them asleep, exhausted from sorrow. ⁴⁶"Why are you sleeping?" he asked them. "Get up and pray so that you will not fall into temptation."

Jesus Arrested

⁴⁷While he was still speaking a crowd came up, and the man who was called Judas, one of the Twelve, was leading them. He approached

---

ᵃ 19,20 Some manuscripts do not have *given for you . . . poured out for you.*
ᵇ 37 Isaiah 53:12   ᶜ 43,44 Many early manuscripts do not have verses 43 and 44.

Jesus to kiss him, 48but Jesus asked him, "Judas, are you betraying the Son of Man with a kiss?"

49When Jesus' followers saw what was going to happen, they said, "Lord, should we strike with our swords?" 50And one of them struck the servant of the high priest, cutting off his right ear.

51But Jesus answered, "No more of this!" And he touched the man's ear and healed him.

52Then Jesus said to the chief priests, the officers of the temple guard, and the elders, who had come for him, "Am I leading a rebellion, that you have come with swords and clubs? 53Every day I was with you in the temple courts, and you did not lay a hand on me. But this is your hour — when darkness reigns."

Peter Disowns Jesus

54Then seizing him, they led him away and took him into the house of the high priest. Peter followed at a distance. 55And when some there had kindled a fire in the middle of the courtyard and had sat down together, Peter sat down with them. 56A servant girl saw him seated there in the firelight. She looked closely at him and said, "This man was with him."

57But he denied it. "Woman, I don't know him," he said.

58A little later someone else saw him and said, "You also are one of them."

"Man, I am not!" Peter replied.

59About an hour later another asserted, "Certainly this fellow was with him, for he is a Galilean."

60Peter replied, "Man, I don't know what you're talking about!" Just as he was speaking, the rooster crowed. 61The Lord turned and looked straight at Peter. Then Peter remembered the word the Lord had spoken to him: "Before the rooster crows today, you will disown me three times." 62And he went outside and wept bitterly.

The Guards Mock Jesus

63The men who were guarding Jesus began mocking and beating him. 64They blindfolded him and demanded, "Prophesy! Who hit you?" 65And they said many other insulting things to him.

Jesus Before Pilate and Herod

66At daybreak the council of the elders of the people, both the chief priests and the teachers of the law, met together, and Jesus was led before them. 67"If you are the Messiah," they said, "tell us."

Jesus answered, "If I tell you, you will not believe me, 68and if I asked you, you would not answer. 69But from now on, the Son of Man will be seated at the right hand of the mighty God."

70They all asked, "Are you then the Son of God?"

He replied, "You say that I am."

71Then they said, "Why do we need any more testimony? We have heard it from his own lips."

23 Then the whole assembly rose and led him off to Pilate. 2And they began to accuse him, saying, "We have found this man subverting our nation. He opposes payment of taxes to Caesar and claims to be Messiah, a king."

3So Pilate asked Jesus, "Are you the king of the Jews?"

"You have said so," Jesus replied.

LUKE 23:1–25

JESUS' TRIAL

Jesus' multistage trial—from the Jewish religious council, to the initial hearing before the Roman governor Pilate, to Herod's court, and finally back to Pilate for sentencing—marked the culmination of a lengthy plot by certain religious leaders to trap and condemn Jesus. After various unsuccessful attempts to undermine Jesus' popularity or frame him for sedition, the elders, chief priests and scribes finally had Jesus in their clutches. They were not about to waste the opportunity. Outraged at Jesus' claim to be the Son of God (Lk 22:70–71), these religious leaders brought Jesus before Pilate and leveled three accusations (23:2), each designed to frame Jesus as a threat to Roman authority. The first charge, "subverting our nation," was a general complaint implying that Jesus was disturbing the peace and stirring up civil unrest. The second and third charges were more directly related to Roman rule: Jesus, they claimed, forbade paying taxes to Caesar (a blatant fabrication; see Lk 20:25) and had declared himself to be the king over Israel. The final charge had an element of truth, but the religious leaders deliberately twisted Jesus' claim into one that usurped Caesar's earthly reign. Pilate himself saw through the unjust accusations, but his repeated attempts to set Jesus free were to no avail. The farcical nature of the trial is just one more indication that Jesus' suffering and death were those of an innocent and righteous man (Lk 23:47).

⁴Then Pilate announced to the chief priests and the crowd, "I find no basis for a charge against this man."

⁵But they insisted, "He stirs up the people all over Judea by his teaching. He started in Galilee and has come all the way here."

⁶On hearing this, Pilate asked if the man was a Galilean. ⁷When he learned that Jesus was under Herod's jurisdiction, he sent him to Herod, who was also in Jerusalem at that time.

⁸When Herod saw Jesus, he was greatly pleased, because for a long time he had been wanting to see him. From what he had heard about him, he hoped to see him perform a sign of some sort. ⁹He plied him with many questions, but Jesus gave him no answer. ¹⁰The chief priests and the teachers of the law were standing there, vehemently accusing him. ¹¹Then Herod and his soldiers ridiculed and mocked him. Dressing him in an elegant robe, they sent him back to Pilate. ¹²That day Herod and Pilate became friends — before this they had been enemies.

¹³Pilate called together the chief priests, the rulers and the people, ¹⁴and said to them, "You brought me this man as one who was inciting the people to rebellion. I have examined him in your presence and have found no basis for your charges against him. ¹⁵Neither has Herod, for he sent him back to us; as you can see, he has done nothing to deserve death. ¹⁶Therefore, I will punish him and then release him." ⁽¹⁷⁾ᵃ

¹⁸But the whole crowd shouted, "Away with this man! Release Barabbas to us!" ¹⁹(Barabbas had been thrown into prison for an insurrection in the city, and for murder.)

²⁰Wanting to release Jesus, Pilate appealed to them again. ²¹But they kept shouting, "Crucify him! Crucify him!"

²²For the third time he spoke to them: "Why? What crime has this man committed? I have found in him no grounds for the death penalty. Therefore I will have him punished and then release him."

²³But with loud shouts they insistently demanded that he be crucified, and their shouts prevailed. ²⁴So Pilate decided to grant their demand. ²⁵He released the man who had been thrown into prison for insurrection and murder, the one they asked for, and surrendered Jesus to their will.

The Crucifixion of Jesus

²⁶As the soldiers led him away, they seized Simon from Cyrene, who was on his way in from the country, and put the cross on him and made him carry it behind Jesus. ²⁷A large number of people followed him, including women who mourned and wailed for him. ²⁸Jesus turned and said to them, "Daughters of Jerusalem, do not weep for me; weep for yourselves and for your children. ²⁹For the time will come when you will say, 'Blessed are the childless women, the wombs that never bore and the breasts that never nursed!' ³⁰Then

> " 'they will say to the mountains, "Fall on us!"
> and to the hills, "Cover us!" ' ᵇ

³¹For if people do these things when the tree is green, what will happen when it is dry?"

³²Two other men, both criminals, were also led out with him to be executed. ³³When they came to the place called the Skull, they crucified

---

ᵃ17 Some manuscripts include here words similar to Matt. 27:15 and Mark 15:6.
ᵇ30 Hosea 10:8

him there, along with the criminals — one on his right, the other on his left. ³⁴Jesus said, "Father, forgive them, for they do not know what they are doing."ᵃ And they divided up his clothes by casting lots.

³⁵The people stood watching, and the rulers even sneered at him. They said, "He saved others; let him save himself if he is God's Messiah, the Chosen One."

³⁶The soldiers also came up and mocked him. They offered him wine vinegar ³⁷and said, "If you are the king of the Jews, save yourself."

³⁸There was a written notice above him, which read: THIS IS THE KING OF THE JEWS.

³⁹One of the criminals who hung there hurled insults at him: "Aren't you the Messiah? Save yourself and us!"

⁴⁰But the other criminal rebuked him. "Don't you fear God," he said, "since you are under the same sentence? ⁴¹We are punished justly, for we are getting what our deeds deserve. But this man has done nothing wrong."

⁴²Then he said, "Jesus, remember me when you come into your kingdom.ᵇ"

⁴³Jesus answered him, "Truly I tell you, today you will be with me in paradise."

The Death of Jesus

⁴⁴It was now about noon, and darkness came over the whole land until three in the afternoon, ⁴⁵for the sun stopped shining. And the curtain of the temple was torn in two. ⁴⁶Jesus called out with a loud voice, "Father, into your hands I commit my spirit."ᶜ When he had said this, he breathed his last.

⁴⁷The centurion, seeing what had happened, praised God and said, "Surely this was a righteous man." ⁴⁸When all the people who had gathered to witness this sight saw what took place, they beat their breasts and went away. ⁴⁹But all those who knew him, including the women who had followed him from Galilee, stood at a distance, watching these things.

The Burial of Jesus

⁵⁰Now there was a man named Joseph, a member of the Council, a good and upright man, ⁵¹who had not consented to their decision and action. He came from the Judean town of Arimathea, and he himself was waiting for the kingdom of God. ⁵²Going to Pilate, he asked for Jesus' body. ⁵³Then he took it down, wrapped it in linen cloth and placed it in a tomb cut in the rock, one in which no one had yet been laid. ⁵⁴It was Preparation Day, and the Sabbath was about to begin.

⁵⁵The women who had come with Jesus from Galilee followed Joseph and saw the tomb and how his body was laid in it. ⁵⁶Then they went home and prepared spices and perfumes. But they rested on the Sabbath in obedience to the commandment.

Jesus Has Risen

24 On the first day of the week, very early in the morning, the women took the spices they had prepared and went to the tomb. ²They found the stone rolled away from the tomb, ³but when

---

ᵃ34 Some early manuscripts do not have this sentence.   ᵇ42 Some manuscripts *come with your kingly power*   ᶜ46 Psalm 31:5

they entered, they did not find the body of the Lord Jesus. [4]While they were wondering about this, suddenly two men in clothes that gleamed like lightning stood beside them. [5]In their fright the women bowed down with their faces to the ground, but the men said to them, "Why do you look for the living among the dead? [6]He is not here; he has risen! Remember how he told you, while he was still with you in Galilee: [7]'The Son of Man must be delivered over to the hands of sinners, be crucified and on the third day be raised again.'" [8]Then they remembered his words.

[9]When they came back from the tomb, they told all these things to the Eleven and to all the others. [10]It was Mary Magdalene, Joanna, Mary the mother of James, and the others with them who told this to the apostles. [11]But they did not believe the women, because their words seemed to them like nonsense. [12]Peter, however, got up and ran to the tomb. Bending over, he saw the strips of linen lying by themselves, and he went away, wondering to himself what had happened.

On the Road to Emmaus

[13]Now that same day two of them were going to a village called Emmaus, about seven miles[a] from Jerusalem. [14]They were talking with each other about everything that had happened. [15]As they talked and discussed these things with each other, Jesus himself came up and walked along with them; [16]but they were kept from recognizing him.

[17]He asked them, "What are you discussing together as you walk along?"

They stood still, their faces downcast. [18]One of them, named Cleopas, asked him, "Are you the only one visiting Jerusalem who does not know the things that have happened there in these days?"

[19]"What things?" he asked.

"About Jesus of Nazareth," they replied. "He was a prophet, powerful in word and deed before God and all the people. [20]The chief priests and our rulers handed him over to be sentenced to death, and they crucified him; [21]but we had hoped that he was the one who was going to redeem Israel. And what is more, it is the third day since all this took place. [22]In addition, some of our women amazed us. They went to the tomb early this morning [23]but didn't find his body. They came and told us that they had seen a vision of angels, who said he was alive. [24]Then some of our companions went to the tomb and found it just as the women had said, but they did not see Jesus."

[25]He said to them, "How foolish you are, and how slow to believe all that the prophets have spoken! [26]Did not the Messiah have to suffer these things and then enter his glory?" [27]And beginning with Moses and all the Prophets, he explained to them what was said in all the Scriptures concerning himself.

[28]As they approached the village to which they were going, Jesus continued on as if he were going farther. [29]But they urged him strongly, "Stay with us, for it is nearly evening; the day is almost over." So he went in to stay with them.

[30]When he was at the table with them, he took bread, gave thanks, broke it and began to give it to them. [31]Then their eyes were opened and they recognized him, and he disappeared from their sight. [32]They asked each other, "Were not our hearts burning within us while he talked with us on the road and opened the Scriptures to us?"

[a]13 Or about 11 kilometers

³³They got up and returned at once to Jerusalem. There they found the Eleven and those with them, assembled together ³⁴and saying, "It is true! The Lord has risen and has appeared to Simon." ³⁵Then the two told what had happened on the way, and how Jesus was recognized by them when he broke the bread.

Jesus Appears to the Disciples

³⁶While they were still talking about this, Jesus himself stood among them and said to them, "Peace be with you."

³⁷They were startled and frightened, thinking they saw a ghost. ³⁸He said to them, "Why are you troubled, and why do doubts rise in your minds? ³⁹Look at my hands and my feet. It is I myself! Touch me and see; a ghost does not have flesh and bones, as you see I have."

⁴⁰When he had said this, he showed them his hands and feet. ⁴¹And while they still did not believe it because of joy and amazement, he asked them, "Do you have anything here to eat?" ⁴²They gave him a piece of broiled fish, ⁴³and he took it and ate it in their presence.

⁴⁴He said to them, "This is what I told you while I was still with you: Everything must be fulfilled that is written about me in the Law of Moses, the Prophets and the Psalms."

⁴⁵Then he opened their minds so they could understand the Scriptures. ⁴⁶He told them, "This is what is written: The Messiah will suffer and rise from the dead on the third day, ⁴⁷and repentance for the forgiveness of sins will be preached in his name to all nations, beginning at Jerusalem. ⁴⁸You are witnesses of these things. ⁴⁹I am going to send you what my Father has promised; but stay in the city until you have been clothed with power from on high."

The Ascension of Jesus

⁵⁰When he had led them out to the vicinity of Bethany, he lifted up his hands and blessed them. ⁵¹While he was blessing them, he left them and was taken up into heaven. ⁵²Then they worshiped him and returned to Jerusalem with great joy. ⁵³And they stayed continually at the temple, praising God.

REMISSION OF SINS

Jesus' power over sin had been called into question early in his ministry. Witnessing the faith of a group of people who made an extraordinary effort to bring their paralyzed friend to him for healing, Jesus said, "Friend, your sins are forgiven" (Lk 5:20). The Pharisees and teachers of the law recognized that only God could forgive sins—and not believing that Jesus was indeed God, they accused him of blasphemy. After Jesus' resurrection, there was no longer room for questioning or doubt. In defeating death, Jesus proved he was neither a pretender nor a blasphemer but the very Son of God. This victory over death signaled his divine authority to forgive sin.

Luke connects the preaching of the life-changing, sin-defeating gospel with Christ's resurrection. The good news of repentance and remission of sins, which the disciples began preaching following Jesus' ascension and the coming of the Holy Spirit in power, is rooted in this fundamental truth: In fulfillment of God's promises in Scripture, Christ suffered and died and was raised to life on the third day. Death is defeated; sin's power is broken. The remission of sins is now available to all who believe in the powerful name of Jesus.

TABLE OF WEIGHTS AND MEASURES

	BIBLICAL UNIT	APPROXIMATE AMERICAN EQUIVALENT	APPROXIMATE METRIC EQUIVALENT
Weights	talent (60 minas)	75 pounds	34 kilograms
	mina (50 shekels)	1 1/4 pounds	560 grams
	shekel (2 bekas)	2/5 ounce	11.5 grams
	pim (2/3 shekel)	1/4 ounce	7.8 grams
	beka (10 gerahs)	2/5 ounce	5.7 grams
	gerah	1/50 ounce	0.6 gram
	daric	1/3 ounce	8.4 grams
Length	cubit	18 inches	45 centimeters
	span	9 inches	23 centimeters
	handbreadth	3 inches	7.5 centimeters
	stadion (pl. stadia)	600 feet	183 meters
Capacity			
Dry Measure	cor [homer] (10 ephahs)	6 bushels	220 liters
	lethek (5 ephahs)	3 bushels	110 liters
	ephah (10 omers)	3/5 bushel	22 liters
	seah (1/3 ephah)	7 quarts	7.5 liters
	omer (1/10 ephah)	2 quarts	2 liters
	cab (1/18 ephah)	1 quart	1 liter
Liquid Measure	bath (1 ephah)	6 gallons	22 liters
	hin (1/6 bath)	1 gallon	3.8 liters
	log (1/72 bath)	1/3 quart	0.3 liter

The figures of the table are calculated on the basis of a shekel equaling 11.5 grams, a cubit equaling inches and an ephah equaling 22 liters. The quart referred to is either a dry quart (slightly larger tha liter) or a liquid quart (slightly smaller than a liter), whichever is applicable. The ton referred to in footnotes is the American ton of 2,000 pounds. These weights are calculated relative to the particu commodity involved. Accordingly, the same measure of capacity in the text may be converted i different weights in the footnotes.

This table is based upon the best available information, but it is not intended to be mat matically precise; like the measurement equivalents in the footnotes, it merely gives approxim amounts and distances. Weights and measures differed somewhat at various times and places in ancient world. There is uncertainty particularly about the ephah and the bath; further discoveries n shed more light on these units of capacity.

ARTICLES

SON OF THE MOST HIGH

When Gabriel announced to Mary that she would have a son, the angel invoked a promise that had echoed throughout the Old Testament. Her son would be called the Son of the Most High and would reign on the throne of his father, David. Those familiar with the Law and the Prophets, including Mary herself, would have quickly begun to connect the prophetic dots.

God had picked David, a young shepherd boy, from among an entire family of brothers and made him the ruler over Israel. God promised to make David's name great. In addition, God promised that after David died, God would raise up one of his offspring to establish the throne of his kingdom forever (2Sa 7:8 – 16).

During his life, as David faced enemies and conspiracy, he sang songs of praise to God for protecting him as God's anointed (Ps 2:1 – 12) and for establishing his line for as long as the heavens endure (Ps 89:19 – 29). David intoned a psalm of praise that contained a phrase that Jesus later quoted to confound his critics: "The Lord says to my lord ..." (Ps 110:1; Mt 22:44). Another psalm affirmed that God, in his promise to David about the duration of his throne, had sworn an oath that could not be revoked (Ps 132:11 – 12).

The prophet Isaiah continued to prophesy the fulfillment of God's promise to David. He wrote that to his people a child would be born, a son would be given and the government would be on his shoulders (Isa 9:6 – 7). Isaiah also affirmed that a shoot would come up from the stump of Jesse, David's father, and from its roots a Branch (referring to Jesus) would bear fruit (Isa 11:1 – 15).

In time, God's plan became clear: he would fulfill this promise through his Son, Jesus. When the angel appeared to Mary, God provided the ultimate update on God's plan to keep his promise. The baby in Mary's womb, conceived by the Holy Spirit though Mary was a virgin, was God's Son who would reign eternally (Lk 1:31 – 33). As a capstone to the astounding declaration, the angel reminded Mary that no word from God would ever fail (v. 37).

The intricate history of God's initial promise realized so fully at Jesus' first coming increases confidence that the rest of God's promises will be fulfilled at Jesus' second coming and after that, into eternity.

ONE MORE POWERFUL

When John began to preach in the wilderness, crowds flocked to see him. He baptized those who confessed their sins but rebuked the pious religious leaders for their self-reliance (Mt 3:7–10). After 400 years without a prophet, people rushed to John, wondering if he might be the Christ, the one for whom they as a people had been waiting for centuries. John pointed them to one more powerful than himself who was to come — Jesus. While John baptized with water as a sign of repentance, Jesus would baptize with the Holy Spirit and fire (Mt 3:11).

The power Jesus demonstrated in his baptism differed from John's to an infinite degree. To observers, their physical actions looked similar. While both used water, Jesus' baptism pointed to an imminent change, the time when God would take up residence in the lives of believers through the person of the Holy Spirit. Each of the Gospel writers reference this distinctive element of Jesus' work (Mt 3:11; Mk 1:8; Jn 1:33), foreshadowing the nature of the Trinity: one God in three persons — Father, Son and Holy Spirit.

During Jesus' earthly ministry, his disciples experienced power for immediate tasks in Jesus' name (Lk 10:17–20). While the disciples relished these experiences, Jesus knew they would soon experience a substantively different reality — something that could only happen when he returned to his Father (Jn 16:7). Before he ascended into heaven after his resurrection, Jesus commanded his disciples not to leave Jerusalem but to wait for the gift his Father had promised, the Holy Spirit (Ac 1:4–5). Once the Spirit came in fullness, the Holy Spirit's filling became the confirmation that God had accepted people by grace through faith in Jesus. This grace extended even to Gentiles who had not kept the Law of Moses (Ac 11:15–17).

Throughout his ministry, John stated firmly that Jesus must become greater while he became less (Jn 3:30). John understood that he was responsible for preparing the way for Jesus, calling people to repentance. Jesus affirmed this role, stating that John was a great man (Mt 11:10–11) who had faithfully fulfilled his purpose. During his life, John never confused his role or ministry with that of Jesus. He knew Jesus was the Lamb of God who would take away the sin of the world — one who was more powerful than himself and greater in all possible ways (Jn 1:36).

JESUS AND THE POOR

Many, if not most, of the people who listened to Jesus' words that day were poor. The difficulties and hardships of their lives drove them to listen to this prophet, Jesus. As those who lacked material wealth, they may have hoped Jesus would tell them more about the kingdom of God — the day when the righteous Messiah and not the cruel Romans would govern them.

From his initial statement, Jesus launched into a series of statements that turned the crowd's perceptions upside down. Jesus' speech contrasted possessions and values with those that flow from a heavenly perspective. In a few sentences, Jesus affirmed that things in this world are not always what they seem and certainly are not what they will one day be.

At face value, it seemed as though Jesus was making a blanket promise of salvation and blessing to everyone who was poor materially. Based on this interpretation, some have viewed the poor as God's chosen people — those who suffer in this world but can expect immeasurable blessings in the next. Those holding this view often advocate that God's people, the church, should prioritize ministry to the poor and in this way advance the kingdom of God.

Others view Jesus' statement as an insight into spiritual poverty, referencing a similar sermon in which Jesus talked about the "poor in spirit" (Mt 5:3). In their view, Jesus was offering great blessing to those who recognize their spiritual poverty before God. Because they acknowledge that nothing they do can enhance their spiritual standing, these people, the poor in spirit, receive God's unmerited favor. So, in this second view, Jesus is not affirming the value of being poor materially but warning against the profound danger of being self-sufficient spiritually.

Since Jesus referenced both the "poor" and the "poor in spirit," the implications of his words can be intertwined. Throughout his ministry on earth, Jesus met the practical needs of the poor — feeding, healing and honoring them. In spite of this emphasis, Jesus refused to place a higher priority on meeting physical needs than on meeting spiritual needs. Through his words and his actions, Jesus demonstrated the divine balance — pay attention to those with physical needs but never forget the priority of spiritual needs.

JESUS AND THE HOLY SPIRIT

One of the cautions in studying exclusively about Jesus is the implication that Jesus was and is separate from the Father and the Holy Spirit. While the truth remains mysterious, the Bible clearly teaches that God exists in three persons, the Trinity. The Bible does not use that term, but it is impossible to understand the Bible's teaching without embracing this reality. Luke, in his writings (Luke and Acts), focused on the Holy Spirit to provide insight into Jesus and the Holy Spirit. Here's an overview:

The Holy Spirit filled John the Baptist in his mother's womb (Lk 1:15–17).

The Holy Spirit was the agent of divine conception with Mary, the mother of Jesus (Lk 1:35).

The Holy Spirit filled Mary's relative, Elizabeth, the mother of John the Baptist, and empowered her to encourage Mary (Lk 1:41–45).

The Holy Spirit filled Zacharias, John's father, so he could prophesy about the Messiah (Lk 1:67–75).

At Jesus' baptism, the Holy Spirit descended in bodily form like a dove as God the Father spoke (Lk 3:22).

The Holy Spirit led Jesus into the wilderness to be tempted by the devil (Lk 4:1–13).

The Holy Spirit empowered Jesus as he began his earthly ministry (Lk 4:14–21).

Jesus spoke of the Father giving the Holy Spirit as he taught his disciples about prayer (Lk 11:1–4,13).

The Holy Spirit filled Jesus' disciples at Pentecost and empowered them to preach the Good News (Ac 2:1–21).

Before his crucifixion, Jesus encouraged his disciples with deep spiritual realities about the Father and the Holy Spirit. He said, "If you love me, keep my commands. And I will ask the Father, and he will give you another advocate to help you and be with you forever — the Spirit of truth" (Jn 14:15–17). Then, as the disciples struggled to understand, Jesus said, "I will not leave you as orphans; I will come to you. Before long, the world will not see me anymore, but you will see me. Because I live, you also will live. On that day you will realize that I am in my Father, and you are in me, and I am in you" (Jn 14:18–20).

JESUS AND THE SABBATH

Jesus clashed with the religious leaders of his day over many issues: religious traditions, associating with sinners, spiritual authority and more. On one issue in particular — the Sabbath — these leaders monitored Jesus' actions scrupulously. The Ten Commandments prohibited work on the Sabbath since it was a holy day set apart (Ex 20:8 – 11). Just as the Israelites were commanded to tithe part of their earnings to God, they were to give him their time as well. Breaking the Sabbath was a grave matter, for God's law demanded death for those who ignored it (Ex 31:14 – 15).

The question, though, was what activities constituted "work." In the years after the temple was rebuilt following the exile (515 BC – AD 70), scribes and rabbis studied the words of Scripture, interpreting every detail. What kinds of work could be allowed on the Sabbath within the Law? For example, according to the Law, no work was to be done on the Sabbath, so that meant burdens were not to be carried on that day. So scholars debated what constituted a "burden." On the surface, the scribes had good reasons for interpreting the Law carefully since they did not want anyone to break it inadvertently. But their interpretations increasingly emphasized external adherence to the Law rather than cultivating an attitude of submission before God. Obeying their own interpretations became a source of pride instead of an expression of love for God. By Jesus' day, the rabbis and scribes had become so strict that they accused Jesus' disciples of breaking the Sabbath because they picked some grain and ate it as they walked through a field on the Sabbath (Lk 6:1 – 2).

Jesus' healings on the Sabbath enraged the religious teachers who classified healing as "work" and therefore prohibited it (Dt 5:15). He revealed the rabbis' hypocrisy with his response.

God had given the Law to encourage the Israelites to love him and to love others (Mk 12:30 – 31). He had never prohibited doing good on the Sabbath. The Pharisees acted as if God had created people so that he would have someone to keep the Sabbath, but Jesus clarified that God had given the Sabbath as a gift to the people he had created (Mk 2:27). For the Pharisees, the Ten Commandments provided great restrictions punishable by death. For Jesus, the Law outlined great freedoms that led to real life (Mt 5:17).

CELEBRATING WHEN THE LOST ARE FOUND

Throughout his earthly ministry, Jesus' association with sinners chafed his religious critics, but Jesus consistently explained that he had come to seek and save the lost (Lk 19:10). To reinforce this truth, Jesus told three stories about a search for lost things.

With each story, Jesus confronted the religious leaders with the truth they kept missing — God is in the business of restoration and celebration (Lk 15:7). These leaders failed to listen with discernment as Jesus confronted them with the fact that they were like the older brother in the third story who had stayed home, served his father grudgingly, judged his brother unfairly, then distanced himself from his father without leaving home (Lk 15:25 – 30).

Jesus came to earth to launch a search-and-rescue mission, seeking and saving those who were spiritually lost. The sinners of his day loved to invite Jesus to their gatherings (Lk 5:29). The Pharisees stood by, scowled and judged. They complained to Jesus' disciples about his eating and drinking with tax collectors and sinners. Jesus responded that it was not the healthy who needed a doctor but rather those who were sick (Mt 9:12).

The Pharisees and other religious leaders loved the trappings of their offices — respectful greetings, sitting in the most important seats and having the opportunity to load others with religious burdens they personally had no intention of carrying (Lk 11:4 – 6). In contrast, Jesus did not come to be served but to serve and give his life as a ransom for many (Mt 20:28). The Pharisees thanked God that they were not needy like the sinners around them. Jesus rebuked them with a story about a tax collector who cried out to God in his spiritual poverty and found salvation (Lk 18:9 – 14).

Earthly concerns clouded the judgment of the religious leaders and caused them to disregard the spiritual truths Jesus taught. Confident that they knew God's will and that God was pleased with them, they resisted Jesus. As Jesus submitted to the grand plan of the gospel, the religious leaders manipulated the political system to ensure Jesus' death. Unwittingly, their actions set in motion all that was required for the lost to be found and for celebration to erupt in heaven.

JESUS AND HELL

Jesus taught more about hell than he taught about heaven. Through the parable of the rich man and a poor man named Lazarus, Jesus provided unforgettable insights into life now and the life to come.

While they lived on earth, a great economic chasm separated the rich man from Lazarus. While the rich man feasted, Lazarus starved. While the rich man lived in pleasure, Lazarus lived in pain. If Jesus had asked his disciples which of these men God favored, they would not have faltered: their answer would have been "the rich man." That's why the disciples were so surprised when Jesus explained that it was easier for a camel to go through the eye of a needle than for a rich man to go to heaven. They exclaimed, "Who then can be saved?" Jesus responded, "With man this is impossible, but with God all things are possible" (Mt 19:25–26).

In the parable, after the rich man and Lazarus died, a great spiritual chasm separated them. While Lazarus enjoyed comfort, the rich man writhed in torment. For these two men, eternity brought about a great reversal. Jesus' story teaches that there is an unbridgeable divide between heaven and hell; no one can travel from one to the other. The good news is that eternity in hell is not inevitable. Choices made in this life impact what happens after death.

The Pharisees and other religious leaders listened that day but clearly missed the point. Later, Jesus raised another man, Lazarus, from the dead. Only God could perform such a miracle. Some placed their faith in Jesus, but others, especially the religious leaders, left and began plotting how and when to kill Jesus (Jn 11:38–53). Jesus had enough power to raise Lazarus from the dead, yet the religious elite pooled their political power to trap, accuse, bring to trial and then crucify Jesus. Jesus confronted them with the truth that they were in league with their father, the devil, and working to carry out his murderous desires (Jn 8:44).

Jesus graciously explained the reality of hell so that people would understand the consequences of their choices. Because of the gospel, everyone can call on the name of the Lord before they die and be saved (Ac 2:21).

CRUCIFIXION

At the time of Jesus' death, crucifixion was the Roman Empire's most brutal and degrading form of capital punishment — a death so horrible it was reserved for slaves and the vilest of criminals. No Roman citizen could be subjected to crucifixion. Indeed, church tradition indicates that while the Jewish apostle Peter eventually was crucified for following Christ, the apostle Paul, who was a Roman citizen, suffered the relatively humane fate of being beheaded.

Crucifixion seems to have taken various forms throughout the Roman Empire, but biblical and historical sources reveal a pattern. First, the condemned person usually was scourged with a flagellum, a whip constructed of leather thongs interwoven with bits of metal or bone. Greatly weakened by the scourging, the victim then carried the crossbeam through a crowd of people to the place of execution, enduring their taunts and jeers along the way. Sometimes a sign specifying the crime was hung around the criminal's neck. At the place of execution, the condemned was forced to lie on the ground with the crossbeam under his shoulders. Adding degradation to suffering, the executioners stripped the victim naked before nailing or binding him with ropes to the crossbeam.

After the condemned had been nailed or tied to the crossbeam, executioners lifted the crossbeam and secured it to a post, with the person's feet hanging above the ground. Archaeological evidence indicates that sometimes a pin or wooden block was placed halfway up the post to provide a seat for the body — allowing the prisoner to rest periodically, further prolonging the agony — and preventing the nails from tearing open the wounds and allowing the body to fall. The feet were also nailed or tied to the post. Finally, as in the case of the two criminals crucified with Jesus, executioners would sometimes break the legs of the crucified. This last brutal tactic sped up death for those lingering on the cross by causing massive shock, loss of circulation and heart failure.

Jesus, completely innocent of all sin and wrongdoing, suffered the ancient world's most horrific and disgraceful punishment. But this was no ordinary case of wrongful condemnation. This perfect man was also the Son of God, and what appeared to be his defeat gave way to the most glorious victory the world has ever known. After suffering and dying for the sins of the world, Jesus Christ rose from the dead three days later. Jesus' glorious resurrection broke the power of sin and death and empowered his disciples to preach the Good News: Through his suffering on the cross and his resurrection, Jesus offers salvation to all who believe in him.

ABOUT THE NIV

The goal of the New International Version (NIV) is to enable English-speaking people from around the world to read and hear God's eternal Word in their own language. Our work as translators is motivated by our conviction that the Bible is God's Word in written form. We believe that the Bible contains the divine answer to the deepest needs of humanity, sheds unique light on our path in a dark world and sets forth the way to our eternal well-being. Out of these deep convictions, we have sought to recreate as far as possible the experience of the original audience — blending transparency to the original text with accessibility for the millions of English speakers around the world. We have prioritized accuracy, clarity and literary quality with the goal of creating a translation suitable for public and private reading, evangelism, teaching, preaching, memorizing and liturgical use. We have also sought to preserve a measure of continuity with the long tradition of translating the Scriptures into English.

The complete NIV Bible was first published in 1978. It was a completely new translation made by over a hundred scholars working directly from the best available Hebrew, Aramaic and Greek texts. The translators came from the United States, Great Britain, Canada, Australia and New Zealand, giving the translation an international scope. They were from many denominations and churches — including Anglican, Assemblies of God, Baptist, Brethren, Christian Reformed, Church of Christ, Evangelical Covenant, Evangelical Free, Lutheran, Mennonite, Methodist, Nazarene, Presbyterian, Wesleyan and others. This breadth of denominational and theological perspective helped to safeguard the translation from sectarian bias. For these reasons, and by the grace of God, the NIV has gained a wide readership in all parts of the English-speaking world.

The work of translating the Bible is never finished. As good as they are, English translations must be regularly updated so that they will continue to communicate accurately the meaning of God's Word. Updates are needed in order to reflect the latest developments in our understanding of the biblical world and its languages and to keep pace with changes in English usage. Recognizing, then, that the NIV would retain its ability to communicate God's Word accurately only if it were regularly updated, the original translators established the Committee on Bible Translation (CBT). The Committee is a self-perpetuating group of biblical scholars charged with keeping abreast of advances in biblical scholarship and changes in English and issuing periodic updates to the NIV. The CBT is an independent, self-governing body and has sole responsibility for the NIV text. The Committee mirrors the original group of translators in its diverse international and denominational makeup and in its unifying commitment to the Bible as God's inspired Word.

In obedience to its mandate, the Committee has issued periodic updates to the NIV. An initial revision was released in 1984. A more thorough revision process was completed in 2005, resulting in the separately published TNIV. The updated NIV you now have in your hands builds on both the original NIV and the TNIV and represents the latest effort of the Committee to articulate God's unchanging Word in the way the original authors might have said it had they been speaking in English to the global English-speaking audience today.

Translation Philosophy

The Committee's translating work has been governed by three widely accepted principles about the way people use words and about the way we understand them.

First, the meaning of words is determined by the way that users of the language actually use them at any given time. For the biblical languages, therefore, the Committee utilizes the best and most recent scholarship on the way Hebrew, Aramaic and Greek words were being used in biblical times. At the same time the Committee carefully studies the state of modern English. Good translation is like good communication: one must know the target audience so that the appropriate choices can be made about which English words to use to represent the original words of Scripture. From its inception, the NIV has had as its target the general English-speaking population all over the world, the "International" in its title reflecting this concern. The aim of the Committee is to put the Scriptures into natural English that will communicate effectively with the broadest possible audience of English speakers.

Modern technology has enhanced the Committee's ability to choose the right English words to convey the meaning of the original ext. The field of computational linguistics harnesses the power of computers to provide broadly applicable and current data about the state of the language. Translators can now access huge databases of modern English to better understand the current meaning and usage of key words. The Committee utilized this resource in preparing the 2011 edition of the NIV. An area of especially rapid and significant change in English is the way certain nouns and pronouns are used to refer to human beings. The Committee therefore requested experts in computational linguistics at Collins Dictionaries to pose some key questions about this usage to its database of English — the largest in the world, with over 4.4 billion words, gathered from several English-speaking countries and including both spoken and written English. The Collins Study, called "The Development and Use of Gender Language in Contemporary English," can be accessed at *http://www.thenivbible.com/about-the-niv/about-the-2011-edition/*.) The study revealed that the most popular words to describe the human race in modern U.S. English were "humanity," "man" and "mankind." The Committee then used this data in the updated NIV, choosing from among these three words (and occasionally others too) depending on the context.

A related issue creates a larger problem for modern translations: the move away from using the third-person masculine singular pronouns — "he/him/his" — to refer to men and women equally. This usage does persist in some forms of English, and this revision therefore occasionally uses these pronouns in a generic sense. But the tendency, recognized in day-to-day usage and confirmed by the Collins study, is away from the generic use of "he," "him" and "his." In recognition of this shift in language and in an effort to translate into the natural English that people are actually using, this revision of the NIV generally uses other constructions when the biblical text is plainly addressed to men and women equally. The reader will encounter especially frequently a "they," "their" or "them" to express a generic singular idea. Thus, for instance, Mark 8:36 reads: "What good is it for someone to gain the whole world, yet forfeit their soul?" This generic use of the "distributive" or "singular" "they/them/their" has been used for many centuries by respected writers of English and has now become established as standard English, spoken and written, all over the world.

A second linguistic principle that feeds into the Committee's translation work is that meaning is found not in individual words, as vital as they are, but in larger clusters: phrases, clauses, sentences, discourses. Translation is not, as many people think, a matter of word substitution: English word *x* in place of Hebrew word *y*. Translators must first determine the meaning of the words of the biblical languages in the context of the passage and then select English words that accurately communicate that meaning to modern listeners and readers. This means that accurate translation will not always reflect the exact structure of the original language. To be sure, there is debate over the degree to which translators should try to preserve the "form" of the original text in English. From the beginning, the NIV has taken a mediating position on this issue. The manual produced when the translation that became the NIV was first being planned states: "If the Greek or Hebrew syntax has a good parallel in modern English, it should be used. But if there is no good parallel, the English syntax appropriate to the meaning of the original is to be chosen." It is fine, in other words, to carry over the form of the biblical languages into English — but not at the expense of natural expression. The principle that meaning resides in larger clusters of words means that the Committee has not insisted on a "word-for-word" approach to translation. We certainly believe that every word of Scripture is inspired by God and therefore to be carefully studied to determine what God is saying to us. It is for this reason that the Committee labors over every single word of the original texts, working hard to determine how each of those words contributes to what the text is saying. Ultimately, however, it is how these individual words function in combination with other words that determines meaning.

A third linguistic principle guiding the Committee in its translation work is the recognition that words have a spectrum of meaning. It is popular to define a word by using another word, or "gloss," to substitute for it. This substitute word is then sometimes called the "literal" meaning of a word. In fact, however, words have a range of possible meanings. Those meanings will vary depending on the context, and words in one language will usually not occupy the same semantic range as words in another language. The Committee therefore studies each original word of Scripture in its context to identify its meaning in a particular verse and then chooses an appropriate English word (or phrase) to represent it. It is impossible, then, to translate any given Hebrew, Aramaic or Greek word with the same English word all the time. The Committee does try to translate related occurrences of a word in the original languages with the same English word in order to preserve the connection for the English reader. But the Committee generally privileges clear natural meaning over a concern with consistency in rendering particular words.

Textual Basis

For the Old Testament the standard Hebrew text, the Masoretic Text as published in the latest edition of *Biblia Hebraica*, has been used throughout. The Masoretic Text tradition contains marginal notations that offer variant readings. These have sometimes been followed instead of the text itself. Because such instances involve variants within the Masoretic tradition, they have not been indicated in the textual notes. In a few cases, words in the basic consonantal text have been divided differently than in the Masoretic Text. Such cases are usually indicated in the textual footnotes. The Dead Sea Scrolls contain biblical texts that represent an earlier stage of the transmission of the Hebrew text. They have been consulted, as have been the Samaritan Pentateuch and the ancient scribal traditions concerning deliberate textual changes. The translators also consulted the more important early versions. Readings from these versions, the Dead Sea Scrolls and the scribal traditions were occasionally followed where the Masoretic Text seemed doubtful and where accepted principles of textual criticism showed that one or more of these textual witnesses appeared to provide the correct reading. In rare cases, the translators have emended the Hebrew text where it appears to have become corrupted at an even earlier stage of its transmission. These departures from the Masoretic Text are also indicated in the textual footnotes. Sometimes the vowel indicators (which are later additions to the basic consonantal text) found in the Masoretic Text did not, in the judgment of the translators, represent the correct vowels for the original text. Accordingly, some words have been read with a different set of vowels. These instances are usually not indicated in the footnotes.

The Greek text used in translating the New Testament has been an eclectic one, based on the latest editions of the Nestle-Aland/United Bible Societies' Greek New Testament. The translators have made their choices among the variant readings in accordance with widely accepted principles of New Testament textu-

al criticism. Footnotes call attention to place where uncertainty remains.

The New Testament authors, writing Greek, often quote the Old Testament fro its ancient Greek version, the Septuagint. Th is one reason why some of the Old Testamei quotations in the NIV New Testament are n identical to the corresponding passages in t NIV Old Testament. Such quotations in t New Testament are indicated with the footno "(see Septuagint)."

Footnotes and Formatting

Footnotes in this version are of several kine most of which need no explanation. Tho giving alternative translations begin with "O and generally introduce the alternative wi the last word preceding it in the text, exce when it is a single-word alternative. When p etry is quoted in a footnote a slash mark ine cates a line division.

It should be noted that references to d eases, minerals, flora and fauna, architectu: details, clothing, jewelry, musical instrumei and other articles cannot always be identifi with precision. Also, linear measurements a measures of capacity can only be approxim. ed (see the Table of Weights and Measure Although *Selah*, used mainly in the Psalms, probably a musical term, its meaning is unc tain. Since it may interrupt reading and d tract the reader, this word has not been kept the English text, but every occurrence has be signaled by a footnote.

As an aid to the reader, sectional headir have been inserted. They are not to be regard as part of the biblical text and are not intend for oral reading. It is the Committee's hope tl these headings may prove more helpful to reader than the traditional chapter divisio which were introduced long after the Bible v written.

Sometimes the chapter and/or verse nu bering in English translations of the Old T tament differs from that found in publish Hebrew texts. This is particularly the case the Psalms, where the traditional titles are cluded in the Hebrew verse numbering. Si differences are indicated in the footnotes the bottom of the page. In the New Testame verse numbers that marked off portions of traditional English text not supported by best Greek manuscripts now appear in brat ets, with a footnote indicating the text t has been omitted (see, for example, Matth 17:[21]).

Mark 16:9 – 20 and John 7:53 — 8:11, although ong accorded virtually equal status with the est of the Gospels in which they stand, have questionable standing in the textual history f the New Testament, as noted in the bracked annotations with which they are set off. different typeface has been chosen for these assages to indicate their uncertain status.

Basic formatting of the text, such as lining he poetry, paragraphing (both prose and potry), setting up of (administrative-like) lists, ndenting letters and lengthy prayers within arratives and the insertion of sectional headngs, has been the work of the Committee. Iowever, the choice between single-column and double-column formats has been left to the publishers. Also the issuing of "red-letter" editions is a publisher's choice — one that the Committee does not endorse.

The Committee has again been reminded that every human effort is flawed — including this revision of the NIV. We trust, however, that many will find in it an improved representation of the Word of God, through which they hear his call to faith in our Lord Jesus Christ and to service in his kingdom. We offer this version of the Bible to him in whose name and for whose glory it has been made.

The Committee on Bible Translation

A NOTE REGARDING THE TYPE

This Bible was set in the Zondervan NIV Typeface, commissioned by Zondervan, a division of HarperCollins Christian Publishing, and designed in Aarhus, Denmark, by Klaus E. Krogh and Heidi Rand Sørensen of 2K/DENMARK. The design takes inspiration from the vision of the New International Version (NIV) to be a modern translation that gives the reader the most accurate Bible text possible, reflects the very best of biblical scholarship, and uses contemporary global English. The designers of the Zondervan NIV Typeface sought to reflect this rich, half-century-old tradition of accuracy, readability, and clarity while also embodying the best advancements in modern Bible typography. The result is a distinctive, open Bible typeface that is uncompromisingly beautiful, clear, readable at any size, and perfectly suited to the New International Version.